Homicide by Horse Show

The Creature Comforts Mystery series
by Arlene Kay

Death by Dog Show

Homicide by Horse Show

Homicide by Horse Show

A Creature Comforts Mystery

Arlene Kay

LYRICAL UNDERGROUND
Kensington Publishing Corp.
www.kensingtonbooks.com

LYRICAL UNDERGROUND BOOKS are published by

Kensington Publishing Corp.
119 West 40th Street
New York, NY 10018

All Kensington titles, imprints, and distributed lines are available at special quantity discounts for bulk purchases for sales promotion, premiums, fund-raising, educational, or institutional use.

Special book excerpts or customized printings can also be created to fit specific needs. For details, write or phone the office of the Kensington Sales Manager: Kensington Publishing Corp., 119 West 40th Street, New York, NY 10018. Attn. Sales Department. Phone: 1-800-221-2647.

Lyrical Underground and Lyrical Underground logo Reg. US Pat. & TM Off.

First Electronic Edition: October 2019
eISBN-13: 978-1-5161-0931-9
eISBN-10: 1-5161-0931-7

First Print Edition: October 2019
ISBN-13: 978-1-5161-0934-0
ISBN-10: 1-5161-0934-1

Printed in the United States of America

To those kind souls who generously give their passion, energy and devotion to animals in need.

Chapter 1

"It's an outrage! Morally indefensible! Outright murder." Babette Croy swept her arms in an arc as she built up a head of steam. When it came to outrage, Babette was second to none. However, on the issue of animal welfare, our passions aligned. Her big brown eyes bulged with emotion as she ticked off the moral failings of her affluent neighbors in Great Marsh, Virginia. "All they care about is property. Their rights. What about the horses? They'll go to kill lots and be slaughtered for dog food. Those selfish prigs don't give a fig about their lives." Tears welled up in her eyes, threatening several thick coats of mascara.

Despite the protests of citizens like Babette, our local town council had recently sanctioned the removal of Cavalry Farms, a forty-acre facility devoted to rescuing horses. The official excuse was community safety, but no one believed that, even after a prominent landholder claimed that the stench and runoff from waste products had polluted her well and contaminated her drinking water. No one had much sympathy for the citizen either, a perpetual whiner who had far too much time and money at her disposal. The local newspaper had been filled with tart comments about her, some of which bordered on libelous.

Our little community valued property above all else and paid exorbitant taxes to prove it. Quite simply, the rescue facility infringed on those most sacred tenets of upper crust society—status and raw profit. It occupied what was now one of the most coveted spots in our town and drew what some referred to as a disreputable crowd, particularly on weekends. Great Marsh residents prided themselves on the exclusivity of their enclave and paid big bucks to maintain it. Businesses and property owners had coalesced into a massive interest group that touted constitutional freedoms and vowed to "re-home" the horses and their rescuers in a more suitable spot, preferably in another universe. Eminent domain was the official tool for change, a tricky strategy that was subject to scrutiny and legal challenge. Several local attorneys argued on both sides of the issue, but to a simple soul like me, equity and compassion superseded everything.

Babette and I commandeered a choice slot in the local coffee house that abutted the town square. She was a regular there, so her histrionics were shrugged off and regarded as nothing special, just a normal part of the scenery. Our server carefully pushed a cup brimming with espresso next to her and fled. No one, no one sane that is, wanted to tangle with Babette on the issue of animal welfare. I leaned across the table and patted my friend's hand.

"Maybe we can mobilize public opinion," I said. "Most people in Great Marsh love horses. After all, we have all kinds of organizations devoted to equestrian stuff. Plenty of little girls and their mamas involved." The equine industry and all the attendant suppliers was a billion-dollar bonanza in Virginia and constituted a good part of my business.

Babette closed her eyes and raked her manicured fingers through expertly highlighted tresses. She was no dilettante, but a serious person who also cared about her appearance and had the money to indulge her needs. She didn't look her age—not at all. Facials, floppy hats and the occasional shot of Juvéderm preserved Babette at a perpetual thirty-nine rather than her actual forty-eight. She always described herself as "thirty-nine and holding on for dear life."

I sported a tailored look more suited to my needs. No manicure. That would be wasted on a leathersmith who spent her time crafting items for dog and horse enthusiasts. Minimal makeup made sense too, although I still had enough girly impulses to apply blush and lip gloss each day. My one point of vanity was my hair, a thick chestnut mane not unlike that of my equine clients. I usually tamed it in a French braid or a twist, but on formal occasions it cascaded down my back in a blaze of glory. Beyond that, my features were regular, and I was a reasonably fit thirty-something—nothing spectacular or hideously ugly. Just call me Perri Morgan, leather artiste and poster child for the average woman.

"You don't get it, Perri. It's a status thing. They say they love horses but only a certain class of them. You know, dressage, jumping, competition thoroughbreds. Cavalry Farms rescues draft horses, farm rejects—nothing that would show up in those glossy magazines they love. These so-called horse lovers see their animals as fashion accessories. Lesser specimens are candidates for dog food or the glue factory."

Babette's sympathies were aroused by almost any animal cause and her perspective wasn't always balanced. Some opposition was indeed based on property values and class distinctions but while many of my friends and neighbors genuinely loved all animals, they differed on this issue. I'd heard the same arguments applied to dog shows by the "adopt don't shop" crowd. Babette and I were both devoted to animal causes, but we also were enthusiasts of purebred dogs and attended shows all over the country. As a purveyor of custom leather goods, my livelihood depended on well-heeled people who spent lavishly on their four-legged friends both equine and canine. Balance was the key to getting things right but there was no sense in telling that to Babette.

She chattered on, happily making plans. "You're so right! I'll showcase it on my next program. Pictures and first-hand accounts. That should throw a spanner in the works." She clutched her cup and sipped greedily. "You can help me, Perri. People listen to you. After all, you're a veteran."

Babette was the eternal optimist, but unlike me she didn't have to support herself or worry about offending customers. That gave her the luxury of time and the illusion that throngs of people actually watched her local television program. Unfortunately, reality differed sharply from perception. Community television shows tended to air at odd hours when most folks were fast asleep.

"I'll do what I can. You know that." My response was weak and feckless but as a small business owner it was all I could offer. Creature Comforts wasn't booming but at least it was operating in the black. That could change in a flash if my clients—the canine and horsey set—turned away from me. High-end leashes, bridles, halters and collars were luxury items affordable to only a few of them or their doting spouses.

"Maybe you should court controversy," I said. "You know, invite the opposition on your show and have a debate. That might stir things up."

Babette drained her cup and gave me a caffeinated grin. "Like who?"

I was playing with fire but what the heck. "What about Glendon Jakes? He certainly has a point of view and he's pretty well known around here."

I hunkered down, waiting for an explosion, but Babette's silence was even more ominous. Jake was her sworn enemy, a buttoned-down biologist whose popular hunting blog, *Bag It*, took every opportunity to excoriate Babette and the causes she espoused. She folded her hands and sighed.

"I get it. Meet the enemy. Bring him into the tent and fight mano a mano. Crafty. You're a genius, Perri! Never met the little creep face to face but I've read enough of his posts to last a lifetime. I'll get right on it. Better still, I'll have Ethel handle that." Ethel, her long-suffering secretary, was a demon of efficiency who could conquer any task.

My cowardice gene immediately kicked in. Babette operated more on emotion than intellect, but she was a kindly soul who would help any creature, human or animal. I did not want to see her hurt or humiliated by a snarky PhD with a penchant for satire. The sticker prominently displayed on his truck said it all: "I love animals. They taste good."

"Maybe you should wait a bit," I said. "You know, build your case. Marshall the facts."

She bared perfectly capped teeth. "Wait? That may mean a death sentence for those horses. Re-home—that's the term they always use. Sounds so much nicer than slaughter. Face it, Perri. Who wants to adopt those old bags of bones, loveable though they may be? Land is expensive anywhere you look."

Before I opened my mouth, Babette continued. "Look what happened at that county animal shelter last year. We picketed, pleaded and blocked the roads like well-behaved citizens but nothing stopped them. Bloodthirsty bastards gassed most of the dogs rescued from Katrina."

Babette dusted off her slacks and jumped to her feet. "Well, it won't happen this time. No sir."

I made a rapid Hail Mary pass, hoping to slow her down. "What about Carleton? He's a good tactician. Maybe he'll have some ideas." Unfortunately, the reference to her former husband had the opposite effect. Babette narrowed her eyes and glared at me, hands on hips.

"Carleton has no interest whatsoever in my activities. My *causes.* That's what he calls them. Can you believe it? Like I'm some silly teeny-bopper crushing on a rock star."

"Sorry. I didn't mean anything." A shroud of invisibility would have come in handy at that point. Anything was preferable to inserting myself into a nasty ex-marital spat.

Babette grabbed the check and patted my hand. "It's not your fault, darlin.' Things haven't been peachy keen between Car and me for some time. It's probably my fault. When the wife holds the purse strings..." She shrugged. "I should've kicked him out when we got divorced but he was so pitiful. Begged to stay until he found another place. That was two years ago and countin.'"

Carleton Croy had impeccable academic credentials, a prominent ego and a perpetual look of gloom. Several of my clients considered him a hunk although the reasons for that eluded me. It wasn't his appearance necessarily. His features were pleasant enough; his body looked fit and his thatch of fiery red hair gave him an air of distinction that was probably merited. As head guidance counselor and drama coach at the prestigious Hamilton Arms School, he held a responsible post and by all accounts was quite good at it. Unfortunately, while pricey institutions charge whopping tuition, they seldom share the spoils with their staff. Thus, every conversation with Carleton was studded with references to his days at Yale, his doctorate, and his many well-heeled pals. The air of entitlement and dashed dreams that surrounded him was almost stifling.

For someone like me who had scraped by paying tuition at a public university with scholarships, loans, and GI benefits, Carleton was an enigma. I was a product of the foster care system. Through luck, hard work, and sheer stubbornness, I had beaten the odds in more ways than one. Despite having a rough start, I felt gratitude, not angst at my lot in life. Things could have gone worse—much worse.

"Are you listening to me, Perri?" Babette fished her keys from her purse and nudged me toward the door. "I'll have Ethel make a few calls. Let's plan to meet up tomorrow morning. My house about nine am. Okay?"

I hated to disappoint her but there was no alternative. "Tomorrow doesn't work for me," I said. "Not the morning anyhow. Got a meeting with a potential client."

Babette's eyes brightened. "What's up? Something lucrative, I hope."

"Could be. A vendor saw those belts I made on Facebook and he's interested. Thinks he could sell a slew of them to the right buyer." I crossed my fingers. "Wish me luck."

She threw her arms around me. "No one can beat you, darlin.' Every time I walk my Clara, people rave about her collar and lead. Stop on over after you finish. We'll have our pow-wow then and toast your success. By the way, give me some more of your cards. I'm fresh out."

Babette was both my biggest booster and challenge. She meant well even when her antics consumed every molecule of air in the room. Three years ago, we had bonded instantly at a charity event for retired military canines. I admired the zeal of this socialite with a conscience. She, on the other hand, was fascinated by my army career and begged for scraps of information. None of my anecdotes were particularly memorable, although after spending three years with the military, I had learned a thing or two about human nature and the use of firearms. Babette had never in her life wielded a weapon more potent than a pen or a credit card. To her, my life was as exotic as the plotline from her favorite thriller. Our friendship had blossomed built on shared values and love for all living creatures, but our circumstances were very different.

"By the way, Perri, I got great news today. You'll die when you hear it. You will not believe it. Guess." Babette steered me to the parking lot where her shiny Mercedes nestled alongside my battered Suburban.

I paused, waiting for the bombshell that she was dying to share. "You know I'm a terrible guesser. Come on. Put me out of my misery."

She shifted from one foot to the other like a gleeful imp. "We did it! Finally got the attention of the mainstream media."

"You're kidding!"

"Nope. Wing called me about it yesterday. That man is just amazing!" Every sentient being in greater Washington DC knew the name Wing Pruett. You couldn't escape him if you tried. The airways were saturated with sound bites and the handsome mug of the investigative journalist. Oversaturated in my opinion. Naturally, I was prejudiced, since Pruett just happened to be my private passion and main squeeze. His name evoked both lust and fear in many of the nation's trendsetters since he had news sources all over the globe. Personally, I was solidly with the lust brigade when it came to Pruett.

"He's covering this protest? I thought he only handled political corruption cases or mob hits. Stuff like that. Things that would get him his next Pulitzer. We're pretty small potatoes to a famous reporter." I kept a smile on my face but inwardly I fumed. Why hadn't Pruett mentioned this to me?

Babette's grin showcased a fetching set of dimples. "I saw him at that benefit for Hamilton Arms last week and I buttonholed him." She fluttered her lashes. "You know how persuasive I can be."

I did know and frankly I didn't care. A recent profile of Pruett in the *Washingtonian* described him as the city's most eligible bachelor, a darling of the "J" School set and per the writer, a man whose social calendar was jam-packed. In my book, he deserved those accolades and more. We kept our relationship on the low burner, but the flame burned brightly just the same.

After animal welfare, Babette's next passion was finding a suitable mate for me. She had wed enough times for both of us, although to be fair, three of her four spouses had succumbed to old age with smiles on their faces as she always joked. Until finding Carleton, she had the foresight or dumb luck to choose extremely wealthy men who doted on her, showered her with cash, and made her rich.

Dating, especially dating a babe-magnet like Pruett, had been the last thing on my agenda, until we connected two years ago. My expectations were low since I assumed of course that he would never be interested in a rather ordinary soul like me. I was above all a realist who adjusted her expectations to attainable goals. That philosophy didn't entail pining for the affections of a society darling like Pruett. I was self-sufficient and determined to stay that way. No ticking biological clock or marriage anxieties engulfed me. I was content with my lot in life. Sounded sensible until I fell hard for him and his adorable daughter, Ella. Now, I buried my misgivings and focused on enjoying every minute I spent with them.

"It's time, Perri." Babette patted my arm. "And a few highlights and some makeup would do wonders for you. After all, it's been four years since you lost Pip. I loved him too, but life goes on. Time you stopped dodging Pruett and settled down. Competition is fierce out there you know."

I turned sideways, ambushed by a sudden mist of tears. Babette meant well but she had no concept of what I had shared with my fiancé or the gaping chasm his death had created in my life. Philip Hahn, "Pip," was the love of my life, a shy veterinarian with a million-dollar grin and a big heart. Melanoma, a cruel and stealthy killer, had taken him from me so fast that at times it still didn't register. What a rebuke to the champion athlete and avid outdoorsman who had shared my life and still consumed my thoughts. Pruett and Ella helped to salve that wound but it still ached at times.

"Oh honey, I'm sorry." Babette seemed close to tears herself. "I never learned to keep my big trap shut. Forgive me?"

I gave her a quick hug and clutched the door handle of my truck. "It's okay. I'll call you after my meeting."

She sped off in her sporty red car oblivious to oncoming traffic or impending disaster. I shook my head, never dreaming what our future would hold.

Chapter 2

Luck was with me. Due to a scheduling change, I met my new client later that same afternoon. Even better, he scooped up the entire stock of belts and ordered four dozen more. I was proud of those belts—English bridle leather, solid brass accents and a convenient pouch for pet treats or keys. Several shops in Great Marsh already carried them and they had quickly sold to the style setters in the community. I downplayed my luck but secretly dreamed of a modest version of hitting the big time. If opportunity knocked, I might expand my reach to DC, Philadelphia, and even New York City. Hot dog!

I plopped down on my sofa, dislodging an outraged feline who considered it her domain. Thatcher—named for the Iron Lady herself—was one very opinionated Maine Coon who couldn't wait to scold me. Pip had rescued her from a heartless client who wanted her "disposed of" because her coat shed on the furniture. Thatcher had adored him, although she barely tolerated me. When his time came, she gently purred Pip into the next world with a tenderness that was both unexpected and mystical. For that, I would always love her no matter how many times she clawed the furniture or ignored me.

The rest of my household included two Belgian Malinois, Keats and Poe, plus Zeke, a cantankerous pygmy goat with bizarre eating habits. They were family more than pets and made sure that I appreciated the fact.

My little homestead didn't compare with the grand estates that dotted most of Great Marsh but that didn't bother me. My hunk of heaven consisted of a comfortable ranch-style house with a renovated barn that served as my studio. Land was at a premium in Great Marsh and local covenants required a five-acre lot for each residence. With all the McMansions springing up, modest homesteads like mine had become an endangered species. Unfortunately, pleasure and pain aligned whenever I considered the bittersweet backstory that accompanied the place. Pip inherited the property from his aunt and when he passed, the home that held so many happy memories became mine. He never really left it though. His spirit inhabited every square foot of our home—always had, always would. That comforted me in the lonely times when I felt Pip's arms hugging me or heard his booming laughter echoing throughout my studio. Pruett understood. At least I think he did. We both agreed to take things slowly and allow our feelings to grow.

I couldn't wait to share my sales triumph with Babette. Unfortunately, Carleton answered the phone and regaled me with a prolonged discussion of his workday, and the usual litany of complaints. Finally, he summoned Ethel McCall to speak with me.

"Babette rescheduled her yoga class," Ethel said. "She's planning some big pow wow tomorrow morning. But I guess you know that."

I explained that I was free after all and would attend the session.

Ethel paused for a moment and laughed. "That's a relief. I'm off tomorrow and Babette needs one of us to keep her on an even keel. She means well, but man oh man that lady can go off like a firecracker."

I pictured Ethel, sensible, faithful Ethel, with her freshly scrubbed face, no-nonsense grey hair and thick glasses. Although she was occasionally gruff, no one ever questioned either her work ethic or her devotion to Babette.

"She invited Glendon Jakes," I said. "Is he coming?"

"Yep. Called him myself." I detected the hint of humor in Ethel's voice. "He sounded eager."

"Anyone else?"

Ethel paused. "Just checking my list. Ken Reedy, Charlotte Westly, Jacqui Parks and Sheila Sands. All confirmed."

I didn't know all of them, but Ken and Sheila were fervent pet people, part of my customer base. "Anyone else?"

"Oh. The pretty one with the wavy black hair. I think you may know him." Now I knew that Ethel was laughing at me. Pruett was a fixture in my life and she knew it well.

"He'll be late. Has some big appearance scheduled on one of those morning shows—*Good Morning America*, I think."

Despite her protests, I knew that Ethel nursed a major crush on newscasters and seldom missed the morning shows. If a fifty-something stalwart could be called a fan girl, Ethel was it.

"Should I bring anything? Food or soft drinks?"

"Got it covered," Ethel said. "I have a surprise for Babette too. Something special to pep up that rally of hers."

I was curious. "What is it? Give me a hint."

Ethel was one tough customer. She chuckled but wouldn't budge. "You'll see it soon enough. By the way, she expects a dozen or so to show up. The usual crowd. There is one thing you could do to help. Maybe you could get here early—eight-thirty or so. Just to make sure everything's set. The rest of the bunch won't be here 'til around nine and half of 'em will probably be late. You know how much this means to Babette. Might make her a tad jumpy."

I did a quick check of my calendar. "I'll be there. Don't worry."

Ethel clucked approvingly. "Good. Want her to call you when she gets home?"

I planned on making and eating a leisurely dinner, then soothing my tired muscles in a hot bath and reading by the fireplace. Babette, bless her heart, would raise my anxiety level to overload by rehashing everything we had already covered that morning. "No need. I'll see her in the morning."

* * * *

I rarely oversleep but that's what happened the next day. If Poe and Keats hadn't rustled around, I might never have gotten up. As it was, I leapt into the shower, turned on my coffee machine and tended to my pets at warp speed. My mop of chestnut hair didn't take much tending, so I clipped it back into a low ponytail and forgot about it. Makeup? Why bother? As I looked into the mirror it suddenly struck me: Pruett was guest of honor at Babette's soiree and he was accustomed to svelte Washington socialites in designer duds. My wardrobe would flunk the *Vogue* test, but I could at least spare a few minutes to apply makeup. A dab of foundation, pinch of blush and a touch of mascara buoyed my spirits and salved my ego. Now I could face the Romeo of the printed page without flinching. No need to downplay my assets.

Poe and Keats leapt into the Suburban without being invited. They were military retirees, heroes of the canine corps, five years old with beauty and brains to spare. As an added bonus, both dogs had also mastered Schutzhund, the three-level training program consisting of tracking, obedience and protection specialties. My boys weren't aggressive, but they were very serious about their mission. I felt safe with them around.

We tore out of the driveway with Zeke giving us the evil eye as he munched hay. That goat had a really bad attitude at times, but who could blame him? He was a pygmy, neutered at an early age and saved by Pip from becoming part of the food chain. Although the literature claimed that goats need others of their own kind to be content, Zeke seemed quite happy cuddling and playing with my dogs. He even maintained détente with Thatcher although each was suspicious of the other. Zeke's talents as a milk producer were another matter entirely and his ambivalence about humans kept me wary of his horns.

I broke a few traffic rules on the ten-minute trek to Babette's place. To be accurate, I drove like a maniac on the deserted back roads. Babette's home was a mansion, a sprawling hilltop heaven set back from the main road behind a spacious guesthouse currently occupied by Ethel. I checked my watch, relieved to find that it was barely half past eight. That gave me plenty of time to tie up any loose ends before the other guests arrived. I zipped into the garage, a six-bay architectural wonder disguised as a farm building. Since it housed a valuable classic Corvette, the garage was typically locked down tight. Not today.

Poe and Keats followed my signal and leapt out to get a bit of exercise. They were immediately joined by Clara, Babette's beloved Border Collie and closest ally. Clara was never left off lead unless she was in a fully fenced enclosure. Border collies run at a blistering pace that no mere human can match, but Babette was more concerned that marauding coyotes might harm Clara. She must have sneaked out amidst the hubbub over the big meeting.

I grabbed a spare lead from my truck, coaxed Clara close enough to slip a Martingale around her neck and stroked her shiny coat. "Here you go, my beauty. Your mama will have a fit if she finds you gone, naughty girl." Clara's normally placid demeanor vanished. She danced about on her toes like a nervous ballerina awaiting her cue.

What in the world could Babette be thinking of? She doted on Clara, lavishing love, attention, and money on her pet. A sense of foreboding swept through me, the same type of early warning system I had felt during my tour in Afghanistan. Those instincts had kept me alive more than once and I valued them. I whistled for my dogs and cautiously approached Babette's house.

The front door was unlocked—nothing unusual about that. Despite my warnings, Babette insisted that Great Marsh was safe, an idyllic place where good will flourished. She was right—up to a point. The town had almost zero crime despite, or because of, the affluence of its inhabitants, but the heroin epidemic that was sweeping northern Virginia left everyone vulnerable.

"Babette? It's Perri. Where are you?" I stepped cautiously into the great room, comforted by the presence of my dogs. Both Malinois went on alert, standing statue-still as their eyes surveyed the terrain. Clara broke free and tore up the winding marble staircase toward Babette's bedroom with her lead trailing behind her. I shivered as I beckoned the Mals and followed. Was something sinister waiting around the corner?

Relax. Take a deep breath. You know how to handle dangerous situations. Been there, done that.

Babette's master suite, a beautifully sculpted three-room space with sitting room and private bath was located at the end of the corridor. I had visited it many times but now something about it seemed sinister.

"Babette!" My voice sounded shrill even to my own ears. "It's late. Better get going." My hand trembled as I clutched the doorknob and knocked. Clara stood at the door, frantically clawing it and whimpering.

I slipped through a narrow opening, leaving the dogs to patrol the corridor. Then I saw it—crimson droplets of what had to be blood, dotting the satin bedspread. Sheets concealed a half-naked female form saturated with still more blood. The chaos contrasted sharply with a neatly folded pile of clothes on the bedside bench. I covered my mouth to suppress the scream building in my throat. She was gone. My friend, Babette. I'd seen enough corpses during the war to recognize a dead body even at a distance. Next to the boudoir chair rested a fire extinguisher covered with still more gore. I didn't touch it, of course. Anyone with a television set knew better than that.

I blinked, forcing myself to approach the bed. Maybe she was still alive. Maybe I could summon help. A blast of cool air from the open French doors assaulted my senses. As I half-turned, a black-clad figure moved forward and struck me down.

* * * *

A chorus of noise not unlike the celestial choir roused me. Actually, those sounds were a cacophony of screams mixed with barks, howls and the sweet sensation of doggy kisses. Was I dreaming? My head sank into downy pillows and an eiderdown throw cosseted me. *What the hell?*

"Breathe slowly, darlin.' Help is on the way."

Either I was dreaming or swirling the drain waiting to die. By some cruel twist of fate, that voice sounded exactly like Babette's. If I hadn't seen her corpse, I might have believed it. I opened one eye and squinted. Which of Dante's circles of hell had trapped me? "You're dead! What's happening to me?"

Ice-cold fingers grabbed my cheek and pinched it. "Persephone Morgan, wake up right now and stop babbling. Do you hear me?"

Very few people knew my full name and only one was crazy enough to pinch a woman in shock. Cautiously—very cautiously—I opened my eyes, looked up, and saw Babette's smiling face. Her makeup was smeared, and her hair was a disaster, but my friend was alive.

"What happened?"

"You tell us." A deep masculine voice that was both familiar and rather snarky assaulted my ears. I reached out, clutching my dogs' soft fur as they formed an honor guard around me. I ignored him and turned toward Babette. "All that blood. I saw your body on the bed."

Babette reached down and squeezed my hand ignoring the tears that coursed down her cheeks. "That was Ethel, honey. I ran out to get supplies and Ethel stayed at the house." Her voice broke when she said her friend's name. "I don't know what in the world she was doing on my bed."

I pulled myself up, balanced on my elbows and turned toward the other person. He was dressed in black just like the blurry figure who almost killed me. Assassins come in all shapes and sizes, but this man was no foe. Pruett held out his arms and hugged me tight.

"Who are you?" I asked.

He laughed. In the midst of murder and mayhem he actually laughed. "Still got that edge I see." His voice was gentler now, almost hypnotic. A lock of thick black hair fell over his eyes as he bent down. Poe immediately went on alert, growling a warning.

"Easy, boy. It's okay." I forced myself to meet Pruett's gaze. "Don't worry. I'm fine."

"Perri, you know who he is." Babette turned toward him. "She's in shock."

The situation felt artificial, more like a third-rate melodrama than a crime scene. Babette was preternaturally calm considering the circumstances. I blinked, hearing other voices just outside the room. "Who's there?" I asked.

"Just friends, honey. Charlotte and Jacqui. Ken Reedy too. Sheila's somewhere around the place and so is Carleton. Haven't seen Jakes, thank the Lord."

My throat ached, and I felt perilously close to throwing up. The enormity of things simply did not register. Murder, assault? Was this a dream?

Pruett said little but focused on me with laser-like precision. Obviously, he was concerned with my welfare, but he also sensed an opportunity.

What better than a first-person account of a brutal murder among the upper crust? It was tailor made for those trashy true crime shows he routinely appeared on.

Deep breaths. Keep your dignity, Perri.

"How did I get out here?" I pointed to Babette's sitting room. "Did I walk?"

"I carried you," Pruett said. "The cops wouldn't appreciate it if you messed up their crime scene any more than it already was." He shuddered. "You're quite an armful my lady."

He was well over six feet tall with the taut body of a dedicated gym rat. More than able to carry me; he'd done it plenty of times before, so I knew he was teasing. A sudden wail of sirens galvanized the dogs into a spate of barking. The cavalry in the person of the local police had finally arrived.

Chapter 3

Fairfax County has a savvy, sophisticated police operation that responds quickly to murder and mayhem at a mansion. By the time I was fully conscious, two squad cars and three detectives from the Major Crimes division had already arrived. After securing the crime scene, a disheveled, slightly tubby white guy with a shop-worn Burberry motioned us down the stairs into the living room.

"Lieutenant Titus Bascomb," he said, flashing his credentials. "Who is the homeowner here?" His tone was all business.

Fear or shock rendered Babette mute. Instead of speaking, she raised her hand like a timid schoolgirl.

Bascomb adjusted his sunglasses and stared at his smartphone. "Mrs. Croy? Did you call this in?"

She shook her head and shivered.

"I did, Lieutenant." Pruett rose gracefully and stood, legs spread wide, facing the cop. "Wing Pruett."

If Bascomb recognized a celebrity in his midst he didn't react. "Okay. Give me the basics."

Even I admired the factual, no-nonsense account that Pruett supplied. His poise emboldened Babette who finally regained the power of speech.

"We all got here about the same time," she said. "Dogs were barking, and the door was wide open. I knew Perri was here 'cause I saw her truck." She pointed to me. "That's Perri. Wing ran up the staircase, but he couldn't get in. The dogs wouldn't let him." Babette blew her nose. "I pushed them aside and opened the door. I thought they were both dead. I've never seen anything like that…" An attack of hiccups rendered her speechless again, and she dissolved into sobs.

Bascomb swiveled around and stared at me. "The paramedics need to check you out. Head injuries are nothing to fool with."

I started to protest until a wave of nausea assailed me. This might be a case of better safe than sorry. Bascomb motioned to his subordinate who put her arm around me and led me from the room. The EMTs were waiting just outside the entryway. They quickly hoisted me on a stretcher and administered a battery of field tests.

"You got a whale of a bump but no blood. We can run you to the hospital for an MRI or contact your own doctor. Do you want to call someone to take you home?" one of the EMTs asked.

A sudden realization hit me with the force of a body blow: I had no one to call. Acquaintances yes, but other than Pruett, Babette was my only real friend. I thought of Poe, Keats, Thatcher and that damn pygmy goat at home. "My pets. I have to take care of my pets."

"Don't worry." The detective was a twenty-something woman with a spindly frame and a kind face. "We'll figure something out. Have you given your statement yet?"

I shook my head. A van with the emblem of the County Coroner blocked the driveway. Two forensic trucks had already arrived. I turned away in case they moved Ethel's corpse out of the house. That was more than I could bear at the moment.

"I can take her home, Officer. I have my SUV parked around the corner, and I've already spoken to the lieutenant." Pruett appeared from out of nowhere and beamed a media bright smile her way.

The cop ignored the charm offensive and turned to me. "I'll tell the Lieutenant. Gotta warn you though he'll want to interview you ASAP. Probably this afternoon. Go home and stay put until you hear from him."

"My dogs…" Was that pathetic whine really coming from me?

Pruett reached down and helped me up. "No problem as long as they don't chew my arm off." He motioned to my truck where some brave soul had already corralled both Malinois. "Throw me your keys and I'll drive you home. I like to know the terrain before I barge into a lady's house, but I suppose you haven't acquired some burly husband since last night."

His wit was totally wasted on me. The dull throbbing ache in my temples was all I focused on. I shook my head and gingerly climbed the running board into my truck. "No worries." I adjusted the GPS for "home" and leaned back in my seat. For once, I was happy to let someone else take charge.

I must have fallen asleep because the next thing I knew, Wing Pruett's hands were on my shoulders gently shaking me awake. "Rise and shine, Sleeping Beauty."

I still felt a bit shaky, so I didn't protest when he lifted me to the ground. Keats and Poe barked impatiently until I opened the hatch and freed them.

"What the hell is that?" Pruett pointed at the corral where Zeke hung his head over the fence glaring balefully at us. "He looks meaner than ever."

"You know how he is. He's harmless."

"Hmm. People say that about me sometimes and they're dead wrong."

"He's neutered. Makes males of any species more docile, or so I hear."

That earned me another chuckle from Pruett, a man who was accustomed to women falling at his feet rather than taunting him. Handsome, brainy guys got used to that treatment. "Think of all the fun we'd miss if you neutered me," he said. "Service with a smile, Ma'am."

"Forget about that, I need some espresso. Interested?" I unlocked the door and deactivated my burglar alarm. "Watch out for Thatcher. You know what an escape artist she is."

Pruett sighed. "You and your pets. No wonder Ella adores you."

Pruett grew up without any pets, but he was slowly acclimating himself to my pet-centric household. His young daughter cheered him on in that effort.

He wrinkled his nose. At that moment, Thatcher appeared and with typical feline logic wrapped herself around his legs, purring loudly.

I waved Pruett toward the living room. "I'll go get that coffee. Make yourself at home." Both dogs escorted me into the kitchen and sat expectantly waiting for treats. Pruett was right behind them.

"Hey. Don't bother with that. You still look shaky. I know how to make espresso. Take it easy. It's not every day that you see a murder or get assaulted."

I gladly sat down at the kitchen table and closed my eyes. "In the army, we saw our share of bodies. You kind of expect that during wartime; but today…"

Pruett moved his chair closer. "Did you know her well? Ethel, I mean."

That impersonal Court TV approach annoyed me. "Yes, I knew her. We weren't confidants or anything, but she seemed like a nice person."

He held up his arms in mock surrender. "Sorry. I didn't mean it. Everything is so nuanced in the media. Has to be. Sometimes it seeps into everyday stuff."

I downed my espresso along with three Advil and tried reconstructing the terrible events of the day. What in the world was Ethel doing in Babette's bed—half-naked no less! From everything I knew of the woman she was a no-nonsense, practical foil to her employer's whimsical ways. Cavorting, whether naked or clothed, was simply contrary to everything she stood for. I'd never seen Ethel wear slacks, let alone her birthday suit!

Until Pruett spoke, I'd forgotten he was there. "You were lucky," he said. "That guy who clobbered you was probably the murderer. Didn't you recognize him?"

"No. I can't even swear that it was a man. Just a tall figure in black." I pointed to him. "Kind of like what you're wearing."

"Now wait a minute." Pruett wagged his finger at me. "Don't try to pin this on me. I was nowhere around there, and I hardly knew this McCall woman. Never really met her."

"You spoke with her. She told me so."

He deflected the tension with banter. "Perri, if I knocked off every woman I spoke to we'd have a damn epidemic. Give me a break, will you?"

Before I responded, someone pounded on the door and my dogs streaked forward barking wildly. Thatcher followed them emitting an angry yowl. I peered out the window at the black sedan with flashing lights. Time to face the law.

* * * *

Lieutenant Bascomb, the slightly paunchy white guy with an attitude and a rumpled suit, strolled into the room, flashed his badge and introduced himself once again. After a quick survey of my living room, he settled right in. "Let's see: Persephone Morgan. Odd name, that. Can't say that I've ever heard it before."

"You must not be a fan of Greek mythology," Pruett interjected. His cheeky remark earned him a scowl from the veteran cop who understood a put-down in any language when he heard one.

"Time for you to leave, Mr. Pruett. My sergeant will show you out." Bascomb pointed toward the door. "We'll be in touch. Boyfriends don't count in a murder investigation unless they're attached to the victim. I presume you and Ms. McCall weren't an item, right?"

Pruett exited the room with a minimum of grace, leaving me to the clutches of a surly cop. Bascomb plopped down in the wing chair and turned on a lamp. "My sergeant got your name and address I see. You run your own business—a leather shop?" His tone and raised eyebrows suggested that my profession was something tawdry.

"Custom leather. Mostly collars, halters and leads for dogs and horses. A few other items for their owners." I reached into my pocket and produced a weathered business card. "I can give you references if you like."

He dismissed my offer with a shrug. "Says here you're a military veteran. What branch?"

"Army." I refused to elaborate and do his work for him.

Bascomb bared a set of uneven teeth in a faux smile. "Human Resources, I bet."

"Not even close. Operations."

He gave me a hard stare. Clearly Bascomb hadn't expected that. "Quite a career change, wouldn't you say? What's your connection to Mrs. Croy?"

I launched into an explanation of the animal rights coalition and the controversy over Cavalry Farms. "Mrs. Croy is a local activist. She's spearheading opposition to the removal petition."

Bascomb folded his arms and smirked. "Now I remember. Didn't she try something during the deer culling too? Got her face all over the local paper when we arrested her."

I nodded. If Bascomb was trying to annoy me, he had succeeded. Political correctness and sensitivity were absent from his skillset, unless this display of boorishness was a deliberate tactic. I studied him carefully. Intelligence radiated from those pale blue eyes and a type of shrewdness I had missed before. His Sam Spade act was shop-worn but calculated. I'd bet my heavily mortgaged farm on that.

My head ached and that made me testy. "Are you always this rude, Lieutenant?"

Bascomb chuckled. "You served in the army, Ms. Morgan. A sergeant no less. Not going to get all girly on me, are you? We need to discuss the victim. Mrs. McCall." He stared at my empty cup. "Any chance I could have some coffee? My sergeant can fetch it."

In my world, canines do the fetching, not female subordinates. I snapped a leash on my temper and asked. "Does your sergeant have a name or only a title?" The woman had been kind to me after my trauma, and I found Bascomb's manner offensive. Truth be told, everything about the man pushed my hot buttons.

Bascomb's lips twitched into a semi-smile. "Well, well. Sometimes I forget my manners. May I present Sergeant Avis Stone?"

She shrugged and when Bascomb bent to tie his shoe, I caught her eye and winked. "Everything's in there," I said, pointing toward the kitchen. "Help yourself. Coffee capsules, sweetener and milk. Quick and easy." I turned to Bascomb. "By the way, Lieutenant, it was Ms. McCall. Ethel never married."

"I stand corrected. Have to be careful these days. No lawsuits for sexism." He gripped the mug that Avis Stone brought and sipped cautiously. "Good.

Much better than what we get at the station. So, tell me what you know about Ethel. She lived with Mrs. Croy I gather."

"What are you suggesting? Ethel was her secretary and friend. Nothing more. She lived in the guest house."

"Hmm. Pretty plush digs for a secretary. What about Mr. Croy? Calls himself Doctor."

"Carleton? He's got a PhD, so I guess he earned the title."

He snorted at that. "Doctor or not, when a half-naked woman is murdered in her employer's bedroom, I get curious. Is he the type to interfere with the help?"

I prayed for patience. Maybe then this pest would go away. "Don't infer anything from that. Babette and Carleton are divorced and have separate rooms. Ethel held strong religious views that didn't include involvement with her employer."

The triumphant look on his face made me bite my tongue.

"Maybe you should explain that for me. Unless of course you need your boyfriend's help."

"Boyfriend?"

Another smirk by Bascomb. "Significant other, then." He held up his hand in faux penitence. "I saw the way you two acted and I just assumed… After all, I am a detective."

"Don't assume anything about my personal life. Mr. Pruett is my friend." I stood and managed to lie without showing any emotion. "If that's all…"

Unfortunately, it wasn't. Bascomb spent another thirty minutes reviewing every aspect of my day up to and including the assault. Despite repeated attempts to wheedle, bully, and cajole me, he finally admitted defeat. Try as I might, I could not identify my assailant except for a vague impression of a black clad figure.

"What about those other folks?" He studied a tattered notepad. Surely even a guy like Bascomb had joined the computer age. Smartphones or iPads were standard issue in the military. He narrowed his eyes as I relayed my meager store of knowledge. I knew Ken and Sheila, but the others were strangers to me.

Bascomb rose and signaled to his sergeant. "I'll get back to you, Ms. Morgan. Maybe the forensic boys will get something. Call me if anything should pop into your mind." He scowled. "This case is complicated, and I hate complications."

Chapter 4

I curled up in my chair and leaned back against the headrest. What a nightmare! Babette's plan to thwart animal cruelty had led to the ultimate abuse—murder. The image of that fire extinguisher and Ethel's pitiful white foot pointed skyward continued to haunt me. Ethel was never vain, but she had always taken pride in her feet. Size six. Women like me with ungainly clodhoppers envied tiny toes that fit comfortably into sample shoes. Ethel always got the best deals because of that. Then it hit me—she'd had a pedicure! Her toes were painted a fashionable shade of red that was totally unlike her. Blood red. I reached for my cell phone and stopped. Bascomb would hee-haw all the way to Richmond if I shared that tidbit, but any woman would understand. Patterns. Someone like Ethel wouldn't change her habits unless she had a damn good reason. Was that reason a rendezvous with some man?

"Feeling better?"

I leapt from my chair as Pruett sauntered toward me. Where the hell were my dogs? Some guardians they were. This was Pip's special room and Pruett knew that. How like him to be strolling around if he owned the place.

"I thought Bascomb sent you packing. Your charm was totally wasted on him."

Pruett pulled a hassock next to my chair and sat down. "I was worried about you. That cop gave you quite a workout."

Most women would have reveled in the attention. After all, he was famous, a major hottie whose deep brown eyes brimmed with concern for little old me. Fortunately, I ignored his routine and focused on the glint of amusement he couldn't quite conceal. This was the patented Pruett technique for coaxing confidences from gullible females. It explained how he got so many scoops.

"You're wasting your time, Scribe Boy. I don't know any more about the murder than you do." I gave him my own version of a steely gaze, which he cheerfully ignored.

"I'm sorry," he said. "Did I say something wrong?" This time his concern seemed genuine.

"I'm not a source, Pruett, and this crime is a tragedy, not a news story. Remember. I know how you operate."

"Forgive me. Reporters get accustomed to asking nosey questions. Crossing boundaries. Manners are a liability in my trade." He showed a set of fetching dimples. "But you're wrong, you know. Every crime is a potential story."

Thatcher jumped into my lap, allowing me to bury my face in her thick fur. I stroked her, eliciting the same throaty purrs that had soothed Pip in his last days.

"What's your angle in this case?" I asked. "Murders are pretty mundane fare for a guy like you."

He pressed his fingertips into a steeple. "I expected a human-interest piece, you know, something light for the holidays. But this has all the hallmarks of a major scoop. Quite simply, since I'm on the scene, I intend to cover it before some hack from the *Washington Post* or, God forbid, *48 Hours* muscles in."

At least he was being honest. I think.

"Lieutenant Bascomb seems very competent. I'm sure he'll solve the case rather quickly."

Pruett raised his eyebrows. It was an eloquent gesture that spoke volumes and reflected my own misgivings. Bascomb appeared to be industrious and intelligent but he faced political pressures to close the case as soon as possible no matter what. Murders in tony towns like Great Marsh were an embarrassment. Anything that affected property values or prestige was anathema to the Powers That Be. There were plenty of power players in our little hamlet—far too many for my liking.

"I could help you," Pruett said. His grin was an ingratiating display of almost perfect teeth—probably a practiced move to keep the ladies in thrall.

"Do what?"

"Investigate. Find the killer." He tapped his foot on the floor as if dancing to some catchy melody. "After all, that's our specialty, and we've done it before. Got rather good at it if I do say so myself. We're a team. Nick and Nora, Lord Peter and Harriet—you know."

Between Bascomb and Pruett, I'd had my fill of overbearing males. "Listen, Pruett. You don't get it, do you? I have a business to run, a livelihood to earn. I want to comfort my friend but that's it. No snooping or detecting."

He must have been used to rebuffs. Either that or he had a major hearing problem. Instead of reacting, he merely nodded pleasantly. "Can you honestly tell me you aren't intrigued? Finding bodies—such a nasty habit but kind of fun."

I considered a dozen crushing replies that would set him straight. Unfortunately, before I could speak, a text message interrupted me. It was a short and simple appeal from Babette. "Help me, Perri. I'm in trouble."

I leapt to my feet and grabbed my purse. "Gotta go. See yourself out."

My dogs thundered through the room heading straight for the front door. So did Pruett.

"I drove you here," he said. "Remember? My car is at Babette's."

The man was a barnacle, so clingy that I could never dislodge him. "Fine. I'll drop you off, but you can't stay at Babette's. She's upset and a snoopy reporter, even one she adores, won't help the situation."

He tilted his head. "Maybe I can help. I'm good at soothing troubled waters. Plus, you probably shouldn't be driving yet. Did it ever occur to you that Bascomb might tag you for the murder?"

"What? That's absurd!"

Pruett crossed his arms. "You found the body and you knew the victim. That moves you to the top of Bascomb's list automatically. Trust me. I know how cops think."

"No need to worry. My conscience is clear. Besides this is a personal crisis that doesn't concern me—or you." I didn't know for certain, but I suspected that Babette's plea involved Carleton Croy prima donna supreme. Bascomb was fixated on Ethel's putative lover and like it or not, Carleton fit the bill.

Poe and Keats leapt into the Suburban without missing a beat. Pruett hesitated then stepped on the running board and climbed aboard.

"Do you suppose she has anything to eat at her house?" he asked. "I'm starving."

"Ask her yourself. Better yet, there's a diner right up the road. Knock yourself out."

Pruett pulled down the sun visor and finger-combed his hair. He had great hair, thick, black and wavy. I care about personal appearance, but a primping male was just too much! For some reason, memories of Pip flooded into my mind. Unlike Pruett, he had zero vanity and scoffed at the thought of excess grooming. I bit my lip, resisting the tears that threatened to fall. Pruett had never seen me cry and he never would. Those girly tactics conveniently called "feminine wiles" were unworthy of me. I simply was not the kind of woman who tried to manipulate men.

"Getting ready for your close-up?" I asked. Sometimes Pruett brought out every snide bone in my body. He also activated latent insecurities about my own looks. Through a supreme effort of will and gritted teeth, I resisted the temptation to check out my reflection in the mirror.

His eyes narrowed as he faced me. "No excuses. I'm in the appearance business. You know that. Have to maintain a presentable façade for my fans. It's a reality of the media obsessed era."

I snorted something impolite and focused on driving and worrying. Pruett was quiet for once as he kept his eyes glued to his smartphone. Poor Babette. She was not the hysterical type but losing a good friend and colleague so horrifically would unhinge anyone. Surely even a terrier like Bascomb wouldn't suspect Babette—or me for that matter—of murder.

"Hmm," Pruett said. "Word about the murder is out on the wire services. Must be a slow news day. Of course, anything that happens within spitting distance of DC makes headlines."

I ignored both him and the posted speed limits. Traffic was horrendous, much heavier than normal for early afternoon and that ratcheted up the tension.

I turned onto Babette's street, prepared to run the gauntlet of cop cars.

Pruett wanted to say something. I could tell by the way he learned forward. Fortunately, a stern-faced trooper with a no-nonsense look approached us.

"Sorry folks. Restricted access. This is a crime scene."

I slid my driver's license from my wallet. "Mrs. Croy asked for me. I'm Perri Morgan."

The trooper consulted his clipboard and nodded. "Right. What about him?"

I was tempted to cast Pruett out, but my better nature asserted itself. "He's with me. His car is up at the house."

A gaggle of reporters in a news van pulled in behind us, just as the cop waved us through. "Go on up and park near the house. You folks be careful now."

I pulled into the garage after dodging several police vans and forensic trucks.

"Your car is at the curb," I told Pruett. "Enjoy your day."

He ignored me and hopped out of the truck. "That espresso went right through me. I need to use the bathroom."

He was quick; I'll give him that. By the time I freed my dogs Pruett had disappeared, Babette was nowhere in sight, and even the police had scattered. I knocked twice on the front door.

"It's Perri. I'm here, Babette."

The first face that I saw was her ex-husband's. He's not ugly, at least not physically, but that air of perpetual petulance renders him unattractive. The man found fault with everyone and everything—especially his ex-wife. Perhaps he saved his charm for the students of Hamilton Arms School and their wealthy parents. Carleton Croy headed the Guidance department and anchored the Theater Arts presentations as well. Several of my clients raved about him, using superlatives like "inspirational" and "empathetic" to describe him. I was hard-pressed to reconcile that paragon with the callous bully-boy I knew.

"Perri, thank God you're here!" Carleton's pristine appearance had suffered a major setback—his thick reddish hair was askew, and crumbs clung to his mustache. He clutched my arm and quickly ushered me into the library. True to form, Carleton the Anglophile called it his study.

"Babette is resting," he said sotto voce.

I couldn't help frowning. "But she just texted me a half hour ago. What's going on?"

The library door burst open, dislodging Babette, Clara, and the ubiquitous Wing Pruett. Carleton curled his lip, a familiar gesture that indicated disapproval, but Babette flung her arms around me and sobbed.

"Oh Perri! What's happening to me? The cops rounded up every one of my guests and gave them the third degree."

I understood her anguish. Finding a corpse was a nasty business especially when the body in question was a dear friend. The memory of poor Ethel's outstretched foot with its varnished nails sent chills through my body. I tried unsuccessfully to blot it out.

"Thank goodness Wing was here," Babette said. "He's agreed to advise me on how to handle the media."

I shot a venomous look at Pruett, which he totally ignored. Instead of guilt, his handsome face radiated a totally underserved look of virtue. Babette might be grateful, but I was not. I knew his game. Pruett planned to isolate her until he was able to consolidate his big news scoop and hit the airwaves. Ethel and everything about her would soon become fodder for the *Washington Post* or a sleazy tabloid.

"They hustled Jakes right into a squad car," Babette said. "Naturally I had to tell them about his behavior. That horrible blog he writes. The man is a vicious beast. Ethel had no use for the man. None at all."

Jakes! I'd forgotten all about the buttoned-down biologist on our guest list. Come to think of it, he was tall and rangy, just like the mysterious figure who attacked me. Had he murdered Ethel in the mistaken belief that she was Babette?

"You've never actually met him, have you?" I was testing my theory that Ethel had been murdered in place of Babette. True, Ethel's hair was grey, but in a darkened room, that might not have mattered. They were about the same size, and any intruder would logically suppose that the woman in the master bedroom was the lady of the house.

Babette curled her lip. "No, but I've seen his nasty little face on television. Reminds me of a weasel. Maybe a wolverine. They're oversized weasels, aren't they?" Her voice rose until it reached the upper registers. I knew all the signs: my pal was working herself into a first-class hissy fit.

Instead of calming his ex-wife, Carleton folded his arms in front of him and turned toward the door. As husbands, and especially ex-husbands went, he was worthless until it came to his spouse's bountiful checkbook. Then Professor Croy was velcroed to Babette's side.

I resurrected the soothing tones used everywhere to defuse volatile situations. "You might be right, Babette, but until we know what Jakes told the police, we're just spinning our wheels. For all we know, he may have already confessed."

Babette managed to eke out a smile.

"I'll nose around the police station and see what I can find out." That was Pruett, being helpful again. I glared at him, but Babette beamed a beatific smile his way.

"Ethel told me she had other plans this morning," I said. "What changed?"

Babette shrugged. "Sheila Sands called and wanted something. Then Ethan Torres emailed all these questions about our project. Ethel offered to stay while I ran the errands." A tear slid down her cheek as she thought of her friend. "Did she die in my place, Perri? I couldn't bear that?"

Some men dissolve when confronted by tears. Carleton went into a snit. "For Christ's sake stop the caterwauling! Grow up, Babette. Ethel's gone and that's that. She probably ran into a burglar and things went bad."

He might be right. Probably was. But that didn't explain Ethel's semi-nude body nestling between her employer's silken sheets. Some servants might enjoy a roll in the hay, but Ethel was fifty and sensible. If she had planned a dalliance it would have been orderly, scrubbed and penciled in at the right time. Ethel was no thrill seeker. Why take chances when her own home was only yards away? Then I recalled that pedicure and Ethel's big surprise.

"Ethel didn't seem like the pedicure type," I said. "Too much of a time waster."

Babette frowned. "Pedicure? Ethel couldn't stand that kind of stuff. Why?" She walked over and put her hand on my forehead. "Are you okay, Perri? You sound disoriented."

I set the scene once again, visualizing Ethel with those pretty painted toes and the lacy chemise.

"Maybe I should drive her home," Pruett said.

"You promised to scout around the cop shop," I reminded him. "Besides, I have a client coming by after supper. At least I hope she won't cancel."

"Who is it, hon?" Babette knew everyone in Great Marsh and beyond.

"Sheila Sands. She rides in the Middleburg Spring Races and she's getting her dogs ready for Westminster too. Wants to update all their equipment." I crossed my fingers, hoping that my wealthy client wasn't too squeamish after today's shock. I could use a quick infusion of cash, and Sheila had plenty of it. She was also a pretty sharp cookie who might have some insights on Ethel's murder. After all, she had been there too.

"Will you be okay?" I asked Babette, giving her a hug. "I'd stay over if it weren't for my pets."

She patted my hand and managed a wan smile. "I'll manage. But keep in touch. The cops keep going around in circles without doing much."

"For Pete's sake, Babette. The crime happened only six hours ago." Carleton was fuming, and it showed. "Don't interfere. You've caused enough trouble with your silly posturing. I forbid you to get involved."

The room grew unbearably silent after his outburst. Even the dogs sat statue-still and stared. Pruett and I locked eyes and for once we were in sync. What kind of man forbids his ex-wife to do something? It smacked of a scene from Ibsen. Victoriana at its worst.

"Ethel was my friend, Carleton, and she died in my bed. I will not rest until the murderer is found." Babette called to her dog and swept up the stairs, showing a type of dignity under fire that heartened me. I took the opportunity to beat a hasty retreat with Pruett right on my heels.

"Wow!" he said. "That was awkward."

"More fodder for your article?" I asked. "The human-interest touch."

Pruett grabbed my elbow until a growl from Keats made him rethink his behavior. "Look. You're suspicious of the press. You have reason to be. I get it. But know this—I do have standards. Solving a murder—now that's up my alley. Marital spats, not so much. Maybe we could work together instead of sparring." He looked sincere and I almost fell for it until a flashbulb nearly blinded me.

"Right on track, huh Pruett." A blowsy blonde with a camera stepped toward us. "You sure know how to work the angles. Come on, mate. Share."

That was my exit line. I broke free, called my dogs and jumped into the Suburban, leaving him and his buddy in the dust.

Chapter 5

I fumed all the way back home, hurling vile insults at Pruett and saving a few for myself. How naive was I to be taken in by his tactics when he was pursuing a story? The Internet brimmed with tales of Pruett's deceit and deception. Anything for a story. There was a duality to the man that I had seen up close and personal. He was a wonderful parent, generous partner and all-around good guy—unless a scoop was involved.

There was enough time before Sheila arrived to feed and brush Zeke and the rest of my pet parade. As usual, tending to the animals soothed my spirit and put things into perspective. They surrounded me in a furry embrace that made everything worthwhile and minimized the trauma of the day.

I did a rapid course correction when Sheila arrived. No more mooning over the past. This was business. Dollars and cents. In addition to being an admirable person, Sheila had the good fortune to be happily married to Ellis, an octogenarian moneybag who funded all her pursuits enthusiastically and without complaint.

"I wasn't sure whether you'd be up to it after today," Sheila said. She parked her super-charged Range Rover Autobiography and hopped out with a vitality that belied her sixty some years. Sheila had kept both her figure and her sense of humor intact. Standing nearly six feet tall didn't hurt her one bit. Not many women of any age could parade around looking fantastic in a tweed hacking jacket, cream jodhpurs, and thigh high boots. Sheila could and did. "I'm still recovering from the shock myself."

I shook my head and waved Sheila inside. "You can bring Cecil in too," I said, motioning to the giant beasty in the back seat. Might help us with our measuring."

Sheila opened the hatch, pushed aside her mountain bike and coaxed the Ridgeback out. "He's kind of shy for such a big boy. Scared of his own shadow half the time." She gave Cecil a nose kiss. "Some lion dog! Of course, he's still a baby."

"Hey, you bully," I called to Zeke who was hanging over the fence with a malevolent gleam in his eye. "Pick on one of your own kind for a change." The last time Cecil visited me, Zeke had thoroughly terrorized the poor pup. It was apparent from the way the dog slinked toward the house that he vividly recalled the incident.

I patted the side of the Range Rover. "That's some snazzy vehicle you've got there, lady. What color is it anyway?"

She shrugged. "They call it Madagascar Orange; can you believe? Ellis was worried that my old heap would collapse and die at one of the shows. Plus, this snazzy number is great for pulling the horse trailer. At least they'll see me coming."

After we shared a laugh at the absurdity of the situation Sheila leaned down and hugged me. "Don't be brave on me now, Perri. You're not that tough. Poor Ethel. Bashed in the head by a fire extinguisher!"

She didn't ask for details. Sheila was far too refined to pry, and besides she didn't have to. I willingly spilled every second of that horrific experience.

"I never got near the body," Sheila said. "The cops cordoned off the entire area before the meeting started."

"So, they never questioned you at all?"

"Not really. Just took my name and license number and sent me packing. I didn't fight them, truth be told. They wouldn't even say who the victim was. I figured Babette finally had enough and clobbered Carleton." Sheila ran her fingers through her shoulder length silver hair. Make no mistake. It was platinum, not granny grey, and Mrs. Ellis Sands looked like a million bucks. Correction several hundred million bucks.

"I was all set to offer Babette a stiff drink and the name of a great attorney. Carleton started playing her for a fool as soon as they got married. He's even worse now." Her expression told me that Sheila was only half-serious.

"I got the full treatment," I said. "That Lieutenant Bascomb made all kinds of aspersions about Ethel and a purported love triangle with Babette and Carleton."

Sheila gave a loud, unladylike hoot as she visualized the scene. "Ethel had more sense than that. Besides, I doubt that Carleton can handle one woman, let alone two. He's such a prissy guy. Having great equipment doesn't count if you don't know how to use it."

I ignored the equipment comment and shrugged. "You'd be surprised how many women consider him a cross between George Clooney and the Dali Lama. More to the point, something made Ethel strip right down to her chemise. I can't for the life of me figure that one out. Come to think of it, Ethel wearing a chemise seems weird too. She was more the sturdy cotton type. Haines all the way."

Sheila grinned. "Honey, people wear all kinds of really weird stuff underneath their clothes. Gives them a sick thrill. Think of all the uptight guys wearing ladies' unmentionables. Remember, I was an ER nurse before Ellis rescued me. Ooh. The stories I could tell you."

Ethel was no weirdo and she was entitled to her little secrets just as we all were. No one knew that I slipped on Pip's graduation ring from Cornell every night before turning off the lights. It helped me to sleep almost as if he were holding me again. It was a harmless ritual, but some might think that was strange too.

Sheila spoke gently to her dog and stepped inside the house. "Maybe that guy in black held her at gunpoint or ripped her clothes off."

Once again, I shook my head. "Doubtful. Her things were neatly folded on the bench in front of Babette's bed. Just what you'd expect of Ethel. She was such a sensible person." I suddenly recalled the pedicure. Sheila raised her eyebrows when I mentioned it.

"That's weird. Ethel once told me what a waste of time pedicures were. That entire Mani Pedi craze made her sick. Downright foolishness she called it. Doesn't sound like her at all—unless a man was involved."

Sheila was a great believer in the power of sex to transform both men and women. Her husband was well into his eighth decade, a sensible, belt and suspenders kind of guy who wore starched shirts, French cuffs and bespoke suits every day, even on weekends. That didn't deter his wife from reading lurid romance books and dreaming. Despite advancing age and immeasurable luxury she still yearned for a steamy love life. Personally, I was ambivalent. Until I met Pruett, I neither had nor wanted physical contact with any man but Pip. Still, I made a note to check with Babette. She would know if any hanky-panky had occurred by checking the sheets. The forensic team had already removed almost everything from the bedroom, but knowing Babette, she would still find out.

"I guess we better get down to business," I said to Sheila. "Let's check your inventory and see where we stand." We spent the next hour discussing show leads, collars, shampoos, and other canine paraphernalia, then switched over to equine gear. Sheila loved Rhodesian Ridgebacks, a brave, formidable breed that suited her just fine. For important dog shows, she employed a professional handler but at local events often did the honors herself. Despite her husband's strong disapproval, Sheila was also an accomplished equestrian who still rode her gelding during competitive shows in the area. Like many riders, she had taken her share of nasty spills. In her one concession to Ellis, she no longer participated in "eventing," the equine equivalent of the iron man challenge, which consumed three days and included dressage, show jumping and cross-country.

Sheila rubbed her hands together. "I admit it, the thought of Cecil winning or even entering Westminster excites me. An impossible dream, sort of like me making the Olympic equestrian team." She grinned. "Still. Ellis and I will be in the stands cheering him on if that miracle happens. That's why I want all his gear to be perfect."

In her case, perfection added up to a tidy sum. I finalized the order and walked Sheila out to her snazzy new ride.

"Is that your latest passion—mountain biking?" I pointed to the grey metal beast nestled in the back of the Rover. "Pretty posh. You better keep it cleaned though. Rust is a bear to get off once it starts."

"Oh that? It's a Fezzari Solitude—does everything but breathe for me. Only the best. You can thank Ellis for that one too. You know what a snob he can be about anything Italian. At least it helps keep me in shape." She opened the hatch and gently helped Cecil into the back. "Come on, you big baby. By the way, Perri, if you hear anything about the murder let me know. I love mystery books and I'm pretty good at solving every one that I read." Sheila sighed. "Let me know about the arrangements for Ethel too. I don't know what Babette will do without her. Ethel was the stabilizer in that household."

* * * *

I spent the rest of the evening working feverishly on my projects. Between the belts and Sheila's order, my finances were looking up for a change. Pip had left me comfortably fixed but I had to work—needed to—to stay sane. I owed it to him and to my own self-respect. I'd lucked into my business. My foster dad did leatherworking as a hobby, but I took an interest in it and got pretty good. Then after college I apprenticed with a leathersmith and branched out from briefcases to custom pet products. Pruett knew better than to expect some sad Orphan Annie tale from me. My foster parents were good people who tried their best. I joined the army out of high school, went to college on GI benefits, and forged a career for myself. Solid and respectable. Nothing dramatic, but very satisfying.

It was peaceful with Poe and Keats stretched out on the floor snoring lustily while I worked the leather into shape. As I sewed the grips, something Sheila mentioned nagged at me. The police corralled her soon after she entered Babette's place, but Jakes had been on the premises too. Bascomb hustled the biologist into a squad car soon after I'd discovered Ethel's body. That suggested Jakes had roamed free for some time, and could well have been my assailant and Ethel's murderer.

Bascomb would laugh at me if I tried to pry information out of him. Babette was probably unavailable, sleeping with the aid of our friend Ambien. There was only one person who might have the answer and even though we were a couple, I dreaded the very thought of calling him. *Don't be a wuss. Act like a professional not a silly little girl.* I grabbed my cell and dialed Pruett's number.

* * * *

Babette and I met bright and early that next morning at the local patisserie. It was formerly a coffee shop that had been sold, Frenchified, and renamed with prices to match. Babette loved it, particularly the croissants and the casual elegance of the décor.

"You look tired," I said, watching her closely. Babette's flawless complexion was splotchy, and her swollen eyes suggested a restless night. "Maybe you should go home and get some sleep."

"Forget it. You wouldn't win any beauty pageants yourself, Missy. Besides, the cops and press are still crawling all over Ethel's place. Who can sleep with that going on?"

I tried not to appear anxious but every time the door opened, I glanced up in case Pruett arrived. He had answered right away last night, promising to join us for breakfast. He sounded amused but slightly sardonic as if he was expecting my call. That generated a storm of self-doubt and humiliation that disrupted my otherwise tranquil evening. Sleep eluded me until very early in the morning.

Nothing escaped Babette. She noticed everything especially when it concerned me. "Waiting for someone, hon?"

I levelled a ferocious glare at her. "Sarcasm doesn't become you. Pruett said he'd join us and I was just checking. After all we have a lot to do today."

Fortunately, just then he sauntered into the café looking casual, elegant and undeniably hot. Some men could pull off wearing shades, jeans and a black turtleneck without looking pretentious. Pruett was one of them. Lustful looks by women of all ages validated my opinion.

"I'm so glad you could make it," Babette said. "Perri was afraid you'd blow us off for some big story."

There was no sense correcting her once she got started. I remained silent and concentrated on the menu.

Pruett kissed the top of my head and turned to Babette. "How are you coping?" He touched Babette's hand. "I know what it is to lose a friend."

That show of sympathy opened the floodgates. Fortunately, Babette's sobs were subdued, lady-like affairs that generated a minimum of tears. Since our table was in a secluded spot, no one noticed that anything was amiss.

"What was she like? Ethel, I mean." His question seemed innocent enough. Pruett didn't know Ethel at all and apparently neither did I. My impression of a prim, conservative matron who doggedly did her duty had obviously missed the mark. If she led a secret life, I knew nothing about it.

"Ethel?" Babette asked. "She was dedicated. I mean, hardworking and loyal. I trusted her."

He leaned forward. "What did she do for fun?"

That stumped me. I had never associated Ethel with the word fun before. She seldom drank and railed against smoking and drugs, even aspirin.

"She loved organic gardening," Babette said, "and crocheting. Ethel was a champ with a needle and thread. And of course, she loved animals. That's why I'm going ahead with our campaign."

"Campaign?" Pruett crossed his arms and waited. I knew the answer even before Babette spoke.

"Why, our stop the eviction campaign of course. Cavalry Farms. You know how close it was to Ethel's heart, don't you, Perri?"

I smiled wanly and sipped my espresso.

"What about men?" Pruett's eyes hardened as he leaned in for the kill. "Your friend was interested in someone—a man or woman. Otherwise she wouldn't have been found that way."

"Remember the pedicure too," I said, "and that bright toenail polish."

Babette gripped the arms of her chair. "I don't know. I just don't know. Ethel never mentioned her private life at all. I thought she didn't have one."

Pruett and I locked eyes. This time I took the lead.

"How come Jakes got in yesterday but Sheila and the others got stopped? Our meeting was supposed to start at ten. The cops nabbed him not long after nine."

Babette shrugged. "That mangy critter probably sneaked in. I never even saw him 'til the lieutenant dragged him out."

That gave me a new and most unwelcome idea. Ethel and Jakes... that might explain why he arrived so early. The same thought must have occurred to Pruett.

"Did Ms. McCall get along with Jakes?" Pruett tried his nice guy grin again.

"Certainly not!" Babette's cheeks flamed. "We both loathed him. Have you read that horrible blog he writes?"

"*Bag It*? I researched it before I came here." Pruett cleared his throat. "Graphic. Dr. Jakes is a big proponent of the second amendment. Loves hunting, apparently."

Babette snorted. "He's a slimy piece of trash and my number one suspect. Ethel probably told him off and he flew into a rage." She leaned toward Pruett. "Some men think owning a big gun makes them a stud but let me tell you. It means squat when it comes to the bedroom."

The bedroom. The grisly murder scene was something that would haunt me for the rest of my life. I would never forget Ethel's neatly folded clothes, the vibrant hue of her nail polish, and the deep dark stain of her blood. The weapon was so mundane—a fire extinguisher for crying out loud! The police call it a weapon of convenience, something the killer found and used for his purposes.

I turned to Pruett. "I don't suppose you found out anything from the forensic evidence? Bascomb was tight as a clam when it came to sharing."

Pruett cocked his head in an insufferably smug pose. "Bascomb wouldn't tell but the coroner's staff had no problems sharing." He crossed his arms. "They're pretty certain that those sheets were clean. No trace evidence to speak of. Of course, that's preliminary."

Babette flushed two shades of crimson and coughed. "Surely you didn't think Ethel was—cavorting with someone in my bed? That's vile and disgusting."

Cavorting? Only Babette could get away with using such an archaic word but somehow it fit. I applied the mental brakes and recalibrated my view of Ethel. Her inner life had obviously been at variance with her public façade. I had to sweep aside my biases and visualize Ethel as a normal woman with needs and desires.

I heard Pruett snickering and glared at him. After all, Babette had suffered a tremendous loss. Contempt was unkind even from a jaded character like him.

"Anything else?" I asked. "Fingerprints on that fire extinguisher?"

Pruett cleared his throat and got serious. "None. They're just kicking around a few theories. Nothing big."

I swallowed before asking. "It was the murder weapon I presume?"

Babette clutched her throat as Pruett nodded. He was hiding something; I could tell by the way he averted his eyes. Apparently so could Babette. She leaned across the table and grabbed Pruett's wrist.

"Tell us. I need to know."

Pruett looked at me and I nodded. "Frankly Babette, they wonder if someone killed Ms. McCall thinking she was you. After all, your house, your bedroom. It makes sense."

My friend bit her lip but didn't falter. "Go on."

"Look. You're an activist and that comes with risks. Calling folks murderers—that's strong language, the kind that can lead to trouble."

I knew that Babette received death threats in the past along with some very unsavory warnings. Ethel handled everything. She had once shown me a thick file neatly clipped and labelled "negative press." Had Bascomb already confiscated it or was it still nestled in Babette's ornate desk drawer?

"Bascomb has the file, I suppose." I kept my tone neutral.

Babette shook her head. "Naturally. But if you're interested, I have copies of everything on my computer. You know how efficient Ethel was." Her voice broke when she said her friend's name. "I'll pull it up on my laptop. It's in my car."

After she trotted off, I cornered Pruett. "Okay. What's the rest of the story?"

Judging by his stony expression, Pruett had aced inscrutability 101 in Journalism school. Fortunately, during my stint in the Army, I learned a thing or two about interrogation techniques myself. I waited patiently, folded my arms and stared him down.

"Geez, Perri, you're a hard case." He looked around the room before answering. "Okay. I heard the cops talking about Babette's ex. Apparently he's quite a player around town."

"Carleton? I don't believe it. He's such a whiner. No woman would have him, especially Ethel."

Pruett shrugged. "I only know what I heard. Actually, I plan to nose around that school he teaches at and see what I can learn. Ella goes there you know. Pre-school. Maybe I'll attend the next parents' partnership meeting." His smile was close to a smirk. "You can go as my guest if you want to. Wednesday. Unless you're afraid to be alone with all those vacuous people."

Rather than smack the sneer off his face I reversed course. "Thanks. Sounds like fun. Count me in."

"On what?" Babette rejoined us, clutching her laptop. It was the latest ultrathin snazzy model from Apple with every possible enhancement. Just seeing it activated a raging case of computer envy. My old desktop barely sputtered through the day.

"Are you two plotting something?" Babette's inner radar had zeroed in on me. I'm a poor liar and an abominable poker player. I pretended to tie my shoe to hide the guilt that suffused my face.

"Nothing. Pruett was discussing Ella's education. Did you find that file?"

She nodded. "It goes back five years or so. Back to that deer massacre."

We refreshed our drinks and set to work. Fortunately, the patisserie was deserted, although with Pruett around that probably wasn't an issue. The hostess, a normally sensible woman, sidled up to him and shyly requested an autograph. He handled it well—just a touch of noblesse oblige—scribbling something on her order pad that made her blush.

"Does that happen often?" Babette asked when she left.

He grinned but didn't answer. I got the message anyway. Pruett was a hot guy and what passed for a celebrity in the nation's capital. The *Washingtonian* had twice tagged him as the sexiest man in the city although competition for that title was pretty slim. Some wag or another once described DC as Hollywood for ugly people, a place filled with powerful men and a few serious women, most of whom wouldn't win any beauty prizes. I gave Pruett a sideways glance while he was hunched over the computer. I had to admit that he was a babe, possibly too much of one for a simple soul like me. Babette chided me, suggesting that a competent therapist could exorcise those doubts. My response was tart and to the point. I wasn't the type of woman who attracted a swarm of men. I didn't need or want that. Maybe in time things would change but until then I was content with Pruett, and the love of my pets and friends.

"Most of these threats are childish," Pruett said, "not to mention anonymous. You sure stirred up a hornet's nest, Babette. Lots of hunters got upset. Gun rights people too who said they don't even hunt."

Babette sniffed. "Half of them weren't even residents. They were yokels from God knows where who used our little community as a killing field."

I thought of my clients and neighbors most of whom were good though misguided people. When it came to anything that threatened the second amendment even peripherally, they went ballistic. Babette's intentions were noble, but her tactics were often scattershot and disruptive. Too often my kindly friend led with her heart and not her head.

"Does Ethel have any family?" I asked. "Nephews, nieces? She never mentioned anyone that I can think of."

"Not really. I think she has a niece somewhere in the Midwest. Chicago maybe. It probably doesn't matter anyway. Ethel didn't have much to leave anyone."

Pruett's ears pricked up when he heard that. "She left a will, I suppose."

"Sure. Carleton and I witnessed it. Ethel left a copy in our safe. Lieutenant Bascomb wanted it but I refused. Let him get a warrant."

That earned her a big smile from Pruett and a fist bump. "Way to go, Babette. Cops should follow the rules."

Apparently, those rules didn't apply to nosey journalists seeking a scoop. Pruett had shown more than once that he had no problem pushing the limits in pursuit of the first amendment, or his version of it.

Before we left, I had one more issue to cover. Pruett ignored my hints and refused to leave until Babette and I did. That left me no alternative.

"Ethel said she had a special surprise for you. Any idea what it was?" I asked.

"No. If it was something in her house the police haven't mentioned it. They took almost everything in my bedroom and packed it up." Babette's eyes narrowed. "Crime scene evidence, they called it. They even pawed through my closet. Very creepy."

Pruett's eyes got a peculiar glint in them that convinced me he was on to something. Something he didn't intend to share with us.

"Let's make a pact," I said, as sweetly as I could manage. "We work together on this and share our findings. Ethel deserves that much."

Chapter 6

That weekend was a busy one for Creature Comforts. I crated my dogs, loaded the Suburban and motored out to Northern Virginia. My goal was strictly business. Although I had a number of private clients, show fanciers and their four-legged charges were the real heart of my business. Dog and horse shows brought out both in abundance. Sunday promised to be even more intense. I promised to staff the rescue booth at the Culpepper horse show in addition to displaying my own products.

I had an ulterior motive as well. Many locals from Great Marsh attended the show both as exhibitors and fans. Typically, they stopped by my booth, cruised the aisles, and exchanged gossip. I knew with certainty that although their horses would be topic number one, Ethel's murder would be a close second. To reinforce that theory, I posted a picture of her with "In Memoriam" prominently displayed.

Soon after I switched on the lights, Becca Tate, a veteran show competitor, barreled through the door. "Perri! Save my life! I need a new bridle ASAP." She glowered at her mount, a gorgeous bay gelding with a jaunty air. "Christopher chewed it to pieces going after a mare. Just what I need before a big show."

"No problem," I said. "Give me a minute and we'll have you set."

"Great! Pay you as soon as I get out of the ring." She swept out the door and vanished into the throng surrounding the competition. Becca was a stalwart, always reliable and a soft touch for any animal cause. She and Ethel had devised our strategy for the farm protest and I hoped she had information that might lead to the murderer.

The pace of my day rapidly accelerated with doting parents studying my fanciest equipment, children shopping for the family pet, and harried horse people searching for consolation. A few equine boosters stopped in to order bridles, halters and the like. The season was heating up in central Virginia and nobody wanted to be caught short.

Some of my customers mentioned Ethel but most looked away from her photo in either guilt or dismay. I forgot about Becca, until almost two hours later when she tapped my arm.

"Here. Let's take a break and sip some tea." My friend wore the satisfied smile of a winner. Christopher, her wayward charge, had acquitted himself well in the ring and that meant professional creds plus a handsome bonus from his owner. My near neighbor, a pet feed vendor, agreed to watch Creature Comforts while I took a break. Keats and Poe stood guard with her.

"Whew! Everyone's running wild today," I said. "By the way, congrats on your win."

Becca grimaced. "I'd feel even better if Ethel were here to celebrate."

"You got to know each other really well, didn't you?"

She reached into her pocket for a tissue and dabbed her eyes. "I called Ethel that morning, you know. Told her I'd be late but to save me a seat."

"Called her? What time was that?"

"Seven-thirty. Both of us are—were—early risers."

Silence is not only golden. Many times, it can be a very effective tool. I squeezed Becca's hand but said nothing.

"Ethel was so excited," she said. "Couldn't wait to spring her surprise on Babette."

A cold chill swept through me. "Surprise?"

"Yeah. Didn't she show you?" Becca staunched a flood of tears with yet another tissue.

I shook my head. It was the best I could do under the circumstances. After taking a deep breath, I finally spoke. "You know when I found her, she had already passed. It was horrible…"

Becca hugged me. "Oh Perri, I'm so sorry. I should never have brought it up."

Another deep breath fortified me. "Tell me. What was this big surprise? It may help explain things."

"You'll think it's silly, but Ethel had a fun side too. We found a horse costume on sale in one of those Halloween shops in DC. She bought it to wear for Babette's event. You know, to make a point but get people laughing too."

I now knew why Ethel had shed her clothes and folded them neatly. Nothing sinister. No sleazy components. She'd planned to surprise Babette and make her happy. That explained a lot, but it didn't address the central question: who murdered Ethel and why.

"You had a pedicure too, I bet."

She cocked her head as if I were speaking Urdu. In Becca's world, horses got their hooves attended to, but serious riders did not. Clearly, she had no idea what I was asking. I felt obliged to fill in the gaps.

"Ethel had recently had a pedicure," I explained. "I saw her toes when I found her, and it seemed so unlike her that I wondered if some guy was in the picture."

"Not that I knew." She lowered her voice. "Ethel—she was a good friend, but Lord knows like most of us she wasn't perfect. Her own life was pretty tame. That's why she poked her nose into other people's business a bit too much."

"Really?"

Becca looked around before answering and clutched her tissue. "She didn't mean any harm. You know how it is. I feel like a heel even mentioning it. Besides everyone suspects that crazy biologist Glendon Jakes. I've had a few run-ins with that guy and believe me, he's got some screws loose."

We exchanged a few more words then returned to work. Becca rewarded her mount with a handful of carrots leaving me in peace to hawk my leather wares.

* * * *

Sunday horse shows had a different rhythm—slower, less frantic and more family oriented. For me, they simulated an almost religious experience as well as a competition. The array of equine beauty, brains, and body types can soften the hardest hearts and change scoffers into believers in a higher power.

The Creature Comforts booth was packed by noon with an eclectic blend of breeders, riders, trainers and sightseers. There was no way to predict which items would be in demand but on this day, my custom braided bridles quickly sold out.

I bent down to restock supplies and when I whirled around, there stood Pruett holding the hand of an adorable tyke.

He didn't look one bit like your average suburban dad—not in head to toe leather. I suppressed all carnal thoughts and focused on his daughter instead.

"Ella," I said. "I missed you." The child jumped into my arms and hugged me.

"You know how she loves animals," Pruett said. "She wants a horse more than anything, but her mom vetoed the idea. Too risky."

I had heard that line before and, in most cases, it was a convenient fiction. Ella's mom was a celebrated photojournalist, probably too busy or selfish to contend with the schedule that an obsessed animal lover generated. I bent down and signaled my dogs. "How about giving Keats and Poe a treat, Ella? It won't spoil their lunch."

Pruett moved closer to his daughter and gingerly patted Poe's silky head. I didn't move a muscle. The touching father-daughter tableau revealed a different side of the man, one that continually surprised me. His devotion was real, not the feigned interest I'd observed from far too many weekend-only parents. How easy it was to judge someone by appearances instead of actions. Ella was a beautiful child, the recipient of gorgeous genes from both her parents. Her long dark hair was thick and curly, and her eyes were a vivid shade of blue. Even better, she was a sweet, unspoiled little sprite who had crept into my heart in record time. Her pointer, Lady Guinevere, was already a Grand Champion and seemed headed for even more accolades. Her handler was grooming her for Westminster as we spoke. Pruett had adjusted to having a dog but hadn't yet transitioned to equine mania.

"This is a local show, you know, mostly hunters and jumpers. You guys can approach any of the riders and ask questions or pet the horses."

Ella was thrilled, although her doting daddy looked less enthusiastic. "Can you go with us?" he asked.

"Sorry. This is a workday for me. But hey," I spotted a bouncy blonde equestrian who had positioned herself in the aisle, staring longingly at Pruett. "I'll find you an expert guide."

Before he could protest, I made introductions and sent them on their way with his escort gabbing a mile a minute.

"She'll owe you her life," Becca said. She had slipped in behind a determined couple tugging a child. "Isn't that the famous Wing Pruett? Girl, you sure hit the jackpot there."

I laughed. "The one and only. He's working the story about Ethel's murder and when anything involves his job he bears watching."

She sighed. "Watching him is no problem."

"I noticed."

"You're not fooling me, Missy. Acting so cool. Besides, looking doesn't mean you have to buy or even sample the merchandise. Right?"

I knew better than to argue. Equestrians are a tough breed, as tenacious as the horses they partner with. Besides, Becca had a point.

"Can I get you anything else?" I asked her.

She clutched my arm. "I almost forgot. Jumpers have switched to ring five and you'll never guess who has his horse entered."

"Not my day for quizzes."

"Glendon Jakes! His mare Cleopatra is already a champion, even if he's not."

My throat went desert dry at the news. Defying all odds, the prime murder suspect had miraculously wandered into my world. I heard opportunity knocking and answered its siren song.

"Watch my store. Please." I can beg with the best of them when the need arises.

She narrowed her eyes. "Perri Morgan, you're up to something. Spill it or I'll walk out."

Sometimes honesty is the best policy—particularly when it's the only option. I swallowed twice to calm myself and hoped against hope that Pruett was under control.

"Jakes was roaming around the day Ethel was killed." I shrank from saying the word murder in front of Becca. It was a cruel, harsh term that no friend needed to hear. "The cops dragged him off for questioning but let him go. I'm not satisfied."

She did a double take. "Could he be the one?"

"Maybe. Either way I want to find out. I owe it to Ethel." I patted Becca's shoulder and sped off before she could stop me.

* * * *

As luck would have it, arena ten was halfway around the fairgrounds. I jogged toward it while dodging excrement, gawkers, and competitors. I arrived just as the first contestants entered the ring.

Jakes was hard to miss. He was taller than most and as rangy as the mare he paraded around the ring. According to the program guide, she was Cleopatra, a golden palomino beauty with a commanding show presence. I had to admit that even Jakes looked respectable in formal show garb. To the uninitiated, he appeared to be a gentleman.

"Looking for a change, Perri?" Ken Reedy, a wizened veteran of the horse and dog circuit raised his eyebrows. "That's the one to beat today. Eight years old and already a contender."

"Wow! Her rider looks familiar too, but I just can't place him."

He curled his lip. "No comment. With the right guidance, Cleo would be an Olympic contender. Count on it. Jakes doesn't deserve her."

"Oh?"

Ken looked around. "He's got a temper, that guy. Threatened a judge when Cleo didn't win the whole shebang. Big dustup."

"Really?" No sane person who wanted to remain on the show circuit did that. It was a mortal sin that could get the owner, rider and horse thrown out of competition and permanently excommunicated. Maybe that was the point—explosive reaction to women in authority. Jakes had an ungovernable temper that exploded into threats and violence. I pondered whether or not to call Bascomb and share the news.

"Quite a sight." Those plummy tones could belong to only one man.

I gave Pruett a baleful glance. "Where is your daughter, Daddy Dearest?"

"Enraptured by what I believe you call a pleasure class." Pruett shuddered. "I decided to take a break. Besides, Ella won't stay away from you too long. She'll be here in a minute."

"Pleasure is a useful art," I said. "You might have learned something."

I hushed him just as Jakes exited the ring looking jubilant. "Be quiet for once and follow my lead. Watch his face."

Jakes was the right height and build to be my assailant, but I couldn't be sure. From what I had just heard, he also had a short fuse. Why not apply a bit of soft soap before testing that theory?

"Great win," I said, patting Cleo.

Jakes was either a top-notch actor or he had no clue who I was. "Goes toward her scores. Cleo's set for the Olympics someday."

I summoned an expression of faux awe. "Wow! Does she do jumping and hunting too?" I expected Jakes to brag about using a gun and horse to mow down hapless creatures, but he surprised me.

"She's a pureblood. I focus on hunting. Nothing too risky for her."

I faked a smile, but Pruett leapt into the discussion and seized the moment.

"Hey, that sounds fascinating. Any chance you'd agree to an interview? I'm a freelance journalist." He extended his hand. "Wing Pruett. And this is Perri Morgan."

Jakes straightened up and stared at Pruett. He didn't give me a second glance. "I've heard of you. You're a network guy. What brings you to this show?"

Deceit was apparently second nature to a journalist, at least if his name was Pruett.

"I'm officially on daddy duty. My daughter's crazy about horses. My friend here was just giving me an earful about ditching my daughter for a while. I'm always on the trail of an interesting story. Occupational hazard, I guess."

For a moment, I pitied Jakes. When it comes to his pet, any animal lover is vulnerable to predators like Pruett. All it takes is a compliment or a willing ear. Then I recalled Ethel's corpse with its beautifully manicured foot pointing skyward. My compassion for Jakes took a quick nosedive.

Chapter 7

Pruett wasn't quite so bold when Cleopatra approached him. He edged toward the railing, kept a respectable distance behind Jakes and left the honors to me. That was no problem at all. Cleo was a perfect exemplar of her breed who looked as if she had just stepped off the pages of *Horses and Hounds.* Like most kids, I'd grown to love Palominos since watching that noble steed Trigger save Roy Rogers's bacon on weekly television.

"She's really lovely," I told Jakes as Cleo nuzzled my pocket looking for treats. "Okay if I give her some carrots?"

He flinched as if I had offered poison. "I'm very particular about her diet."

"Understood. I have apples if she prefers those."

"Ugh!" Pruett said. "Pretty poor snacks if you ask me."

"Not to a horse." After Jakes nodded, I held my palm flat and fed Cleo her treat. Jakes smiled as she licked her lips and he relaxed enough for the interview to proceed. Pruett started slowly, asking innocuous questions about Jakes and Cleo's history. I studied his face, marveling at the expressionless mask that overlaid his features. Pruett gave nothing away. Not a smile or a frown.

"You say you're a biologist, Dr. Jakes? Your name sounds familiar to me, but I can't quite place it." Pruett leaned in. "*Got* it! I'm a fan of your blog. *Bag It.* Isn't that the name? A fascinating piece."

Glendon Jakes was only human. Praise from a celebrity left him tongue-tied and totally disarmed. He sputtered a quick thank you.

Pruett immediately capitalized on his advantage. "Say, weren't you on the site of that murder last week? The animal rights activist. Babette somebody or other."

"I got there late," Jakes was another facile liar. "Traffic, you know. The cops asked for my help. Practically begged for it. They're in way over their heads."

Bascomb begging? That's one scenario I would pay to watch.

"My friend was there too," Pruett said pointing to me. "Actually, she found the body."

Jakes narrowed his eyes and studied me. "Why was she there?"

I'd had enough of Pruett's sleazy tactics. It was time for some truth telling. "I'm a friend of Ms. Croy's, and for your information, the dead woman was her secretary Ethel McCall."

"Sorry. Didn't know the lady." Jakes sucked his cheeks in as if he were eating a lemon.

Pruett stepped closer and put his arm around me. "She's still quite emotional about it. I'm sure you understand." They exchanged men of the world glances that set my teeth on edge.

Pruett averted an explosion by embracing me, whispering a warning in my ear as he did so. "Go along with me, Perri. Just this once."

I should have pulled away. Should have stomped on his foot or done something, anything except savor the faint scent of his cologne and the touch of his lips. I was out of practice and out of sorts.

"Were you able to help the cops at all?" Pruett asked. "They haven't told the press anything."

Jakes thrust out his chest, peacock-style. "I gave them a tip or two. That group of harpies was bound to stir up trouble. Impinging on the Second Amendment like they do, or try to do. As for Cavalry Farms, those old nags at that farm have no business occupying valuable real estate. I'm a biologist and believe me, I know a thing or two about that. Genetic stock is important."

Pruett leaned in. "I understand that Mrs. Croy got plenty of threats, but this Ethel person was kind of a nobody." He lowered his voice. "And she was almost naked."

Jakes hooted as if that were comic gold. "That old bat? Believe me. No man would look twice at her body, naked or not."

Pruett pivoted deftly and faced him. "I thought you said you never met her?"

Bullseye! "Ugly women always join those protest movements. That's the closest they get to a man," Jakes sputtered. He lunged toward Pruett. "What's your game? You said this was about my horse."

I had to hand it to Pruett. He stood his ground even after Jakes clenched his fists. I expected a brawl or at least a shouting match. The biologist was red-faced and out of control, but the journalist appeared to be enjoying himself. Looking at them, I gave Pruett the edge. He had a black belt in some form of martial arts and I'd seen him in action before.

An unlikely peacemaker arrived on the scene and immediately diffused the tension.

"Daddy! Where have you been?" Ella Pruett, accompanied by several other little girls, grabbed Pruett and hugged his waist. "Oh!" She ran up to Cleopatra and held out her hand. "She's beautiful."

The mare obliged by nuzzling Ella's hand.

"I love her! Daddy, can we bring her home?"

Pruett's horrified expression was priceless. I enjoyed watching him squirm, but I had to intervene.

"Cleo already has a home, Ella, and Guinnie takes up a lot of your time. Ask Mr. Jakes. He'll tell you all about her."

Jakes managed a smile and bent down to speak with the little girl. "Sit over here. I'll show you pictures of Cleo when she was just a foal."

Pruett and I locked eyes as yet another side of the biologist emerged. Call me easy, but any man who loves his horse gets my vote. Provisionally.

When Pruett joined his daughter, I made my escape. He raised an eyebrow but waved me on. Ella and Jakes were so engrossed in discussing Cleopatra that they never even noticed my absence. I power-walked across the field to Creature Comforts just as Becca started to lock it up.

"Just in time, Ms. Persephone. I've got a prospective client waiting for me outside ring six and he does *not* like to wait."

She had a point—why pick a fight especially when a fat fee was in the offing? I hugged her as she breezed past me. "You're a real pal. I owe you."

The next two hours flew by as I filled orders, measured harnesses, and restocked the bins. None of my customers mentioned Ethel, alluded to Babette, or discussed Cavalry Farms, even though the memorial photo was prominently displayed by the cash register. When the show wound down at five, I signaled to Poe and Keats, and began the arduous process of loading my stock into the van. Most of my fellow vendors had vanished and I was glad for the canine company. Ethel had been struck down with an ordinary object, not an exotic weapon. Dog and horse shows were full of potentially lethal implements, a fact that made me eager to finish the task and get home. My back was turned when Keats growled, a low, menacing sound that raised the hackles on his neck. I whirled around, ready to stand my ground and fight. It was an automatic reflex, a throwback to my military training that came in handy during a physical confrontation. I was confident but not cocky—neither Wonder Woman nor weakling.

"Whoa, Morgan. Stand down. We swung by to help you." Pruett stood well behind me, staring fixedly at my dogs. Ella had no such reservations. She ran over to the Malinois with a mile-wide grin on her face and threw her arms around them. Pruett's eyes widened as if he were envisioning the dogs making a meal out of his precious child.

"You finished your interview?" I asked.

His smirk returned. "Our wayward biologist clammed up and left the area in a huff. Apparently, my legendary charm deserted me this time. Go figure."

I'm not too proud to accept help even when it comes with strings attached. Pruett obviously saw the shows as a conduit to Babette and a source for Ethel's grisly murder. How else to explain his show of interest and sudden appearance? I pointed toward the boxes. "Thanks. Just grab one of them. Maybe Ella can watch the pups for me."

The little girl clapped her hands. "Can I, Daddy? Please."

Pruett was an easy target. He obviously adored his daughter and would give her anything. "Okay. But be careful."

We emptied out my stall and dismantled the booth in record time. The sunset was magical, a multi-colored tribute to the master painter of the universe. Pruett and I both stood there savoring it until one of the security trucks circled around and asked us to leave. I whistled for the dogs and slid open the door of my van. Pruett put his hand on my shoulder. "Wait a minute, Perri. Ella and I are starving, and I'll bet you could use some dinner too. Come with us to Applebee's." A flush crept across his cheeks. "It's Ella's favorite place, as you well know. I promised her."

I bent down to face Ella. "You have good taste. I love Applebee's too, Ella, especially their boneless wings."

"Yum," she said.

"We'll do it some other time. I have to get home and feed Thatcher and Zeke. You know how they get when they're hungry."

"Just like kids," Ella said.

"Exactly." The idea of a pygmy goat had always fascinated the little girl, prompting a flood of questions that alarmed her father. Pruett had no desire for a goat to spoil his elegant Georgetown address.

Pruett finally intervened, playing the daddy card. The contrast between his typical sardonic manner and stern parental pose was highly entertaining.

"Time to go, Ella. I can taste those wings even now."

I nodded and bid them a final good night.

* * * *

Babette was waiting for me when I got home, and she was wired. A mournful tune by Adele blared from the car as my friend and the loyal Clara swayed to the music.

"You're late. Where in hell have you been?" Her voice quaked when she spoke.

Babette was close to tears and to my surprise she tossed a cigarette butt out the window. She'd quit that noxious habit three years ago, or so I thought.

"Calm down. Culpepper shows were on today and yesterday. I told you. Remember?"

She covered her face with her hands and sobbed until I fished a tissue from my backpack and handed it to her through the open window.

"Here. Blow."

"Forgive me, hon. I'm so frazzled I can't think straight. This nightmare turned me into a big witch."

I opened her car door and coaxed her out. "You? Never. Come on. I have some wine in the fridge from that Virginia vineyard you like so much." I felt rather than saw Zeke's evil grin emanating from his enclosure. "Tell you what. You feed the dogs and Thatcher and I'll tackle Zeke. Then we can relax."

Babette was a worker. Give her a task and she forgot her problems and pitched right in. In short order, my pets were fed and we were sipping wine and nibbling on cheese.

"Okay," I said. "What's up? Tell me what happened, and I'll fill you in on some very interesting developments." I expected a tale of marital discord or police harassment but that was not the case.

"My committee. They all quit."

It took me a minute to process what she said. "You mean the Save the Farm group?"

Babette sniffled. "They think I did it, Perri. Can you believe that? I've known those people for years. Why would they think I'd hurt anyone, let alone murder Ethel?"

That puzzled me. Babette was many things but anyone around her also knew her kind heart and generous nature. She had rescued Ethel from financial ruin, given her respectability, a job and a spacious place to live. It didn't compute. Unless...

"Maybe it's not you they suspect." I kept my voice neutral and spoke quietly.

"You mean?"

I nodded. "You know how small towns are. Rumors fly, especially when the victim is found naked."

Babette clasped her hands in front of her and sat quietly. I expected harsh words and a quick denial but didn't get them.

"Has Bascomb been talking to your friends?" I asked. "He's very blunt. Not the most tactful person you could meet."

At first, she smiled. Then Babette dissolved into peals of laughter. "That's absurd! Ethel and Carleton. Honey, I can tell you that when he cats around, he chooses some sweet young thing who thinks he hung the moon or an heiress who just doesn't care. Ethel saw right through him."

She had a point, one that I had no intention of arguing with. As Carleton's former spouse who still allowed him to live in her home, Babette was hardly a disinterested spectator. My strategy was to serve up Jakes as a suspect. With his unpleasant personality and perpetual sneer, he was easy to dislike. There was only one problem: I couldn't for the life of me think of a plausible motive.

"We had quite a crowd at the show," I said, "and I found out why Ethel shed her clothes. It was actually very innocent."

"What?" Babette clutched Clara in a grip so firm that the Border Collie yipped.

When she heard about the horse costume, my friend broke down into sobs. It took almost superhuman willpower to avoid joining her. A moment of levity had caused poor Ethel to risk her reputation and lose her life.

I focused instead on following the facts. "Tell me. Did Lieutenant Bascomb find that costume?"

"He never mentioned it if he did. Let's call him and ask."

I shook my head. "Not yet. That wasn't the only thing I found out."

Babette gasped when I mentioned Pruett and Ella. The news about Jakes made her choke. "That sidewinder has a horse? I can't believe it."

"Relax. He might still be a murderer even though Cleopatra is quite a charmer." I shared Jakes's comments about Ethel and Ken Reedy's warning about Jakes's temper. "Jakes knew who Ethel was, no matter what he said. But why kill her?"

Babette furrowed her brow. "It doesn't make any damn sense. Jakes hates me but that's mutual. Ethel never fought with anyone. You know how smooth she was."

Smooth? Inoffensive maybe but not exactly smooth. I thought about the complicated woman who was Ethel McCall. She was so unobtrusive that when she first moved to town three years ago, I barely noticed her. Pip met her through the no-kill shelter and invited her over for a drink. He sipped bourbon, but Ethel was strictly a diet Coke girl. Even her facial features were uniform and unremarkable. Grey hair styled in a short smooth bob, rimless glasses, and nary a touch of makeup or jewelry. I am no style setter but next to Ethel I felt like a supermodel. I pondered that for a moment. Maybe that was the point.

"How well did you really know her?" I asked. "Did Ethel ever mention her home or family?"

Babette hesitated, carefully parsing her words. "She came from the West Coast. Oregon or California. One of those states. Didn't talk much about her past but I got the idea that her ex-husband abused her."

That wasn't much to go on, but it was something. If Bascomb wouldn't keep us informed, we had to develop our own sources. I walked over to my computer and punched in Ethel's name and Oregon. A general Google search yielded absolutely nothing of interest. There were a number of Ethel McCalls, most of them elderly, others long deceased.

Babette looked over my shoulder and shook her head. "Time to bring in the big guns, hon. Try PrivateEye.com, then take a pass at the Mugshots website. You wouldn't believe the folks you see. I've got an account with both of them." She flinched when I squeezed her arm. "I feel disloyal even suggesting it about Ethel, but we have to know."

PrivateEye.com listed a number of Ethel McCalls, none of whom fit our age criterion. The Mugshots website was even more problematic. If the name was an alias, combing through that sad collection of losers was an exercise in futility.

"I give up," Babette said. "Spying on someone isn't exciting at all. It's tedious!"

She seemed reluctant to go home but I was exhausted. It took a great deal of effort to avoid dozing off in mid-sentence.

"You're welcome to stay in the guest room tonight," I said. "This weekend was rough, and I can barely stay awake."

"I better mosey on home or Carleton will be positive that I've been arrested." Babette called to Clara. "Come on little darlin.' Let's make tracks." Before opening the door, she swung around and pointed my way. "We're just spinning our wheels. Call Pruett tomorrow and get some help. No excuses."

"What about you?"

She grimaced. "Tomorrow I'm going to take the bull by the horns and go mano a mano with Lieutenant Bascomb."

Chapter 8

I seldom avoid tough choices. All my life, until I met Pip, I've had to stand up for myself. There was no one else to fight my battles and I did what was necessary in order to survive. Procrastination was foreign to me—until now. That next morning, I lagged behind doing every conceivable chore twice just to fill the time. Why did I avoid calling Pruett, particularly when the subject was business not personal? Such girly behavior was illogical and unacceptable. I detested wimps especially when I was the wimp in question. Wing Pruett had information about Ethel's murder. Plain and simple. He was an investigative reporter with all kinds of sources for heaven's sake. His motives were beside the point. I had agreed to accompany him to parents' night as part of our inquiry and his idea to work as a team had its appeal. It was not a competition between us, at least not on my part.

I called his cell, hoping that my message would go directly to voice mail. As luck would have it, Pruett answered on the first ring.

"Perri! What a surprise. I was just thinking about you." His voice was deep and sultry, custom-made for seduction. I swallowed my pride and soldiered on. "Babette and I were discussing the murder last night and we need your help with something."

"Anything. Just ask. Sometimes I think you don't realize what you mean to me. Ella spent the entire time at dinner talking about you, your pets, and Lord save me, horses." Pruett waited half a beat. "We're already like a family."

I hesitated and swallowed the lump in my throat. "She's a great kid. You're lucky to have her and so am I." That part was true. He was lucky to have an endearing child who so obviously loved him. Fortune had shined on Pruett most of his life according to everything I knew about him. If that left him spoiled, entitled, and a touch arrogant, it was perfectly understandable—unacceptable but understandable. We were working on that, and progress was noticeable. Pruett said that he loved me, and Lord knows, I felt the same way about him. It frightened me, made me want to burrow under the covers and hide.

A no-nonsense, business-like approach was called for. I summarized our concerns about Ethel and the need to do some digging. Pruett stayed silent at first as if he were evaluating the request. Against my better judgement, I tried to explain.

"Babette and I tried Google and the other search engines. No luck. We figured you might have other sources."

"You're presuming that Ethel, not Mrs. Croy, was the target. Is that what the police think now? Bascomb was sold on a grudge killing when last I spoke with him."

I hated to admit that our strategy was based on pure speculation.

"Babette is meeting with the police this morning. Maybe she'll find something out. She can be quite persuasive." I'd seen my friend worm intimate information out of the most unlikely people. Bascomb might succumb to her charms as well.

"I'll see what I can do," Pruett said. "Get me Ethel's social security number if you can and don't forget our date at Hamilton Arms tomorrow. We can stop for dinner afterwards to compare notes."

"Okay. Where should I meet you?"

"Perri—get real. I'll pick you up at six. Parents mingle before the big show and we don't want to miss that. By the way, I suggest you invent a sister or niece as a potential student. It works every time. They'll fall all over themselves to be friendly then."

I had plenty to think about after he hung up.

Long ago, I found that hard work was the best tonic for an uneasy mind. With that thought, I took Poe and Keats for a five-mile jog, turned off my cell phone, and devoted the balance of the day to crafting ten leather belts. They were an affirmation, tangible proof that I had accomplished something worthwhile, beautiful, and lucrative. The work absorbed me so completely that I blocked out every other sound. Fortunately, my Malinois were on the job. Their heads and ears went on alert as they swarmed the door. Since they didn't bark, I knew my guest was someone they knew and approved of.

Sure enough, Babette with Clara in tow swung into the driveway and bounded toward my office, tossing her hair gleefully.

"I presume you were successful," I said as she greeted my dogs and plopped down in a chair.

"Damn straight! Bascomb didn't know what hit him. I buttered him up. You know, the old feminine wiles stuff."

"Skip the preamble. What did he tell you?"

"Okay, spoilsport. First of all, he still thinks I was the target. Probably a hit man who didn't know what I looked like. Some gun crazy with a Second Amendment fetish."

I took a deep breath. Babette hadn't gotten very far with Bascomb. He was craftier than I gave him credit for.

"He has proof of that, does he?"

That deflated her high spirits. "Proof? Not exactly, but he was very confident."

"What about the horse costume?"

"Oh that. His guys seized it with the other stuff." She shrugged as if it were nothing important. By the way Babette ducked her head, splaying her fingers through Clara's shiny coat, I knew that she was avoiding something.

Time to summon my tough Army persona. "Will he check Ethel out? That's nothing extraordinary for crying out loud. Just good, solid police work. After all, she was the victim."

"Cool it, Perri. I have complete confidence in Titus."

"Titus!" It took effort to control my voice and avoid screeching. "You two got awfully chummy, Mrs. Croy. Did he ask you anything about Carleton?"

My pal's cheeks morphed from pink to crimson. "Nothing too personal. Just the general stuff. You know, how happy was our marriage, why was he still hanging around if we were divorced—blah, blah, blah."

It appeared that Lieutenant Bascomb had peeled Babette like a grape without any reciprocity at all. I took a deep breath and kept that opinion to myself.

"What about Jakes? Surely that came up."

Babette's confidence blossomed. "That was the best part of all, Perri. Get this. Jakes is a big fat fraud! Titus says Jakes doesn't even hunt. No guns registered to him either. How about that?"

I was stunned, gobsmacked, thrown for a loop. Suppose Ethel knew Jakes's big secret? He might clobber her in a fit of panic if she threatened to tell. *Bag It* was an important credential for a wimpy guy like Jakes. He had probably spent his adolescence being the last kid chosen for every sports team. Now, as the champion of hunters and gonzo gun freaks, he had the chance to redeem himself.

I was curious about Jakes's personal life too. Did he have a wife, girlfriend or both? Despite his claims, he may have been involved with Ethel. As my drill sergeant often said, still waters run deep and muddy. Ethel was a quiet one who seldom revealed herself. Leading a double life made that a wise precaution.

"Earth to Perri. What did Pruett have to say?"

I explained that he agreed to check his sources. Somehow, the subject of our date at Hamilton Arms never arose.

Babette bounced from foot to foot as she watched me. "I knew it!"

"What?"

"Pruett. He's in love with you. Don't deny it. I can tell these things. Has he asked you to marry him yet?"

A flush threatened to engulf me, but I played it cool. "You're nuts. Forget your romantic fantasies and focus on the important things. Ethel's murder. Remember?"

Babette was a SCUD missile locked on target and harder to deflect. "Your love life is important too. I've heard that he's dynamite in the sack." She smirked. "Jacqueline Parks shared a moment with him last year and she said—"

"Stop. You're as lurid as a tabloid, for heaven's sake. Privacy matters. I refuse to discuss that stuff with you." When Poe nuzzled my palm, another thought occurred to me. "Ella loves animals, but Pruett doesn't. To his credit, he's working on it though."

She fluttered her lashes, playing the coquette. "Maybe so, darlin,' but I say relax and enjoy the ride while you can. Definitely worth it."

I changed the subject to horses, something that my friend was equally passionate about. Soon Babette was absorbed in a discussion of the need for therapy horses for children and the opportunity to use our rescues for that purpose. I added my two cents' worth about my love for the beautiful Raza, an Arabian mare and current resident at Cavalry Farms. The hour passed without a single reference to Pruett and his physical prowess.

Later that evening I grew restless. Sleep eluded me, and my thoughts strayed to long forbidden subjects. *Am I lonely, horny or losing my sanity?* None of those choices seemed appealing. To complicate matters, Thatcher's throaty purrs were a Greek chorus, chanting the word *traitor*. In a fit of desperation, I crawled over to Pruett's side of the bed, grabbed his pillow and cried my eyes out.

* * * *

The next day I busied myself by doing mundane chores—things that were tedious but had to be done. It took discipline but somehow, I forced myself not to watch the clock or count the hours until six pm.

I spent more time than usual getting ready, even making the supreme sacrifice by blowing dry my hair and applying makeup. Glamour was foreign to me and always had been. I was far more comfortable in jeans and a sweater than pantyhose and a dress. Still, I told myself I was doing this for Babette, Ethel and maybe a bit for myself.

When he arrived, the glint in his eyes told me that the effort had been worth it. Pruett gave a slow, disbelieving shake of his head and smiled. "Wow! You clean up nicely, Ms. Morgan. Beautiful."

It wasn't hard to return the compliment. No leather jacket tonight. He wore a navy pinstriped suit, red tie and a crisp white shirt with French cuffs.

"What's your cover story?" he asked. "These people are pretty sharp."

I was proud of the scheme I concocted. It evoked forgotten times from my army days when I was pressed into undercover sting operations. I squared my shoulders and grinned. "I am acting as an agent for my sister who has two pre-teen girls who love horses. No names of course but that should open conversation about Carleton. He teaches junior high and above according to Babette."

Pruett nodded. There was a glint of surprise, even admiration in his eyes. "You have a talent for deception. I'll have to remember that." He edged away from my dogs and led me to his car. Tonight, in acknowledgement of the occasion, he drove a black Jaguar sedan.

"Quite a car," I said. "Jags have always fascinated me."

"What about the men who drive them?" he asked. "Any opinions?"

"None. By the way, doesn't Ella's mother attend these events?"

Unknowingly, I had killed the mood. Parental neglect was apparently a sore point between the two celebrity parents. Pruett hunkered down, gripped the steering wheel and glowered. "Monique is doing a shoot somewhere in the south of France. She's a big believer in laissez-faire parenting. I am not."

After that, I knew enough to keep my big mouth shut. In lieu of commenting I merely changed the subject. "I've never been to Hamilton Arms. Passed by it several times but I had no reason to go in. According to the website, their equestrian program is top notch. Boarding stables, riding rings, the whole shebang."

"It's impressive. Should be with what they charge for tuition. It's a Quaker school so they expect participation by parents in addition to shelling out the big bucks. Service they call it."

I closed my eyes, envisioning Pruett, or the fabulous Monique Allaire, performing mundane chores like peeling potatoes. Just the thought of it made me smile.

"Something funny that I missed?" he growled.

"Nope." A sudden thought made me bolt upright. "We won't run into him tonight, I hope. Carleton, I mean."

Pruett waved a hand in dismissal. "Already handled. Tonight is exclusively for K through six classes. Ella enters second grade this year. Now remember. Our man Croy deals with upper form students. I suggest we split up as soon as the reception starts. Women won't discuss another man with me standing there."

I agreed, since whenever Pruett appeared, women tended to forget that other men even existed. Fortunately, Babette avoided most school functions even though as a former faculty wife she would have been welcome. If she blundered into the room, our plans would be ruined. I'm not much of a drinker but I rued the fact that this event was strictly non-alcoholic. Booze, the ultimate social lubricant, has the capacity to loosen the lips of even the most reserved matron. Far easier to spark a candid discussion of Dr. Croy and his habits if my new acquaintances had a cocktail or two under their belts.

Pruett swung into the valet lane, surrendered his keys, and helped me out of the Jag. He frowned and gave the young parking attendant a tight smile as though envisioning his vehicle being savaged.

"Something bothering you?" I asked.

"That kid looks barely old enough to drive. Let's hope he doesn't take the Jag on a joyride."

Seeing Pruett lose his cool was curiously satisfying. On the other hand, I had never owned a car worth worrying about. No one runs amuck with an ancient Suburban.

"Ready?" he asked. "Remember our objective."

His arrogance rubbed me raw. I was no rube in need of handholding or stage direction. Instead of responding, I settled for a curt nod and moved briskly into the reception hall. Pruett was immediately surrounded by a scrum of fawning females led by a buxom blonde with flowing locks. As she locked a proprietary arm around Pruett, I recognized Babette's friend Jacqui Parks from last week's meeting. This was the woman who had reputedly shared a moment with Pruett. Whatever they shared must have been memorable since Mrs. Parks practically salivated on the shoulder of his Savile Row suit.

I headed straight for the punch bowl and easily faded into the background. Several women milled about the table and one of them, a petite redhead wearing thick glasses, took pity on me.

"You're Babette's friend, right? Part of the committee." She lowered her voice to conspiratorial levels. "You found her body, didn't you? Ethel, I mean."

I nodded. "Perri Morgan. We met once before at Sheila Sands's house."

She flashed a vague smile my way. Obviously, I had failed to make an impression. "I'm Charlotte Westly. Girls in grades one and eight."

Despite a feeling of guilt, I responded with my cover story. "My sister asked me to check out things in the high school for her, but I feel out of place." That part was true at least.

Charlotte lowered her voice again. "Want the scoop on what really goes on in the upper form? My husband's on the Board of Trustees so believe me, I've heard it all." Mrs. Westly's candor surprised me and I wondered if she often got the chance to dish the dirt.

I used an unassuming, tentative voice. "It's just that Penny—my niece—is very naïve. More comfortable with horses than humans. Vulnerable if you get my drift. She'll be living with me and—well one hears such dreadful things about predators in schools these days."

Charlotte nodded. "Understood. But don't worry. Hamilton has a first-class guidance department. You probably know that the head counsellor is Dr. Croy, Babette's better half—or rather former half." She sighed. "He's dreamy. All the mothers adore him. Such a personal touch. Your niece will be in good hands with him."

"He's not around much but I understand his credentials are impeccable." I sighed. "Let's hope that murder doesn't spook people. Guilt by association, you know."

Charlotte leapt to Carleton's defense. If she wondered why a relative stranger would broach such a sensitive topic, she chose to ignore it. After patting my arm, Charlotte said. "Oh that. Dr. Croy had nothing to do with it. He only joined in because of Babette. Besides, Ethel wasn't anyone important. Just a secretary. Probably a love triangle or drugs." She shrugged. "They're all over the place these days. Not at Hamilton Arms of course but elsewhere."

Duplicity does not come easily to me, but the memory of poor Ethel's corpse spurred me on. I swallowed my misgivings and focused on the goal. "It's just that I'm all alone and raising a teenager is such a responsibility without a man to help."

Charlotte took off her glasses and wiped them on a cloth she had plucked from her purse. Without thick lenses shielding them, I could see her eyes clearly. They were small and glittering with malice.

"You're in luck, dear. Lonely females, married or not, are Carleton's specialty. All shapes, shades and ages too, even ones you'd never expect. Results guaranteed. But I'm sure you know that."

My senses went on full alert. "Surely not with the children though. My niece is only fifteen."

My new pal stiffened. "Carleton has absolutely zero interest in kids. He likes money, perks and fine living. Guess Babette kept him on a pretty short leash and a man like that needed his space. Next time you see him, just ask about Hamilton. You'll see."

At that moment, a stubby man garbed in tweed, took the microphone. "Oops. There's my Lord and master," Charlotte said. "Call me." She slipped me her card and vanished into the crowd.

Chapter 9

Pruett edged over to me when the program began, all the while scanning the crowd. He wore a hunted look as if he feared being ambushed by his admirers.

"Whew! I thought I'd never escape."

I resisted the obvious and took the high road. "You don't look any worse for wear. Mrs. Parks must be a very close friend."

"Acquaintance." Pruett moved closer—too close for my taste. The faint scent of his cologne stirred my senses and aroused an uncomfortable stab of desire. I shook it off immediately. "Easy, boy."

"What about you," he asked. "Any luck?"

"Some. Let's discuss it afterwards."

Charlotte's husband droned on for far too long extolling the virtues of Hamilton Arms, its moral compass, emphasis on equine sports, and the role of activist parents in shaping their children's future. By the end of his monologue, I was prepared to embrace the virtues of tough DC schools and gang tattoos over the "Hamilton Way." Pruett stood so motionless the entire time that he was either transfixed or comatose. When the painful program finally concluded, he clutched my elbow and steered me toward the entranceway.

"Let's make tracks before someone corners us."

"I'm perfectly safe," I said. "It's your virtue that's in danger around here."

He rolled his eyes but kept on moving. The valet sprang into action as soon as Pruett waved a five-dollar bill his way.

"We're not allowed to accept gratuities," the young man said with downcast eyes.

"Take a risk, son." Pruett pressed the bill into the youth's hand.

"Corrupting the flock," I muttered, sotto voce.

Pruett stared down at me with a dazzling smile. "I'd rather corrupt you, Perri. We can skip dinner and head back to your place if you like."

Despite being a grown woman and military veteran, I blushed and turned away as heat rose to my cheeks. Why did I feel so vulnerable around this man? Relax, I told myself.

"I'm ravenous," I said. "For food. Didn't you say something about dinner?"

He shook his head and fired up the Jag. "You're no fun at all. My reputation is in tatters."

"Deal with it."

He cruised up Connecticut Avenue into Georgetown, turned on to New Hampshire Avenue, and valet parked in the Four Seasons Hotel garage. "Come on. The restaurant is right across the street."

Most of my time was spent in Great Marsh, but Pip and I had hit the DC spots for special occasions. Pruett's mouth fell open when the Maître'd at La Chaumiere greeted me by name.

"How come he knows you?"

I gave him a saucy grin and sailed into the dining room. "You're not the only one around here who likes French food. Don't be so conceited."

"Touchy, touchy. I live around the corner on P Street," Pruett said. "This is my neighborhood watering spot and I've never seen you here before. I'm surprised, that's all."

I loved Georgetown, but the upscale shops and astronomically priced real estate were far beyond my ken. Just another reminder of the vast economic chasm that separated Pruett and me.

He ordered wine and scanned the menu. "Any suggestions?"

I always order the same thing—pike dumplings, food of the gods. Pruett would scoff at such humble offerings but so be it. I am neither a gourmet nor a gourmand and don't pretend to be. In my world, meals were for sustenance, not showing off.

He pored over the menu, debating the merits of duck versus medallions of beef. The cow lost the contest.

"Tell me what you learned," Pruett said after sipping his wine.

I shared the nuggets of information provided by voluble Charlotte Westly. That made me think. Maybe I was too picky about men. Hard to believe, but to some women, creepy Carleton Croy was actually a sex symbol. As Babette would say, there must be mighty slim pickings out there.

Pruett tugged a lock of his hair as he considered the information. "Okay. Carleton is a player. That doesn't make him a murderer, especially since he's on the market now. Hell, they'd have to indict half the men in DC using that standard. We need proof and a motive. Babette has bucks, but why kill Ethel? He certainly knew what his ex looked like, so it couldn't be an accident."

Pruett made some valid points, but I wasn't about to concede that. Instead, I doubled down. "Okay. What did you find out besides the fact that Mrs. Parks is still hot for you? She told her friends all about you by the way. Highly complimentary. Top marks."

For a moment, Pruett was speechless. He lowered his eyes and took another slug of wine. "There is no bad publicity when it comes to romance. Maybe my satisfied customers will sign testimonials? Publish them in the *Post*."

Then he turned serious. "As it happens, my friend Mrs. Parks was a font of information. It seems that Ethel was a pearl of great price. She served on a number of committees attending to the tedious details nobody else wanted to do. All the virtues of an indentured servant without the cost.

"Except—Jacqui, Mrs. Parks, had some misgivings about dear Ethel. Nothing that jumped out right away, but there were unexplained shortages in some of the funds—sizable but not huge sums. Nothing that set off alarms. At the time, they chalked it up to sloppy record keeping. Now, it makes you wonder."

What was the definition of sizable? For me, five hundred dollars would be catastrophic but in their social set, thousands were no big deal. I always assumed that Ethel was a woman of modest means and few wants.

"I'll get Babette to check out Ethel's finances."

Pruett curled his lip. "No offense, but Babette? Doesn't seem like her sort of thing."

"She's a demon when it comes to money. Watches every penny like a hawk. Drove Carleton crazy. Besides, Babette is the executrix of Ethel's will and has legal status. Even Bascomb can't argue with that."

When our entrees arrived, I dug into my pike dumplings with zest. Detective work made me hungry. Unrequited lust didn't help much either. I noticed Pruett watching me with a snarky grin plastered all over his face. Pip had always applauded my healthy appetite. If Pruett felt otherwise, he kept it to himself.

"I had one of my contacts researching Ethel's background. Problem is, her records only go back ten years. Before that time, Ethel McCall was a ghost." He frowned. "If she was in witness protection we're screwed. Nobody can crack that system."

He was right of course, but if Ethel had been a con woman, she might have left traces elsewhere. Suddenly it dawned on me. Sheila Sands! Her moneybags hubby presided over a huge conglomerate that included an insurance company and a private security force. Maybe Ellis could help. He would do anything to please his wife.

"Let me think about it," I said. "I have a few ideas we haven't tried yet."

They lowered the lights and the rosy glow of candles enveloped the restaurant, bathing each table with a special splash of color. He was watching me, staring as if he had never before seen me. Pruett was too sophisticated to propose anything crude, but I knew at that moment what he wanted. I was awash in ambivalence, yearning for love, but wary of being hurt.

"Oops!" I checked my watch. "I didn't realize what time it was. Better get going."

Pruett reached across the table and took my hand. "Don't worry, Cinderella. You won't turn into a pumpkin yet. My place is right around the corner."

I looked down, unable to meet those dreamy eyes. "I can call Uber if you'd rather not drive. My pets…"

He laughed as if we shared an exquisite private jest. "Persephone Morgan that's the damnedest excuse I've ever heard. Husbands, boyfriends, kids—yes. But pets?"

"It's true," I said. "Zeke will shout down the neighborhood if I don't tend to him. The dogs have their needs too."

Pruett held up his hands in mock surrender. "Okay. I give up. Ella would never forgive me if I inconvenienced your pets." He flung money on the table and helped me with my chair.

"Wait a minute," I said. "Let me pay the tip."

"Perri, Perri, Perri." Pruett shook his head. "What am I going to do with you? Like it or not, I go old school. When I invite a beautiful woman to dinner, I pay."

I was speechless, overwhelmed by conflicting emotions. He gently ran his finger over my lips and nudged me toward the door. "We better head back to your menagerie. I can already hear that goat calling."

We rode back to Great Marsh in companionable silence, cosseted by the Jaguar's soft leather seats and a soothing stream of jazz. When we stopped at a red light, I closed my eyes and, to my abject humiliation, fell fast asleep. Before long, we were back in Great Marsh and Pruett was gently shaking my shoulder.

"Wake up, Sleeping Beauty," he whispered. "Your subjects await."

"Some sleuth I am," I said. "Sorry for sleeping. Missed the chance to review the case."

The interior light shone directly on his face. Lord, he was handsome! Most women would jump at the chance to share even a fraction of his life. What was wrong with me?

"I can make coffee," I said. "Do you have to leave?"

Pruett shook his head. "Rain check. I have some stuff to do when I get home. I'll call you." He insisted on walking me to my door, even though he flinched when Keats and Poe streaked out. Before leaving, he took my hand and kissed it. When he said my name, he pronounced all four syllables slowly and sensuously.

"Sleep tight, Persephone. You'll find out soon enough. I don't give up easily."

Chapter 10

Babette battered down my door the next morning, oblivious to Zeke's shrieks or the chorus of barks from the Malinois. I stared at the clock through sleep-laden eyes, astonished to see that it was nearly eight am. Guilt overwhelmed me. I was a bad pet mother, neglectful of their most basic needs and doomed to pay for it.

"I'm coming in," she trilled. "Are ya decent?"

I sent a prayer of thanks to St. Nickolas the patron of bad girls everywhere that Pruett was nowhere to be found. For good measure, I tipped my hat to St. Lawrence too. He was the patron saint of tanners, an unfortunate martyr who had suffered a grisly death by being roasted on a spit. Those details were way too much to contemplate early on a weekday morning with my best friend grinning down on me.

"Big night?" she asked. "I know you were with Pruett. Don't lie. My pal Jacqui told me all about it." Her smile put Cheshire cats to shame. "Here." She thrust a venti latte made just the way I like it at me. "I stopped at Starbucks on the way. Now tell me everything."

Babette plopped down on the edge of the bed and giggled. "I'll bet he was even better than they say."

Dignity and guilt don't always mix. Unfortunately, I had nothing to repent except a few licentious thoughts. "What's wrong with you," I scolded. "This isn't high school. Nothing happened. We were trying to get information—about the murder. Strictly business."

Most people not named Babette Croy would back off. My friend upped the ante. "Listen, Perri. Jacqueline is no fool and she was all lathered up after seeing him. I understand he looked hotter than hell." She took a deep breath and a gulp of espresso. "Anyway, Jacqui made absolutely no progress. She said he never took his eyes off you the whole time. So there."

Suddenly it was my turn to inhale my latte. Had Pruett really looked for me? If so, he was probably trying to escape the amorous Mrs. Parks. I forced myself to regroup and filled Babette in on the gossip. She gasped when she heard about the missing funds.

"Ethel a thief? She only volunteered at Hamilton to help me out. That woman never took a penny from me, Perri, and she had plenty of chances. It was probably one of those kleptos from the committee. Too much money, not enough to do and always bitchin' about being bored."

I recalled Charlotte Westly's beady little eyes, glittering with malice. When I mentioned her name, Babette stiffened.

"That horny heifer! What a laugh. She's always trying to seduce someone, even Carleton, if you can believe it. Everyone knows about her. They joke about getting entangled in Charlotte's Web. A little literary pun but what can you expect from that crowd."

Candor was the only possible reaction even if it wounded my friend. I respected Babette too much to lie. Evasion was pointless.

"Charlotte seemed very interested in Carleton. She hinted that he was a favorite of lots of the mothers." I lost my nerve and began to backslide. "She was probably lying. Seemed like the type."

Babette jumped up and tossed her coffee cup into the waste bin, narrowing missing Thatcher who stalked off in a huff. "Perri. How dumb do you think I am?"

"What do you mean?"

She strolled over and flung her arms around me. "Honey, I know all about Carleton and his little romances. That's why I watched the money like I did. I didn't begrudge him some fun, but I'll be damned if I'd finance it. When it got too much I called in my lawyer."

My mouth opened but no words emerged. What does one say to a betrayed wife? I was torn between shock, shame and awe.

"Did he and Ethel...?" I couldn't complete the thought

"No way! Besides Ethel wasn't his type. He never came on to you, did he?"

"Nope. If anything, Carleton avoids me like the plague." I hunched over my latte and sucked it dry. "What's your point?"

Babette squeezed my shoulders. "Money, honey. My dear ex-husband, hound that he is, finds women with bucks irresistible. Why do you think he chased after me?" She bit down on her bottom lip and preened. "Hard to believe with all this feminine pulchritude staring him in the face, he hadn't touched me in months before our divorce."

She didn't cry even though her lips trembled. In fact, Babette folded her arms in front of her and set her jaw tighter than a bank vault. I was torn between offering comfort and following her lead. I chose door number two. Anything that helped Babette to salvage some dignity was a harmless deception.

"I'm sorry," I said. Simple sentiment but vivid enough to release a flood of feelings inside Babette.

"Funny thing. It started when I got a cold. Carleton slept in the guest room because my coughing kept him up." She rolled her eyes. "Or so he said. Pretty soon, he was yapping about my snoring. And on and on. After a while I didn't even ask. Why bother? When a man doesn't want you it's fairly obvious."

As if she sensed the tension, Clara sidled up to Babette displaying female solidarity at its most furry.

"What's your plan?" I asked. Planning was her strength. It kept Babette sane.

"Life at the Croys is no Hallmark card," she said. "Hasn't been for some time. I should have kicked him out a while ago when we got divorced but I kept putting it off."

"Because of money?" I asked.

No one can snort as well as Babette. Her distain was vivid and truly world class.

"I take my finances seriously as well you know. Before we said 'I do,' my lawyers drew up a prenup tighter than a hangman's noose. Carleton got practically nothing in the divorce."

My curiosity overcame good breeding. "Why then?" I expected her to cite loneliness or even love but my pal was way ahead of me.

"Okay. Fasten your seatbelt." Babette hesitated. "Carleton has hidden talents. You get my meaning?"

"What?" I gasped at the very thought of it.

"You betcha! Why else would I keep him around? Not for his disposition, that's for damn sure. He's smart enough, but basically boring. Until you get him into the sack."

I'm not naïve but that information floored me. All I could do was gape at Babette as I tried to visualize Carleton the sex magnet, swinging from a tree branch.

Her chin trembled as she gathered her thoughts. "Guess I need to come to terms with things now that he's no longer putting out. Too bad."

Timing is everything in life. If Babette sent him packing now, Bascomb and every citizen of Great Marsh would assume that he was a murderer or that his wife thought he was. A disquieting thought popped into my mind. If Babette died would her ex-husband benefit? Asking was awkward and downright rude but it couldn't be helped. I chose my words carefully.

"Carleton can't be a suspect if he doesn't inherit."

Babette trained her big brown eyes on me. "Nope. He left our little union pretty much the way he came into it. Particularly when I played the adultery card."

"You did?"

"Honey not only did I, but I planned to name names. Trust me. None of those floozies who fooled around with my husband went unscathed." She heaved a big sigh. "Matter of pride."

I pictured Charlotte's smug face pasted all over the tabloids and the visual made me smile. Big time. As satisfying as that prospect was, it did nothing to explain Ethel's murder. Had she threatened someone, or was Ethel merely in the wrong place at the wrong time? Collateral damage as they say. Babette was a high profile hard-charging type of gal who collected foes and wore them as badges of honor. Jakes was a prime example of that, but there were plenty of others. If Carleton was a playboy, one of his sweeties might have used extreme measures to eliminate the competition. Had Ethel interrupted a murder in progress and paid the price?

"Hold on, Babette, I just thought of one more thing."

She glared at me, hands on hips, as though daring me to speak.

It took all my courage to broach the issue, but I had to know. "If something happened to you, who would inherit? You're a woman of substance after all."

My persistence paid off, but it didn't endear me to my pal. Babette bent down and gave Clara a big smooch before answering my question.

"You are way behind the curve. The cops asked me that first thing, Perri. Bascomb is sharper than you think. He's actually quite impressive. Better brush up on your detective skills if you plan to do any good."

I winced but didn't back down. "So?"

"My entire estate goes to charity—animal charities of course. The horse farm and the animal shelter especially. I named you to head up the Babette Croy Foundation. Satisfied? No one benefits from losing little ole me unless they add you to the suspect list."

That left me gobsmacked. Babette had never mentioned a foundation or my role in one before. Just another reason to wish my friend a long and healthy life! What did I know about managing a foundation? Furthermore, how many other people knew about her scheme?

Babette spoke slowly and deliberately as if I were an addled child. "In case you're wondering, Ethel knew all about it. Helped me set up the whole thing with my lawyer." Babette didn't taunt me outright but came fairly close to doing so.

I stared into space, contemplating the many sides of Ethel. Obviously, I had underestimated the woman. By blending into the scenery, Ethel had managed to escape scrutiny and remain an enigma. What else had she been up to?

"Why was Ethel at your place the day she was murdered? She told me she had other plans."

Babette shrugged. "Beats me. We had a pretty loose arrangement. The way friends do." She stifled a sob. "I cared about her, Perri. Ethel was like an older sister—wise, kind of bossy but good-hearted. She wasn't a criminal. I know it." Babette fetched a lacy handkerchief from her bag and noisily blew her nose. "If she died because of me, I... just couldn't bear it."

My irrepressible friend was a changed person, laid low by Ethel's murder. I had to do something—anything—to help her. When I outlined my plan to involve Sheila, Babette immediately brightened. Suddenly I vaulted back to hero status with her once again.

"I forgot about ole Ellis," she said, giving me a hug. "Perri, you're brilliant!"

"You're too generous," I said. "Come on. Help me with the pets and then we'll call Sheila. Deal?"

She slapped my hand and skipped toward the door with Clara by her side. "Deal!"

* * * *

Zeke gave us a hard stare as soon as we entered his enclosure. He eyed the bucket of corn and oats I carried, sniffed the alfalfa, and backed against the stall as if preparing for a fight.

"Calm down, big guy," I whispered. "Eat up and then I'll groom you." Zeke is a glutton, so food offerings mollified him somewhat. Before eating, he plunged his head in the water pail and drank lustily. When I left him, he was satiated, shiny and relatively happy. I considered it a good omen that he neither nipped, bit, or butted either one of us.

"Pip was nuts to bring that goat home," Babette said. "He eyed me like I was an appetizer."

"Just foreplay," I said. "He'll settle down once the dogs are with him." I never even dreamed of exiling Zeke. For better or worse, he was part of

Pip's legacy and I would never let him go. It would be akin to discarding Pip himself and that would never happen.

I linked arms with Babette and nudged her toward the house. "Ah forget about it. Let's bring Sheila in on this. She always has good ideas." Keats and Poe responded instantly to my whistle and trailed behind us. Clara brought up the rear.

"If we're lucky, Sheila will be home. You know how she obsesses about mysteries. Thinks she's a cross between Jessica Fletcher and Miss Marple. I'll make some espresso to go with that shortbread you brought. Looks yummy."

Babette's eyes sparkled. "I had to sneak it out of the house. Carleton pitches a fit if he sees me eating sweets. Says it makes me fat." She grimaced. "Not that it's any of his business now."

I refrained from commenting about men who played the body-shaming card. Most women were sensitive about their weight, even ones like me who had always been called skinny. Some of the most unlikely men felt entitled to comment on so-called female imperfections. It was the ultimate power game. I scowled thinking about Babette's supercilious ex-spouse. Carleton was no prize package no matter what hidden assets he might possess. To his credit, I had never heard Pruett make those disparaging comments.

"You look great and you know it," I told Babette. "Lieutenant Bascomb appreciates those curves. I saw the way he looked at you."

She flushed with pleasure. "Even at my advanced age, a compliment makes me feel good. Still seeking approval from a man, I guess."

"Big deal. That's just being human, and you my friend deserve the attention." I winked at her and led the way into the living room.

Fortunately, we caught Sheila just as she was leaving the house. After hearing our plan, she immediately agreed to cancel her appointments and join us.

"Funny thing. I've been thinking a lot about Ethel lately," she said. "Who knows what will happen if we put our heads together? The power of three you know."

My thoughts exactly. Self-restraint and discipline have always been my watchwords. No wonder I was often described as dull, reliable, nose to the grindstone Perri Morgan. I caught myself just as I reached for the cell phone to call Pruett. No matter how often I vowed that it was strictly business between us, my internal truth detector pinged a very different message. My only option was to relax and enjoy.

Sometimes my pal can almost read my mind. Babette tilted her head to the side and grinned. "Pruett really should join us. Don't you agree?"

I shrugged with as much nonchalance as I could muster.

"Call him, Perri. You have his number."

I busied myself arranging shortbread on a fancy plate. "Later. After the three of us talk."

Babette peered out the window as the dogs began a cacophony of barks and growls. "Oops. Looks like it's too late. Unless I'm mistaken, and I seldom am, the man himself just pulled into your driveway right behind Sheila." She strutted toward the door. "Guess you better make enough espresso for four."

Chapter 11

Our planning committee turned into a coffee klatch with four adults, four dogs and one highly agitated feline. Pruett captivated Sheila right away by focusing his considerable charm squarely upon her. He even feigned enthusiasm for Cecil although he kept a safe distance from the Ridgeback pup.

"Beautiful animal," he said. "My daughter is dog-crazy, so we've studied every breed. She feels the same way about horses. Takes lessons every week."

Sheila launched into a soliloquy about animal companionship and the therapy provided by horses. "They're not the right choice for everyone," she said. "Rather a lot for novices to handle but worth it."

Babette heaved an enormous sigh. "We all need love."

I leapt to my feet and played hostess in order to stave off another bout of melancholia by my friend. "Why don't we start by sharing information? That way we'll all be on the same page." I gave Pruett a hard stare. "Needless to say, this is all off the record."

Babette gave an exhaustive and somewhat exhausting account of her interview with Bascomb. Although she didn't mention it per se, her infatuation with the police chief was obvious—flushed cheeks and head tosses gave her away every time.

"No kidding," Sheila said. "I always pegged him as the village idiot. You know, Inspector Clouseau without the Gallic charm."

"Certainly not!" Babette bristled. "Titus zeroed in on the fact that I was the likely target instead of Ethel. He asked me all about my will and those nasty emails too." She curled her lip. "Believe me, he took old Jakes very seriously as a suspect, especially since the creep is a big phony too. Doesn't even own a gun!"

Pruett's eyes met mine and he nodded. I told my tale about our horse show exploits, focusing on Jakes and his angry outbursts.

Sheila leaned forward with her elbows planted firmly on her knees. "Wow! So that guy is a misogynist and a creep! Quite a combo. Too bad he's an animal lover. Normally that's such a good sign."

"Admittedly the guy's a loser but unless we find a link to Ethel, it doesn't mean anything." Pruett described our undercover operation at Hamilton Arms, clearly and concisely, omitting his encounter with the amorous Jacqui.

Once again, Sheila's mouth flew open. "Ethel a thief? Mousey little Ethel McCall who faded into the woodwork? I don't believe it."

"It kind of makes sense," said Pruett. "Ethel was the invisible woman, there but never noticed. An amiable drudge. Maybe she used it to her advantage. How many embezzlers are quiet, industrious ladies who nobody suspects—until it's too late?"

"She never took a penny from me," Babette said. Emotion mottled her normally flawless skin as she leapt to her feet and began pacing. "Those broads are a bunch of gossips. I told Perri that and it's true."

I stroked Poe's back and zoned out as they debated the pros and cons of the issue. Suddenly something new occurred to me—something that might explain the Ethel enigma.

"Maybe Babette's right," I said. "Maybe you're all right. What if Ethel wasn't a thief? Sheila said she blended into the woodwork. Remember? Someone like that hears everything because people forget that she's there. What if Ethel heard incriminating information and acted on it?"

Pruett shot a snarky grin my way. "Of course! Blackmail! That's perfect. Check out her bank balance and safety deposit box. She had to stash it somewhere."

"Maybe it wasn't about money," Sheila said. "Some people like power over others. Nothing is more powerful than holding secrets."

As the executrix of Ethel's estate, Babette had access to all her records if she chose to study them. Unfortunately, loyalty had clouded my friend's normally incisive mind. She refused to even consider anything that implicated Ethel.

I poured each of them another espresso and gingerly suggested another approach. At first there was only a deafening silence. They were a tough trio to read: Sheila, wide-eyed and excited; Babette, tense and unresponsive; Pruett, totally inscrutable.

"Think about it," I said. "We've got dual tracks here. Either Babette was the intended victim, or Ethel was. Each possibility leads to entirely different motives and suspects. I say we divide up and explore each one independently of the other."

Instead of the explosive reaction I'd anticipated, the room became tomb silent. It was uncomfortable and somewhat insulting, but I waited patiently for their verdict.

"I'm in," Pruett said. "Perri and I make a pretty good team so let's stick with that."

Babette shot me a sly look of triumph before grudgingly agreeing to do her part. "Okay. But I refuse to investigate my own possible murder. Sheila and I can rifle through Ethel's life for all the good it'll do."

"One of Ellis's companies has an internal security branch," said Sheila. "I'll put them on Ethel's past. Unless you can pry the info out of Bascomb." I visualized Sheila wearing a deerstalker cap and brandishing a magnifying glass. Not a great visual but close enough. "There's one other possibility," she said. "Maybe it was a random attack. You know, an intruder. What if Ethel was just in the wrong place at the wrong time?"

Pruett had the solution to that approach. He offered to check the police logs for reports of burglaries or robberies in the Great Marsh area within the past six months. It was a good idea although I suspected that some minion—probably female—would do the legwork for him. There was also a simpler way to get the data. If Bascomb was half the wizard Babette claimed he was, he would have already scanned the files for the same information.

The next hour was a productive one as we sketched out a plan of action. Pruett and I agreed to tackle the irascible Jakes again at the first opportunity. I fired up my computer and checked the registrants for the weekend show in Leesburg. One name immediately caught my eye—Cleopatra was competing with Jakes astride her. I hadn't rented a stall for that day, but another vendor had agreed to sell some of my products, so no one would be surprised if I were to turn up.

"I'll swing by the show this Saturday," I said. "Jakes is registered in the hunter class that afternoon."

Pruett curled his lip before I had even finished the sentence. "Hold on. Is that your definition of teamwork, Perri? I'll go too. Lord help me, Ella will be thrilled at another animal outing. Besides, that Jakes guy has a nasty temper. You might need reinforcements."

Sheila turned away, hiding a half-smile. "We'll have quite a little party then. One of my jumpers is competing." She frowned. "I'm not riding this time. Just cheering my trainer on."

Another task demanded our immediate attention. A visit to Cavalry Farms was a necessity. Who knew what that horsey crowd might know about Ethel?

"Change of plans," I said. "I'll amble over to the horse farm and chat with them. Ella might enjoy a trip too if you guys are free."

"Don't need to ask," Pruett said. "That kid will be over the moon."

I expected a reaction from Babette, but she stared out the window as if she were a million miles away. She had agreed to get Ethel's will and with Bascomb's permission, to access her safety deposit box as well. Both of these essentially personal tasks would be difficult for her. I flashed back to the time when I had fulfilled the same sad duties after Pip's passing.

"I'll go with you," I said, taking Babette's hand and squeezing it. "We can do this together just like we did before."

She closed her eyes and nodded. "Tomorrow. Let's do it tomorrow."

After dividing up our various tasks, the committee dispersed. Sheila grabbed Cecil, waved jauntily and hopped into her Rover while Pruett hovered over his cell phone.

"I just got another assignment for Saturday," he growled. "Looks like I can't make the horse farm."

"Don't worry. I'll connect with Sheila and text you if anything turns up," I replied.

Pruett narrowed his eyes and stared at me for a moment as if he were puzzled. "Okay. But be careful."

When he left, Babette doubled over with ill-concealed mirth. "Honey, you made my day. That man just got the shock of his life. Bet he hasn't met too many women who brush him off like you did. Not looking the way he does. No ma'am!"

"You're delusional. Pruett and I understand each other. That's all. We're both busy professionals, not joined at the hip." I folded my arms and glared as if that settled everything. "Now I've got work to do and you need to set up an appointment with Lieutenant Bascomb for tomorrow. Make it early if you can. I promised to deliver some belts out to Middleburg in the afternoon."

Babette saluted and sped off with Clara at her heels. Gone were her doldrums and teary rants. She was clear-eyed and firmly focused on the prize.

* * * *

Bascomb looked the worse for wear when we met him the next day. His shabby suit had seen better times and his wrinkled shirt badly needed the services of a dry cleaner. His manners could have used improvement too. Despite Babette's attempts to vamp him, Bascomb glowered at us and gestured brusquely toward the faux leather couch in his office. Perhaps he was not a morning person. More likely, he resented the interference of civilians in an active murder investigation on his turf. Either way, his days with the welcome wagon were long since gone.

"Make this quick, ladies. I have a meeting with the mayor in one hour."

Babette's dimples immediately went on display. "We won't need much of your time, Lieutenant. The bank manager is waiting to open Ethel's safety deposit box for me and I wanted to clear it with you." She preened a bit. "I'm her executrix, you know."

Bascomb's hands, larger than a Smithfield ham, blocked out the sunlight. He held them in front of our faces in a "stop" gesture. "Hold on, Mrs. Croy. Halt right there. You can't open that without a police witness and I need a court order to do so." His repressive frown stopped Babette in her tracks, but it only inspired me.

I trotted out my customer friendly techniques. "Maybe we can both get what we need. Since Mrs. Croy has a key and power of attorney, she can give permission for you to witness the contents and seize anything relevant to your investigation. No need for a warrant."

He gave me a speculative look and pursed his lips. "Why are you here, Ms. Morgan? Recall anything more about your assailant?"

My smile widened. "Unfortunately, no. I'm only here to support Mrs. Croy. You know how difficult it is to do these things."

He grunted and checked his watch. "Ms. McCall used the SunTrust down the street you said?"

Babette nodded.

In a rare gesture of cooperation, Bascomb agreed to follow us to the bank. "Make it snappy though. I'll need to inventory everything in there." He loped through the door and into his cruiser, leaving Babette and me far behind. Fortunately, her flame-red sports car was parked right at the curb.

"Titus certainly was cranky," Babette grumbled. "It must be you, Perri. He was a lamb when I met alone with him."

Babette's fragile emotional state saved her from a tongue-lashing. Normally I would have mentioned her impaired judgement where men were concerned, citing chapter and verse starting with her ex-spouse. Today, I merely rolled my eyes. Bascomb was as tough as an old Army boot, but my dear friend was too naive to sense that. Lamb, indeed!

"Let's just get this over with," I said. "You know the bank manager?"

"Darlin' when you have my kind of money, bank managers know you. That's their job." She gasped and put her hand over her mouth. "I'm sorry. That sounded bad. Maybe those stuck-up heifers at Hamilton Arms are rubbing off on me."

She swung into a space in front of the bank, right next to Bascomb's cruiser. He was slouched on the fender, scowling as usual. Come to think of it, I had never seen the man smile. Had some genetic quirk made him incapable of it?

Smiling was not a problem for the bank manager, however. His fulsome grin, a tribute to her hefty account balance, was a beacon beaming directly at Babette. With a minimum of fuss, he escorted her and Bascomb into the secure area that housed the safety deposit boxes. I stood guard in the lobby while checking my email. When the trio emerged, I got an unanticipated shock. Babette's face was ashen, Bascomb's grim, and the bank manager's positively frozen.

"Are you okay?" I asked. It was an automatic, essentially worthless question, especially since I knew darn well that something was wrong.

Babette grasped my arm with fingers colder than a Yukon night. "Wait'til we get out of here." She tossed me her keys. "You drive. We have to go back to the station."

I fired up the Mercedes and followed Bascomb in a somber procession back to the cop shop. Babette sat staring silently, stonily, into space. After sixty seconds, I lost control and cracked.

"Tell me what happened right now, or I swear I'll run this fancy hunk of metal into a post." The look on my face must have convinced her, but instead of speaking, Babette began to sob—big, honking sobs, that attracted attention. Instead of comforting her, I pulled over to the side of the street and glared.

"Oh, Perri," she said. "It's horrible."

"Skip the drama and fill me in before Bascomb sends out an APB for us. What was in that box? Drugs, cash—what?"

Babette hiccupped, wiped her eyes and blew her nose almost simultaneously. "None of that stuff. There were four drivers' licenses, birth certificates and passports in four different names." She paused. "And they all had Ethel's face on them."

Chapter 12

I drove the two blocks to the police station on autopilot. I felt hollow and strangely disconnected. A dozen possibilities flew through my brain, none of them good. Was our late friend a spy, confidence woman or criminal on the run? After wedging the sports car into a parking spot, I turned to Babette. "What else did you find? I presume Bascomb scooped the lot."

Babette swallowed twice and dabbed at the mascara under her eyes. "There was a bankbook too and some jewelry—a watch and a couple of rings. Stuff she never wore in front of me. And bankbooks—I didn't even know they had those things anymore. Of course, it was a foreign account, so they do everything differently."

"What country?" Patience and persistence were essential when Babette veered off track.

She gulped once more. "The Cayman Islands. And Perri, it gets worse. Ethel had over half a million bucks in the account. Can you believe it? She said she was broke. I paid for her food."

At that point I was willing to believe almost anything especially if it involved a certain murder victim who had deceived us all. Like it or not, Ethel was probably a blackmailer at the very least. A wealthy community like Great Marsh overflowed with potential victims who could and probably would pay to keep their secrets safe. Those solid citizens might also kill to protect their interests. Babette released her seatbelt and scrambled out of the car.

"Come on," she wailed. "Get the lead out. Titus is waiting for us."

I waved her on and waited while she disappeared into the maw of justice. Something important was burning inside me. I grabbed my cell phone and dialed Pruett's number.

* * * *

That afternoon, good, hard work saved me from obsessing about Ethel. I tidied up my office, attended to my pets, and focused on perfecting the shipment of belts that had been ordered. I admit that I primped a bit while getting dressed but that was professional pride. Nothing more. Subdued makeup, a spritz of perfume and my best silk slacks were merely tools to lift my spirits. Pruett wouldn't even notice.

When Babette swung by at six pm, I was seated on the porch, calmly reading *The Washington Post*. She gave me one look and hooted. "All gussied up, aren't you, hon? Guess I can't blame you. One night with Pruett could make a girl's entire year."

"What are you babbling about? Besides you look pretty spiffy yourself." Posh jewelry and a dreamy red pantsuit lent Babette a glamorous air. Her high-heeled boots upped the sex appeal to a new high.

Compliments usually sidetracked her, but this time was different. I ignored her contemptuous snort and plugged in the GPS. Since car thefts in Georgetown had reached epidemic proportions, we decided to take my old Suburban. As an added precaution, I loaded Keats and Poe into the back seat. Anyone trying to steal my ride would get a rude awakening when that Pretorian Guard sprang out at them.

Clyde's was a favorite watering hole for Georgetown style-setters, and the crowd hovering outside the door reflected that. We slowly worked our way up to the maître'd without much hope of ever getting seated. Then Babette uttered the magic words: Wing Pruett.

The server's face was wreathed in smiles as she nodded. Mr. Pruett was waiting for us in his booth. *His booth?* Although there was no metal plaque on it, the choice spot was clearly reserved for Pruett, bon vivant and general hottie. When he saw us, he rose and waved merrily. "Ladies. Welcome. You both look lovely. Have a seat. Please."

He looked jaw-droppingly handsome himself in tight black jeans and a white turtleneck. Fortunately, dignity triumphed over lust and I forced myself to turn away rather than gape. Babette showed no restraint at all. She seemed intent on slobbering over him and swilling alcohol with equal abandon.

"Looks like you own the place, Wing," she trilled. "This your regular hangout?"

For a moment, I thought that he blushed, but I was mistaken. The amused glint in his eyes dispelled that notion. Charming female admirers was second nature to this Beltway bad boy, a practiced art in which he excelled. I stared at the menu to collect my thoughts.

"I'm sure Pruett is busy, Babette, so let's get down to business."

He raised an eyebrow at my brusque tone but said nothing. Leave it to Babette. She downed her cosmopolitan and blundered right in without giving it a second thought.

"Don't mind her. Perri and I had a hard day what with the bank and the cops too." Babette's dimples deepened as she pinched my cheeks. "She'll perk up when she has a drink. Let's order."

"Hot stuff," Pruett said after Babette had filled him in about the safety deposit box. "What about the jewelry? Any initials or identifying marks?"

Babette shook her head. "A gold Rolex, and two nice sapphire rings with diamonds. Possibly Art Deco. Pretty standard stuff. Nothing worth killing for." Since my pal was almost a pro when it came to the glittery stuff, I trusted her assessment.

"Hmm. No letters or disks, I guess. Too bad. Of course, extortion can excite a bunch of emotions. Sometimes just the thought of getting ripped off is enough."

"Blackmail is such a low crime," Babette growled. "I'd kill her myself if Ethel were still alive." Her exuberance attracted the attention of several diners. She lowered her voice after I hushed her. DC was filled with tipsters and newshounds determined to satisfy the public's unending appetite for gossip.

I knew both crimes were bad but wasn't sure if blackmail and extortion were the same thing. Fortunately, Pruett the know-it-all supplied the answer.

"Extortion," he said, grinning. "In Virginia statutes, there is no blackmail. Just extortion. Kind of interchangeable, actually."

"I forgot that you're an attorney too," Babette simpered. I really hated it when she did that. Luckily it only happened around the limited supply of presentable males who came her way.

Pruett shrugged. "A failed law student. Family thing, you know. My mother insisted but it bored the pants off me."

I closed my eyes and recreated today's scene at the Great Marsh police station. Lieutenant Bascomb's reaction had been priceless. The man just about combusted once he realized that his suspect pool had tripled and now included some of the town's most prominent citizens. Quiet, inoffensive Ethel had cut quite a swathe through the community. Her selfless service to so many worthy causes was now tinged with the taint of corruption.

Pruett prattled on about something forgettable that entertained Babette and bored me. I came to attention when he mentioned Ethel's suspicious bank balance.

"That's a nice chunk of change, but really not a lot of money." He stared into space. "Not for extortion in a well-heeled community like Great Marsh. What price respectability, huh?"

I analyzed the situation calmly and clearly. Perhaps Ethel was an intelligent criminal who realized that even wealthy housewives—and I believed most, if not all, her victims were women—might have trouble gathering huge sums of money. Relatively paltry payments on the other hand were much more sustainable.

"Maybe she was more interested in smaller, steady payments than one big score," I said. "And don't discount the elements of power and control in the equation. That's a lot of ego balm for a clerical worker."

Pruett nodded and asked what Bascomb's plan of action was. I suspected that while we enjoyed the comforts of a Georgetown eatery, the poor cop was busy sussing out the many faces of one Ethel McCall.

"I checked reported burglaries in the area," Pruett said. "Not too many. Casts doubt on that theory. After what you guys learned today it's even less likely."

"At least he doesn't think I'm in danger anymore," Babette said. "Ethel had plenty of her own enemies."

Pruett got a peculiar look on his face that roused my suspicions. When we locked eyes, I understood everything. Ethel's criminal past was a two-edged sword. Babette's personal danger had lessened, but she had just graduated from potential victim to prime suspect.

* * * *

We left shortly after eating our dinner. Pruett escorted us to my car but leapt back as Keats and Poe launched a spate of growls and barks.

"Got your guard dogs with you I see." His expression was more smirk than smile. "Don't they know this is America not a war zone?"

"Sometimes it's hard to see the difference," I said.

Babette ignored the subtext of his comments. "Those dogs are crazy about Perri. Lord help anyone who tries to mess with her." She swayed a bit causing Pruett to grasp her arm and help her into the Suburban. I vowed immediately to prevent her from driving home. Bascomb would lock her up and throw away the key if she were nabbed for DUI.

Pruett nodded. "That's for sure." He stepped back then pivoted sharply. "Text me if you get anything useful from Jakes. I'll work a few angles from my end. And be careful. Both of you."

The drive home seemed endless as Babette chirped nonstop about the glories of Pruett. Nothing, not even the small matter of her dear friend's murder, deterred her from weaving alcohol fueled romantic fantasies. All of them ended the same way with Pruett and I joined in wedded bliss.

"You're not listening to me, Perri," she griped. "You know my instincts about these things are always on target."

That statement was too ludicrous to even comment on. Besides, Babette meant well, however misguided she might be, and anything that lifted her spirits was okay with me. As we pulled into her driveway, I grew anxious. Her estate was shrouded in darkness. Swaying tree limbs and swirling leaves lent an ominous air to the place.

"Where's Carleton?" I asked her. "Isn't he usually home on a weeknight?"

"Don't ask me. He doesn't punch a timecard. We have our own "don't ask don't tell" policy."

A sudden noise startled me, causing my dogs to bark. "What was that? Sounded like a door banging."

I could tell from the way Babette's eyes widened that she was frightened. "It's coming from Ethel's place," she whimpered. "Oh, dear Lord. I have to find Clara." She bolted out of the Suburban and sped toward her front door.

I reached under the seat for the powerful torch I had carried since my army days. It was military grade, a tactical flashlight with a strobe designed to immobilize any person or creature that posed a threat. Personally, I preferred it to a gun, although I had one of those too.

Keats and Poe were already on alert. As soon as the hatch opened, they bounded toward the sound with their hackles raised. I followed close behind them, activating the strobe feature of my torch.

"Babette! Stop! Wait for us!"

She disappeared into her house, switched on the lights and emerged with Clara hugging her side. I shone the floodlight toward the garage windows where Carleton's black BMW was clearly outlined. Babette saw it too; bent over and made a keening sound like none I had ever heard before. She was clearly terrified, and I didn't blame her. She froze in place as rigid as a stone sculpture.

"Call the police while I check out Ethel's place." I walked toward the guesthouse feeling braver than normal because of my dogs. Both Keats and Poe had faced danger many times and never failed. If only I could match their courage.

The unlocked screen door, mired in crime scene tape, rattled on its hinges. Perhaps the police had forgotten to fasten it. There must be a dozen different explanations, all of which eluded me as I stood there.

"Perri, wait. I called the police. They'll be here any minute." Babette and Clara edged toward us.

Her words made sense. No sane person would barge into a darkened home, no matter what type of training or skills she might have. For some reason common sense deserted me. I forged ahead with the Malinois at my side and stepped over the threshold. Babette and Clara made it a party of five. Once again, I activated the strobe and panned the hallway that had led to Ethel's space. Babette's scream pierced the night like a siren.

There at the bottom of the stairwell lay the crumpled form of Carleton Croy.

Chapter 13

Despite the blood, he wasn't dead. When I bent over Carleton I felt a faint pulse throbbing in his neck. I reached for my cell phone and dialed 911 again, knowing that Babette would be no help at all. She had fainted dead away the moment she saw her ex-husband, put down for the count by a morbid fear of blood and bodies, combined with an inordinate amount of alcohol. Doggy kisses from the faithful Clara ultimately revived her, although until the paramedics arrived she remained groggy and incoherent.

Lieutenant Bascomb was first on the scene. His cruiser roared into the driveway at the same time that the ambulance arrived. The top cop's scowl showed more annoyance than concern. He wore the morning's wrinkled shirt and shiny suit and his disposition was foul.

"What the hell's going on?" he growled, pointing to Carleton's form on the stretcher. "This place is a damn body farm." As they loaded Babette in beside Carleton, Bascomb exploded. "Her too? You have a lot of explaining to do, Ms. Morgan. Both of you do."

Ethel's house was now filled with lights and law enforcement—no need for my trusty torch. Bascomb gave an impatient snort and motioned me toward the living room sofa. He plopped down beside me as though prepared to stun me with his version of the third degree. Funny. I had curled up on that sofa a dozen times in the past sipping tea and listening to Babette and Ethel plot their projects. The plump down cushions and overstuffed chintz chairs were very English manor house, fitting tributes to Babette's exquisite taste and bountiful checkbook. How different everything looked today. The presence of Bascomb and his minions immediately dispelled any illusion of comfort. Bascomb's outsized limbs splayed over the sides of the delicate furniture in an ungainly pose that did nothing to improve his disposition. I had dealt with bullies many times and the path to victory lay in blanketing them with smiles and good cheer. It drove him mad.

"What's wrong with you?" he barked. "Two friends of yours were just carted away in an ambulance and you sit here grinning."

I reached down and ran my hand through Poe's thick fur. Keats gave me a doggy smile and wagged his tail. The dogs were the constants in my life. Bascomb could just wait until I was ready. I revisited every minute from the time I left his office to the ghastly discovery of Carleton's body. Bascomb said little. He folded his arms and stared as if he were an oracle who knew damn well that I was lying.

"What time did Mrs. Croy get to your place?"

I counted to ten in my head—twice—before answering. "As I mentioned, she arrived around six pm."

"You're sure of that, are you?"

"Absolutely. I checked my watch while I was sitting on the porch. Why is that such a big deal?"

His smile was probably intended to be enigmatic, but it came off as third-rate burlesque. Good thing Bascomb had opted for law enforcement over comedy. Suddenly it occurred to me that he was more interested in Babette's movements than mine.

"Surely you don't think Mrs. Croy attacked him? She was with me all night. Ask Mr. Pruett if you don't believe me."

Bascomb curled his lip. "Who knows when it happened? She could have clobbered him before joining you. When a husband runs around..." He raised his eyebrows. "Wives tend to react."

He gave me the cop's stare—the one that separates the innocent from the guilty. In my case, seeing it was déjà vu all over again.

"Need I remind you that the Croys are divorced? Quite amicably as it turns out." I rose and brushed off my slacks. "I'm going to the hospital," I said, in a tone so frosty that Bascomb blinked. "If anything develops, you can find me there. But for now, Mrs. Croy needs me." Without saying another word, I corralled Clara, whistled to my dogs, and headed for the Suburban. George Washington University Hospital was ten miles away, a short enough distance at this time of night. As I fired up the engine and switched on the headlights, my cell phone buzzed. Sheila had a police scanner and the bad news about Carleton travelled fast. Bad news always moved through small communities with lightning speed.

"What's going on?" she asked. "Is Babette okay?"

My voice quivered as I shared the story with her. Funny. Until then I hadn't noticed that my hands were trembling.

"You sound shaky," Sheila said. "Wait a minute and I'll come pick you up. We don't need another neighbor in the hospital."

Her plan made sense until she realized that I had three dogs to attend to. Fortunately, Zeke was in his stall at home with an ample supply of food at his disposal. Like most goats, he was an unemotional old cuss. Food was his primary focus.

Sheila agreed to stay home only after I promised to call her as soon as I got an update. I toyed with calling Pruett but texted him instead. It was late, and as much as his presence would have comforted me, I saw big danger signs flashing. No sense in clinging to something that might soon vanish.

* * * *

Like most institutions of its kind, George Washington University Hospital was a city unto itself, filled with white-coated healers and their cohorts striding purposefully about. This particular hospital had successfully treated Presidents and dignitaries of all kinds without batting an eye. Carleton and Babette were in very good hands.

A helpful receptionist directed me to Babette's cubicle on the far side of the emergency room area. My pal was a drama queen at the best of times, so I steeled myself for the worst. After seeing Carleton's bloody body, tears, tantrums, and hysterics were probably on the menu. To my surprise Babette was sitting up, dried eyed, calmly sipping orange juice. She was not alone. Pruett stood there with his arm around her speaking softly.

"Perri! I told Pruett you'd be here."

I murmured something soothing and asked what I most dreaded. "Carleton. How is he?"

"Still in surgery. No word yet but the staff was optimistic. They've been wonderful, Perri. Everyone. So many nurses stoppin' in to see me."

Normally Babette was laser sharp, but I suspected she had been pumped full of happy juice. I locked eyes with Pruett and got my answer. Those helpful employees were more interested in seeing his sexy self than in comforting Babette. That's the way celebrity worked in DC and like it or not Pruett was a certified star.

He glided my way and took my arm. "How are you doing? You look beat." An electrical blast jolted me the moment that his arm touched mine. I stepped back to avoid the heat and swallowed twice before answering.

"I didn't expect you to come here. I just wanted to let you know what happened. For your story and all." At first, he said nothing. Just gazed down at me, letting those dreamy eyes do the talking. I raised my face upward, forcing myself to remain calm. Then Pruett gently stroked my cheek as if we were alone in the universe. "You know better, don't you? This is more than work. Has been from the beginning. Persephone, after all this time I don't know how to convince you. So much for objectivity. I just violated every tenet of the journalists' code. Blame yourself, Belt Babe."

Me, Persephone Morgan, a temptress? Talk about your unfamiliar roles! Babette had dozed off, so I felt emboldened and quite unlike myself. "I won't tell if you don't," I said.

The sudden appearance of a doctor broke the spell. She was garbed in surgical gear—cap, mask and gloves. Her manner was grave as she approached Babette and I shuddered, fully expecting to hear the worst news possible.

"Mrs. Croy? I'm Dr. Hightower, your husband's surgeon." She gently shook my friend's shoulder.

Babette dribbled juice on the bed, watching helplessly as it slowly seeped down her chin. Her movements were stiff, totally out of character for my animated pal. I left Pruett and walked quickly to her side. Babette was glassy eyed as she watched the surgeon. She seemed to be waiting for a cue.

"The news is good, Mrs. Croy." Dr. Hightower assayed a slight smile. "He's not totally out of the woods yet but the signs are promising."

"Can I see him? When can I see him?" Once the floodgates opened, Babette spewed forth an endless stream of chatter. The surgeon waited for it to subside before answering.

"He's sedated. Come back tomorrow morning and you can stay with him. Cheer him up." She reached for a towel and mopped up orange juice briskly and efficiently. "There we go. No need to get this sticky stuff all over you. We want you to brighten up Mr. Croy."

Knowing Carleton, I doubted that cheer or brightness was on the menu. Still, at least this time he had a legitimate gripe rather than his usual litany of petty grievances. For Babette's sake, I was happy. Despite his folksy ways, Bascomb was nobody's fool. He had anointed her as the prime murder suspect and another corpse on her property would only complicate her situation.

"Come on," I said. "I'll take you home. You need your beauty rest."

Pruett quickly intervened. "No need. My place is just down the street. Stay in my guest room tonight and I can drop you off first thing tomorrow. It's easier. Avoid the traffic that way."

Babette wasn't firing on all cylinders, but she wasn't oblivious. She blinked and looked up at Pruett. "Really? You're sure?"

He nodded.

I stayed neutral, not wanting to admit that it was actually a pretty good idea. A kind gesture too. "Pruett's right. Don't worry about Clara," I said. "She's in the back of my truck with the others. I'll take care of her."

"That invitation included you," Pruett said. "It's after midnight and you look exhausted." He raised his eyebrows in an exaggerated leer. "Don't worry. Your virtue is safe. I'm too tired to do any damage."

"Please, Perri." Babette gave me the wide-eyed look. "Don't leave me."

I shrugged helplessly. "I've got three big dogs with me and Zeke has to be fed by sunup or he goes berserk."

"Call Sheila. She'll take care of everything. She has keys to both of our places and besides she actually likes that goat." Babette's spirits seemed to be rising. She managed to eke out a smile as she spoke of Zeke.

Pruett leapt to his feet. "Come on, ladies, we could all use a good night's sleep. Let me check with the nurse." He returned accompanied by a beaming hospital worker pushing a wheelchair. After helping Babette off the cot, the aide led the way to the elevator chattering all the while to a bemused Pruett. He didn't say much, just did a lot of nodding and smiling, followed by an autograph signing. Whatever. I was too exhausted to notice or even care. The thought of driving back to Great Marsh was enough to knock me out and Pruett's offer was more welcome than I was willing to admit even without the normal fringe benefits.

"I'll get the Suburban and follow you," I said. "You're sure the dogs won't bother you?"

Pruett lied bravely. "Not a bit. Wait'til Ella hears about it. I'll be her hero."

He already was his daughter's hero. Anyone who saw the two of them together figured that out right away. Who could blame a little girl for idolizing a glamorous dad who so obviously returned the favor? Instead of railing against Pruett's brash, take-charge manner, I found it comforting. On occasion, even a strong woman like me needed someone to lean on. Pip knew just how to do that without compromising my independence. Fortunately, Pruett knew that too.

Chapter 14

Pruett's townhouse was one notch short of spectacular. For someone like me, who fancied historic homes with high ceilings and original woodwork, it was very close to perfect. My observations were limited of course. We had neither time nor energy for a house tour that evening, just enough to sip a brandy in the walnut paneled study. The three dogs gathered at our feet as we collected our thoughts.

"What if Bascomb comes looking for me?" Babette fretted. "He'll think I've gone on the lam." She was barely coherent, so exhausted that she punctuated each sentence with a yawn.

"Don't worry. I already left a message for Bascomb." Pruett grinned. "Can't risk a SWAT operation at this hour, can we? Come on, ladies." He moved cautiously under the watchful gaze of our canine guardians. "Let me show you to the guest rooms. The beds have clean linens on them and if you check the closets you should find some nightclothes."

He reddened as I gave him the gimlet eye. "It's not what you think. My housekeeper has everything fully stocked with men's and women's stuff. That way she's prepared for any guests."

"Personally, I don't care. Lead me to the bedroom before I drop." Babette had passed the time for social niceties. A tidal wave of grief and fear had swept away her party manners and laid bare her emotions. I sympathized since I was almost there myself.

We formed a solemn processional both human and canine as we dragged up the stairwell to our rooms. Each was beautifully appointed and boasted its own private bath. Babette called Clara and staggered off to bed without saying another word. Any other time I would have scrutinized everything in the place but that evening I managed only to nod and summon my dogs.

Pruett lingered outside the door for a moment. "Not quite how I envisioned this scene," he said ruefully. "But as you know timing is everything. You've already seen the master bedroom."

Watching his perfect profile, I felt a sudden stab of desire. How comforting it would be to have someone's arms around me all night—someone like Pruett. I spun around and faced him.

"You've been very kind to Babette. Thanks."

He brushed aside a wing of my hair and moved closer. "Kindness had nothing to do with it, Perri. I'll always be there for you. Someday you'll come to accept that."

After bidding me goodnight, Pruett pivoted and disappeared down the hallway whistling a cheery tune.

* * * *

I slept so soundly that only the cold noses of my dogs awakened me the next morning. Their unerring internal clocks told them that it was past time for me to rise and shine. Besides, they had needs to address too.

I leapt out of bed, quickly dressed, and crept down the staircase hoping that Pruett had deactivated his alarm system. Instead of seeing him, I came face to face with a middle-aged Hispanic woman wearing an apron and a big smile. Her eyes widened when she glimpsed Poe and Keats although she showed no fear.

"Excuse me," I said. "Is Mr. Pruett here? I'm Perri Morgan, and you must be Alma. Ella speaks of you often."

"He left with the other lady an hour ago. Come into the kitchen when you are ready, por favor. I have espresso and breakfast for you and your friends." She extended her hand. "We haven't met before, but I've heard all about you, especially from Ella. I live at home on the weekends."

I hitched up Clara and the Malinois for a quick outing and introduced myself. "Be right back."

The dogs were not urban dwellers, but they quickly adapted to the new terrain. After two turns around the block, the four of us returned to Pruett's house and Alma's hospitality.

"My dogs won't hurt you," I said. "They're very gentle."

She bent over and stroked the dogs. "They are beautiful. I love dogs and so does Ella." Her face softened when she said the little girl's name. "Mr. Pruett—not so much." Alma filled bowls with roast chicken and placed them on the floor. Poe, Clara and Keats immediately showed their gratitude by gobbling up the treats. I sipped espresso and nibbled a bit of toast while the housekeeper reminisced about Ella and her exploits.

"You should eat," Alma said. "Mr. Wing he likes strong, healthy girls."

I turned away to hide the blush stinging my face. "I'm not hungry," I said. My tone was unconvincing even to my own ears. Perhaps it was illusion, my personal fantasy. More likely it was wishful thinking. Alma knew Pruett's famous ex. It didn't take a mirror to draw the contrast between an international celebrity and a country mouse like me.

The housekeeper was easy to talk to and over a second espresso I found myself sharing an abbreviated version of the murder. Alma mentioned that she had been with Pruett for eight years. Her tone was affectionate, more akin to that of a favorite aunt than an employee.

"You like Mr. Pruett, don't you Alma?"

"I came from Mexico," she said. "Mr. Wing got me a green card. Gave me a new life. With his help, now, I am American citizen. He is a good man, Mr. Wing."

I thanked Alma, gathered the dogs and headed for my Suburban. Babette phoned just as I reached the car.

"Come get me, Perri. I need to go home." Her voice sounded tense and once again I feared the worst.

"Everything okay?" I asked.

"Fine. Just come get me. I'll be outside by the curb."

I inched my way through Georgetown, hoping to find the ever-elusive parking space near the hospital. Home sounded like a good idea for both of us about now. Sheila had texted me earlier to report that Zeke had been fed and watered and that Bascomb had stationed a deputy in front of my place. I groaned. Facing the dour detective was not on my hit parade this morning. I had neglected my business long enough.

As I neared the front of the hospital, Babette charged out and flagged me down. She looked remarkably rested and relatively carefree despite her ordeal.

"Hop in before someone runs over you," I grunted. "I've had my fill of hospitals."

"No kidding. Carleton's still unconscious but he is 'resting comfortably,' whatever that means. They say his vital signs are good." Babette exhaled forcefully. "The cops are stationed outside his door. Can you believe it? One of them stayed in the room with me when I tried to see him."

I shrugged, unwilling to state the obvious. Until he proved otherwise, Bascomb regarded Babette as a potential murderer.

"Where did Pruett go?" I tried to act nonchalant, but Babette caught on right away.

"Maybe I should ask you. He didn't slip into your bedroom last night, did he?"

That made me laugh. "Hardly. With two guard dogs around me Pruett wouldn't dare. He's brave but not crazy."

She didn't answer, but the look on her face was decidedly smug. Even last night's tragedy couldn't dim her romantic fantasies—at least as they pertained to me and Pruett. Her own love story was more complicated. It pained me to even think it, but Babette acted untroubled by Carleton's situation, somewhere between indifference and complacency.

"When will they release him?" I asked. "Carleton, I mean."

"Not for a couple of days. The cops have to question him first. Bascomb probably has his handcuffs ready for me."

Gallows humor was contrary to Babette's sunny nature and indicated just how worried she really was.

"I'll drop you off first," I said. "I need to stop by Sheila's place. She may have some ideas about this mess."

Babette clutched my arm so firmly that I nearly lost control of the car. "Take me with you. I don't want to be alone." Her voice was shaky, and her nails were chipped and bitten to the core. Her normally pristine pageboy was in disarray.

"No problem." I handed her my cell phone. "Here. Call Sheila and make sure she's home. No sense in wasting a trip."

After a brief conversation with Sheila, Babette confirmed that our friend was indeed anxious to see us. Apparently, she had been nosing about and had some progress to report. The next twenty minutes seemed endless as Babette chattered aimlessly about every topic except the murder case. I focused on driving, with the occasional nod and noise of encouragement as if this were just another casual road trip.

When Arcadia, the Sands manse, came into view I heaved a sigh of relief. The house was spectacular in the understated style that had long served Virginia's moneyed classes. It sat high upon a hill, buttressed by majestic columns that stood in judgement of lesser structures and beings. Eighty acres of rolling land gave the Sandses maximum privacy and then some. A stone fence and paddock area housed a majestic structure that served as a kennel for her Ridgebacks and barn for their show horses. Despite his age, Ellis Sands still rode his favorite gelding regularly and Sheila was a demon for competition.

Sheila shrugged off any mention of their wealth as a lucky accident. Ellis had made a fortune in his thirties, raised a family in his forties, survived his spouse's death in his fifties, and found Sheila, the love of his life, in his sixties. In a world fueled by perpetual entitlement and planned obsolescence, he was that rarity—a very happy man. His wife was a big part of that and as far as Ellis Sands was concerned, she could do no wrong.

Sheila must have been on the alert for us. She flung open the front door and charged outside as soon as we turned into her driveway. As usual, her attire was impeccable—jodhpurs and a cream turtleneck with burnished knee-high boots. She bounced from side to side and beckoned us into the house scarcely able to contain her excitement. After enveloping Babette in a tight hug, Sheila recalled her hostess duties and offered us tea.

"I could use something stronger," Babette said. "Scotch. Straight up. Double."

I refused the offer of alcohol, thanked Sheila for feeding Zeke, and settled for tea.

"You said you made progress," I prompted her. "Tell us."

After some hemming and hawing, she came to the point. "I hope you're still going to the show on Friday because we have work to do. Jakes will be there."

That was hardly newsworthy. Jakes attended almost every show in the area. He was pushing hard to amass enough points to wow the judges at the regional shows. Babette took a slug of scotch and began another frenzied rant about Jakes. I had heard it all before—too many times. Apparently, Sheila had too. She held up her hand and stopped Babette in mid-epithet.

"Here's something you didn't know. Jakes said he'd never met Ethel, right? Well he was lying." Sheila looked inordinately pleased with herself. A very becoming flush colored her cheeks.

"Lying?" I leaned forward, slopping a bit of tea into my saucer.

"Yep. I had lunch yesterday with the Ridgeback Regulars. You know, my local breed club. Anyhow, Lucinda Croft mentioned that Jakes and Ethel had a loud quarrel last month outside the refreshment tent at the jumping competition."

Babette drained her scotch and slammed the glass on the table. "No kidding!"

"Was she sure it was Ethel?" I asked. "I never saw her at a show."

Sheila lifted her head skyward. "You missed the one in Fredericksburg last month."

"You mean Northern Neck?"

Sheila nodded. "Now that I think about it Ethel was there. She volunteered to staff the rescue booth, the one for retired farm horses. Don't you remember, Babette? You asked her to cover for you."

Babette's eyes widened, and she covered her mouth with her hand. "Oh God! Of course. I forgot all about that."

My mind was working overtime. Bascomb should hear about this right away. On the other hand, knowing his attitude, he might not take the whole thing seriously. Unless. Unless we learned something more specific. Something incriminating that could tie Jakes to Ethel's murder.

"What were they fighting about?" I asked.

Sheila grimaced. "She couldn't hear anything but raised voices. Threats were made though. She said Ethel kept her cool and Jakes just stalked off. You know how volatile he is."

My thoughts raced as I considered the possibilities. Someone else must have witnessed that scene. The dog and horse world were rife with intrigue, and rumors spread like a bad rash. Come to think of it, my old pal Ken Reedy was usually tuned in to all the show gossip and Rebecca knew everyone on the circuit. I vowed to chat them up this weekend when they visited my shop.

"Earth to Perri. Are you still with us?" Sheila cocked her head and smiled.

"I was trying to hatch a plan. Believe me, anyone who knows about that scene between Ethel and Jakes will be there this weekend. Our job is to find out something specific."

Babette argued that she should join us, but we stopped her cold by dropping Bascomb's name. From what I'd observed, he was a conservative man with very traditional beliefs about marriage even when the parties were divorced. Babette's role in our little drama was to play the devoted female and hover over Carleton. Sheila and I would do the detecting.

Chapter 15

For the next three days, I worked feverishly to fill orders and replenish my stock. Show customers were an impatient lot who demanded that vendors instantly fulfill their needs. Horse enthusiasts were even edgier. Better to be overly prepared rather than to risk being abandoned for a competitor. I also gathered some surplus gear for the equine beauties at Cavalry Farms. They might be castoffs, but they deserved a bit of primping too. During that time, I heard not one word from Pruett. No email, voicemail, telephone or text. Naturally, I refused to initiate contact unlike the fawning, slobbering females he was accustomed to.

Babette brought Carleton home and feigned a devotion I never dreamed she was capable of. She answered all Bascomb's questions but was wise enough to retain one of the best criminal defense attorneys in DC as backup.

Unfortunately, Carleton had absolutely no information to offer about his assailant. He had seen a light in Ethel's house, gone to investigate and been clobbered by person or persons unknown. The experience was not unlike my own, although his injuries were more severe. According to Babette, a steady stream of students and their mothers had trickled in to comfort their fallen hero, bearing cakes, casseroles, and kisses. Lots of them. Carleton bravely bore up under the strain and vowed to return to his teaching duties as soon as possible.

That Friday, I loaded up my truck, popped Keats and Poe into their crates, and headed for the horse show. When he saw his buddies leave, Zeke hung his head over the fence and emitted a strangled cry of either anger or frustration. His water trough was filled to the brim and his hay supply was plentiful, but his emotional needs for companionship were unfulfilled. I had toyed with the idea of getting another goat but quickly abandoned the thought. One Zeke was more than I had bargained for. Two would put me down for the count. I blocked all thoughts about having Raza, the Arabian beauty, keep Zeke company, even though horses and goats coexisted peacefully on many farms.

As I eased into the vendors' area, I saw Sheila with Cecil at her side waving madly to me. Most stores didn't open until mid-morning, but I liked plenty of time to set out my stock and relax before hordes of frantic horse fanciers descended. Sheila made herself useful by loading bridles, stirrups, and one saddle into the cart and pulling them toward my stall. Cecil valiantly masqueraded as guard dog and general factotum. Since he was still a pup and timid by nature, the impact was more theoretical than practical. Keats and Poe, on the other hand, were effective sentinels who sat silently and calmly surveying everyone who passed by.

"What's our strategy?" Sheila asked. "Should we confront him? Jakes goes in the ring at noon. I checked."

I had no intention of confronting Jakes or anyone else. This was strictly reconnaissance, an information gathering mission that required finesse and a delicate touch. Since Sheila was masterful at chatting up her pals, I suggested that she start there.

"Try to find a witness. Someone who actually heard something. If we ask Jakes directly he'll only brazen it out. He told Pruett that he never even met Ethel." I winced when I said his name, even though I told myself it was no big deal. "You're zoning out again," Sheila said. "Are you sure you're okay?"

I busied myself with arranging woven leather leads by length and color and pairing them with padded collars. "Just thinking. You schmooze the owners and I'll take the rest. If you see anything let me know. I'm set for tomorrow at Cavalry Farms."

Sheila saluted and tugged Cecil out toward the exercise pen. "You can count on me. This is so exciting. My first detective mission."

"Be careful," I warned. "Your husband would go berserk if he knew what you were up to." I shuddered to think what Ellis Sands would make of the whole scheme. He was highly protective of his bride and extremely jealous. If ever a man was besotted by his wife, Ellis was it.

She laughed. "My life is pretty dull these days, you know. At his age, Ellis isn't exactly Mr. Excitement even though he tries, bless his heart. Forget those television commercials. That little blue pill can only do so much."

Sheila checked her watch. It was a clunky-looking thing, a Rolex Cosmograph. For some reason, she preferred the men's version originally designed for race car drivers. To me it looked big and bulky, but it suited her taste and needs not mine. She had the solid gold men's version too, although I hadn't seen her wearing it for some time.

"Whoops! Got to run. My gelding goes on in thirty minutes and I have to check with the farrier. Thought he was favoring his right hoof a tad." She winked. "My horse, not the blacksmith! Don't worry. I am on task."

I busied myself with the mundane matters of show life, pricing my items and arranging a sale bin. Customers always loved that even though the discount was often miniscule. It caught their attention and drew them in. The first lesson of retail strategy was reel them in then clinch the sale.

My first customer was really just a visitor. Rebecca, aka Becca, limped in wearing a black jacket with patches displaying her client's emblems. It was a sophisticated choice but a challenge to keep free of hair.

"Save me, Perri," she cried holding up her right shoe. "Some idiot didn't clean up after his mount. God, I hate that!"

Becca was always high drama but this time she had a point. For everyone's sake, owners and riders had to clean up after their charges or someone else paid the price. They knew the rules and most scrupulously obeyed them. I guided her to a seat, gingerly picked up her shoe and gave it a thorough cleaning with a baby wipe.

"There you go," I said. "Now tell me, what's new?" Becca kept her ears open at all times and was an invaluable source of show scuttlebutt. Horse people trusted and confided in her.

She shrugged. "Nothing much. Just the usual drama."

"I heard that Jakes and Ethel had it out the week before she was murdered," I said. "Know anything about that?"

"Oh that. Yeah. I did hear something about it."

"A lovers' quarrel?" I asked.

"Are you daft? It was about something important—horse shows. Whatever Ethel said to him about Cleopatra made Jakes crazy. He got all red-faced and started shouting until one of the officials shut him down."

It wasn't hard to picture that scene. Jakes had reacted the same way toward Pruett.

"What about Ethel? That must have shaken her up too."

Becca thought about it for a bit. "That I can't say, but I saw her not long after and she was at the Cavalry Farm rescue booth looking cool as the proverbial cucumber."

That sounded like the woman I thought I knew. Cool, calm and collected. Nothing fazed her, even Babette's manic periods. Of course, I didn't know at the time that she was a blackmailer with a hefty bank balance. That could have a calming effect on anyone.

"Funny thing," Becca said. "I asked Ethel about it and she said something strange, like if you want to get under someone's skin find his passion and go for it. She got a big grin on her face and just laughed. Never did explain what the hell she meant."

After Becca left, I thought long and hard about what she had said. Was Glendon Jakes passionate about anything? He was certainly fervent about his blog, *Bag It*. For a wimpy man, a chance to rub shoulders with macho gun-toters had to be exhilarating. If Ethel knew that he faked everything, she might blackmail him, but somehow it just didn't seem important enough. Not life and death important.

An influx of customers occupied me until lunchtime when I hastily closed the shop and sprinted toward ring twelve. Jakes and Cleopatra had a ring call at noon and I planned to be there, front and center. What had Becca said? If the quarrel between Jakes and Ethel had something to do with Cleo maybe that was the answer. Winning meant a lot to a man like Jakes. Had Ethel somehow threatened that simple pleasure?

My self-absorption almost caused a collision with a family group. Luckily, Ken Reedy reached out and pulled me from harm's way.

"Whoa there, Perri. You're in a fog." Even though he was codger-age, Ken radiated a type of confidence and masculinity that made him a useful ally.

"Sorry. I didn't want to miss the hunters," I said. "Why are you here instead of at Cavalry Farms? Not giving up on those horses, I hope."

Ken smirked. "I've got energy enough for both, don't you worry. It's you I wonder about. Got a crush on Glendon Jakes or something? I thought that news guy was more your type."

I was used to his teasing. "Ha. Ha. I doubt any woman has ever had a crush on Mr. Jakes although I did hear that he and Ethel McCall were close."

"What? Who told you that?" He chuckled. "They went at it hammer and tongs at the Fredericksburg horse show. Thought we were going to have to call the cops."

"Really? That's weird. Wonder what it was all about." I did my best to look disinterested, but Reedy wasn't fooled. He shot a quizzical look my way and folded his arms.

"Still playing detective? Watch your step, Perri. This isn't some silly television show. People get hurt in real life. Thought you'd know that by now."

I opted for truth telling. It was the best defense I had. "This is for Babette. The police suspect her and I'm worried. Glendon Jakes was on the premises the day that Ethel died, and it appears that she was...well...

unethical enough to blackmail people. I just can't figure out what she found out about Jakes."

Reedy paused for a moment. In another life, he had been a hard-charging prosecutor. I got a taste of that by looking into his eyes. They were cold and calculating, a glacial blue. "Look. This is only rumor and innuendo so take it for what it's worth."

"Okay."

He lowered his voice. "People say some judges will rule in your favor for the right price. You know how subjective the whole process is anyway."

He was right of course. Objective standards were used to assess jumping, but hunter classes were based on a judge's personal view of the horse and rider's deportment and style.

"Bribes?" It shocked me but then again it also made sense in a warped sort of way. I recalled Jakes's intensity in the ring and the way he bragged about Cleopatra. The equine world would act immediately to snuff out any whiff of scandal and Jakes would be banned for life. Poor Cleo would suffer too. Who knew what Ethel, the mousey matron quietly observing everyone, could have heard or surmised?

My conscience began to bother me. I felt obliged to share information with Bascomb, but his attitude annoyed me. The solidarity of the thin blue line felt remote in the chilly confines of the Great Marsh police station. Bascomb acted as though I were a meddler, or even worse, an amateur. Besides, I really didn't know anything for sure. As Ken said it was only rumor and innuendo. Dog and horse shows were rife with conspiracy buffs who attributed every loss to vendetta, favoritism, or malfeasance. If only Pruett were around. I could use a sounding board, a dispassionate listener to bounce theories off. I was honest enough to know that there were other reasons I wanted him around too. I immediately blotted out any thought of Pruett. Those matters were better left to lonely evenings by the fire surrounded by my pets.

As the hunters lined up, I studied Jakes. The man's intensity bordered on mania and his demeanor was one notch north of twitchy. He had the whole psychotic thing going for him—bulging eyes, pursed lips and heightened color. Beautiful Cleopatra shared none of her master's traits. She trotted calmly and confidently into the ring and turned in a winning performance. No doubt in my mind that the lady deserved to win her class.

As he exited the ring, Jakes saw me and glared. Had smoke belched out of his ears, I would not have been at all surprised. Instead of basking in his win, he dismounted and stalked up to me.

"You again! What do you want?"

I decided to take a risk. After all, I could handle myself in a fracas and I knew how to vanquish bullies. "Congratulations on your win, Mr. Jakes. As for me, I want the same thing Ethel McCall wanted. No more. No less."

Jakes clutched Cleo's lead so tightly that she balked. An adjacent rider immediately leapt to her defense.

"Hey, cut that out. You're hurting her."

Jakes loosened his grip. "Mind your own business if you know what's good for you." He then pointed a finger my way. "And that goes double for you."

He didn't frighten me despite the nasty scowl distorting his face. I had faced too many drunken soldiers to worry about one adenoidal biologist. Instead of cowering, I cackled. "Wow! Big, tough man. Just remember what I said if you know what's good for you." I turned on my heel and strolled away as coolly as Cleopatra herself.

Chapter 16

The remainder of the day passed uneventfully, though profitably. Winners stopped by to gloat and lesser lights commiserated with other losers. Delighted show devotees dove into the sales bin and unearthed treasures for their mounts while I tried unsuccessfully to worm information from my colleagues. Most of them felt Ethel and her murder were old news. Equine crimes such as awarding points to unworthy specimens held their interest. Human misdeeds were irrelevant unless they concerned double-dealing owners, shifty trainers or biased judges.

I had all but abandoned hope when Rebecca bounced into view. "Where's your sexy friend?" she asked with a wink. "I have more to show him."

"Pruett was busy today," I said, ignoring her provocations. "How did you do?"

"I did okay. Big deal. Might as well sit home if Cleopatra hits the ring."

I decided to stir the pot a bit. "She is lovely though. Can't say the same for her owner. What an unpleasant man!"

Becca hooted. "He's a class A jerk and a wimp too. Do you know he actually tried to make time with me last year? Ugh! Probably has scales instead of skin, not that I plan to find out."

"I guess the rumors aren't true," I said. "You know. About Jakes bribing judges?"

She raised one brow and gave me a speculative look. "He's capable of trying anything but only an idiot would risk that with a winner like Cleo. She's spectacular. Does all the work herself and makes even a clod like Jakes look good."

After some more chitchat, Becca left but not before pressing her card into my hand. "Give this to Pruett when you see him," she said, "unless you claim dibs on him."

I held up my hands in surrender. "Not at all. I will definitely pass it on."

* * * *

Sheila zoomed in just as I was closing up shop. Cecil trailed behind her cringing every time a stranger lunged his way. Someday Cecil would realize that he was bigger and stronger than almost any competitor, canine or human, but for now he was merely a pup in a big dog's body.

"Well," Sheila asked, "did you find out anything interesting?"

"Maybe. At the very least, I confirmed that Ethel had something on Jakes, or thought she did. He snarled at me when I mentioned her name."

"Interesting. My buddies said that Ethel was sitting on the fringes when they were sharing snacks. Didn't say much, but absorbed everything like a damn sponge. You know how people talk in those things, Perri. Everyone lets her hair down."

The women at Hamilton Arms said the same thing. Stolid, unobtrusive Ethel was the sort of woman who handled chores efficiently and volunteered for more. She had certainly fooled me and everyone else in Great Marsh. I pictured her sitting quietly in the corner, spinning her web, hooded eyes alight with malice. Just waiting for someone to slip. If Carleton had money, he would have been Ethel's perfect victim. On the other hand, that was awfully close to home and Ethel had a good thing going thanks to Babette's kind heart. Perhaps Ethel focused on Carleton's lady friends instead. After all, they had money and secure social positions. Dowdy Ethel would get plenty of satisfaction from bringing pampered housewives to heel.

"Want to stop for dinner?" I asked Sheila.

"Love to, but Ellis has something special planned for tonight. That man is such a romantic."

I brushed aside a pang of jealousy. Sheila was a good friend who didn't deserve that. "Nice that after ten years of marriage he still idolizes you. You're lucky."

Sheila yawned. "I suppose. Sometimes it gets tiresome though, being so perfect." She rolled her eyes. "I guess it's just my cross to bear." She winked at me as we exited the exhibit hall. "Tomorrow is another day. Who knows. Maybe my boy will win his class. I'm riding him myself so anything's possible." She waved a jaunty purple ribbon, the kind that every participant receives, in the air as she trotted toward her car. "Enjoy your time at the farm. Give those horsies a big nose kiss for me." She reached into her bag and produced a check. "Here's a little something extra for them. Hay money." I glanced at the amount and gasped. Sheila's idea of hay money would keep those rescues fed for a month.

Keats and Poe heeled by my side as we strolled toward the Suburban. Most everyone had left, and I had parked near the far side of the building to facilitate loading and unloading my truck. Advertising was fine but tonight I cursed the big red letters saying, "Creature Comforts Custom Leather." They were a neon sign beckoning anyone who wished me harm to step this way. Thank goodness for my dogs. I couldn't ask for braver more steadfast companions than these military veterans. Talk about terrific backup! Suddenly, as we neared the back of my vehicle, Poe stiffened and issued a low growl. Immediately Keats joined in. Their angst became mine as I peered into the darkness, trying to see what they saw. I issued the "stay" command, *Bleib*, not wanting to endanger my precious dogs. Besides, it might be a panhandler or even a harmless pedestrian. No need to panic. I brushed aside memories of Ethel's corpse, my assault, and Carleton's bloodied head. This was a public space. Surely other people would come along soon.

A noise from behind the dumpster spooked me. I unlocked the Suburban, secured the dogs in the back hatch and walked swiftly toward the driver's side door. As long as no gun was involved I would be fine. I switched on the engine, activated the high beams, and reached under the seat for the can of mace I kept there. *Deep breaths, Perri.*

Whoever lurked in the shadows was in for a shock if he or she advanced further. I am neither a victim nor a fool. I prepared for a quick getaway knowing that retreat was always the best course of action whenever possible. Any tactician knew that.

The drama was over in a minute, leaving me wary but sheepish. Lights flashed, foot traffic increased, and the hum of show life continued minus the sinister overtones. Had I imagined it? I am not subject to fantasies, but a palpable air of menace lingered in the air. I trusted my dogs. If they sensed danger that was good enough for me. Before I backed up, someone rapped on the driver's side window.

"Everything okay, Perri?" Ken Reedy was the perfect antidote to terror—solid, dependable, and no nonsense.

I rolled down the window and smiled at him. "Yep. Still a bit jumpy I guess. How are things at the Farm? I thought I'd swing by tomorrow with a few bridles and doodads. Finally finished repairing those saddles too."

Ken volunteered at Cavalry Farms and was handling the legal challenge to its status. "They'll appreciate it. Now go on home and have a brandy and I'll see you tomorrow. Always works for me." He rapped the side of the car and stood watching as I exited the parking lot.

* * * *

Ken was right. Brandy and a warm fire did the trick helping me to unwind and reassess my fears. As I sat watching the flames, clad in Pip's flannel robe with my pets surrounding me, the idea of a creeping menace seemed more and more absurd. Something—probably a guy using his own public urinal—had frightened me and alerted my dogs. No need to panic now. I had lived by myself for most of my life even when I most regretted it.

I must have dozed off because only the frantic barking of the Malinois roused me. I'm brave enough. Responsible risk-taking is part of my makeup and always has been. I reached into the end-table drawer and slipped my old service weapon, a Glock-9, into the pocket of Pip's robe. I hoped never to use it but was prepared to do so to protect my life. The rapping on the door continued. I switched on the outdoor light and peered through the peephole. There illuminated in the harsh glare stood Pruett.

Chapter 17

Pruett pressed forward, momentarily forgetting about my dogs. "I had to see you," he said. "Had to make sure you were safe."

I stammered something wholly unoriginal and inadequate. "Why?"

"I had this feeling you were in danger." Pruett looked a bit shamefaced. "Silly, I know, but I care about you. More than you'd ever realize."

I took his arm and drew him closer. Poe and Keats held their position, watching and waiting for my signal. Thatcher strolled up to him immediately, chirping a greeting.

"Please. Sit down by the fire and have a brandy. I could use another one myself."

He sank into the plush sofa cushions and waited as I poured his drink. "You didn't answer your phone and Babette said you weren't with her. I guess I panicked."

Of course. In the mad dash to get inside, I'd left my cell phone in the car. How careless could I be! These last few weeks had really taken their toll. I was normally the poster child for routine, the dull, reliable exponent of predictability.

"That was stupid of me," I said. "Careless." I glanced down at the tatty robe and scuffed slippers I wore, and the bulge of the Glock in my pocket. Hardly the stuff of seduction, so much closer to farce that the contrast was ludicrous. Firelight heightened Pruett's good looks making him look even more desirable than before. Never had any couple been more mismatched. Under other circumstances, I would have laughed. Instead, I gulped before saying a word. Might as well tell him what happened. He deserved an answer.

"Your instincts were on target. Today was a very strange day." I forced myself to meet his eyes, unwilling to admit how very lost and vulnerable I had felt. "I'm glad you came. I needed you."

Pruett leaned down and touched my cheek, slowly and gently. His fingers were exceptionally long and slender. Why had I never noticed that before?

"Kindness had nothing to do with it, Persephone. I shouldn't have barged in like this," he said. "I can go now if you'd rather be alone."

It didn't take me long to respond. Somehow things felt right, even in this room that held so many memories. I was lonely, tired of being the strong one. Since Pip passed, I'd been mired in grief, living a cautious half-life bereft of love or male companionship—until I met Pruett. My need for him exceeded logic or reason. It was an exquisite combination of love leavened with a pinch of lust.

"Don't leave," I whispered. "Please. Stay with me tonight."

He doused the lights and gathered me in his arms.

* * * *

Some things were just meant to be. That was my feeling the next morning after awakening from a glorious night with Pruett. I tiptoed across the room, freed my dogs from their crates and headed outside to do chores. Zeke was hungry and not at all pleased. He shot a malevolent look my way and thrust his head into the hay bin. Goats get lonely too, so I left Keats and Poe to keep him company while I made breakfast for my entire crew. I readied the coffee, set the table, and slipped up to the guest bathroom to freshen up. Today I remembered to wear my belt with the sterling silver buckle. It was good advertising and a useful weapon besides. When I returned, Pruett was there sitting at the kitchen table sipping coffee and wolfing down eggs. His right-from-the-shower look was stunning even though he wore last evening's clothes.

"I made myself at home," Pruett said. "Hope you don't mind." He pointed to the frying pan. "Plenty of eggs for two in there."

He put down his fork and stretched in a movement as feline as any from Thatcher herself. "Last night was special for me. You finally admitted that you need me, Perri, and that was a first. My only regret comes every time I leave this place."

A silly smile was all I could manage. Pruett said exactly what I hoped he would say.

I clutched my coffee mug as if my life depended on it. "Busy day today. A dressage show in New Kent and I plan to visit Cavalry Farms before going. What's on your agenda?"

"I have to collect Ella but we'll both swing around to the show in the afternoon. Don't leave without me. Okay?"

I tried nonchalance, but failed miserably. "Don't worry about me. I'll have one of the other riders walk out with me at closing time."

He crossed his arms and looked toward the ceiling. "Lord, you are one stubborn woman. Look. I know you can take care of yourself, but a little backup never hurts. Right?"

It was hard to resist the gleam in his eyes, so I didn't even try. "Okay. Guess I'll see you there."

He rose and caught me as I headed toward the door. "Persephone. I won't hurt you. Just trust me, okay? Besides, you promised to eat wings with Ella at her favorite restaurant. Don't forget."

"Sounds good." I gave him a little half wave and went to collect my dogs.

* * * *

Cavalry Farms was a ramshackle spot and like most rescue outfits it operated on a shoestring budget. Any comparison between these weatherworn stalls and Sheila Sands's palatial stables was merely a fantasy. The two dozen residents it housed ranged from retired draft horses to abandoned pleasure horses whose former owners no longer wanted them. I marveled anew at the callous cruelty displayed by some humans who regarded living things as disposable items. That cruelty was matched, however, by the kindness of volunteers like Ken, Babette, and Sheila who donated time, energy, and love to these hapless creatures. Many were rescued from "kill lots" where they would endure more suffering before being shipped to Mexico or Canada for slaughter. The very thought of it made me shudder. Today the horses were in the paddock, munching on grass and in a few instances kicking up their heels. Boxer, a gigantic roan Percheron named for the beloved equine in *Animal Farm*, lifted his head and whinnied at me. Despite his size, Boxer was biddable and affectionate. I marveled at how a creature over seventeen hands high could maneuver so gracefully around his frail human caretakers, as if he knew how easy it was to injure us. Some of his buddies were less careful. I'd learned to be wary of Plato, a fiery quarter horse with a tendency to literally bite the hands that fed him, and Disraeli, a loveable Clydesdale who planted his huge hooves perilously close to human feet. Like many of us, the horses had unique personalities, not all of which were pleasant.

Ken and I had floated the idea of repurposing Cavalry Farms to serve some community needs for returning veterans or handicapped children. Plenty of success stories celebrated the magical effects of the human-equine bond. Even the entitled citizens of Great Marsh would think twice about severing that connection.

I unloaded my truck and freed Keats and Poe to join in the fun. Both dogs enjoyed the equine family but were properly respectful of those sharp hooves. I stood at the fence armed with a supply of cut apples and carrots and called out. Immediately Raza, my special favorite, loped toward me with her ears pricked. Raza was my fantasy horse, a beautiful bay with the delicate features and sweet nature that Arabians were known for. She accepted the treats like the aristocrat that she was and nuzzled my hand.

"Riding today, Perri?"

Ken Reedy wore jeans, a flannel shirt and well-loved Wellingtons. The pitchfork he carried told me that he had been policing the horses' living quarters. For a man past sixty he looked fit and rather fetching.

"Probably not," I said. "Couldn't resist seeing my princess, though. I made a special bridle for her." I dangled a red braided leather bridle with fancy brass studs. Custom made for a special girl.

He smiled. "Sure, that pasture at home doesn't need a horse? Raza's only ten, you know. Plenty of life left in that girl."

"Don't tempt me. I'm on the brink." Logic told me that I didn't need another mouth to feed, but emotion pushed me to include Raza in my little family. Soon. "Maybe I'll ride for a little while after all."

Something about his voice made me scrutinize Ken's face. "How are things going?"

He stretched to his full height. "Holding our own. Powerful interests aligned against us, though. These forty acres have everyone salivating. Townhouses. Just what Great Marsh needs more of, right? Not much appetite for housing a bunch of refugees like these guys. Not when profits are involved."

"What's our next move?" I asked.

Ken's smile was beguiling and in it I saw the ghost of the fierce litigator he once had been. "Oh, we still have a few tricks left in our grab bag. Ellis Sands may weigh in, and that is a very big voice."

Sheila had never mentioned it, but help from a moneybag like her husband would mean a lot in our status-obsessed community. Good news indeed. "That reminds me. Sheila ponied up a little hay money today." I waved the check in front of his face and studied his reaction.

"My lucky day," he muttered. "We just need another hundred public spirited citizens to do the same."

As we carried my box of bridles, martingales, and cinches toward the barn, I quizzed Reedy about scandals among the rich and famous in Great Marsh. He knew just about everyone in Virginia's horse and dog world and I was curious about his take on Ethel the mystery woman.

"Okay, Perri. Out with it." His sardonic grin told me I was a very poor poker player indeed. "It's about Ethel, right?"

I nodded. "Everything I thought I knew about her was wrong. She had me completely fooled and I don't like that. Dull, respectable Ethel was a charade. She didn't exist."

He stood silent, his grin never fading.

"You're not surprised?"

"Nope."

"How come?" My patience was rapidly fading as this round of twenty questions continued. "I don't play games, Ken. Never was any good at them."

He sat down on a stool and gestured toward one for me. "Ethel—or whatever her real name was—dabbled in scandal. The messier the better. And she wasn't shy about demanding money."

"Blackmail! Are you sure?"

"Positive. I know because she tried it on me."

Good thing I had a firm grip on the stool. Otherwise I would have toppled right off into the straw. Reedy's grin broadened but he kept his counsel, waiting for me to question him.

"Okay. I give up. What could Ethel ever blackmail you about? You're an exemplary citizen—Mr. Public Spirited incarnate."

He reached into his pocket for a package of gum. "You know I used to practice law."

I nodded.

"Ever wonder why I stopped?"

That question left me dumbstruck. "I just figured you retired."

Reedy got up and sorted through the box I had brought. "Not really. I guess lawyers are like marines—never totally give it up. You weren't here when my wife died. Rosemary was the sweetest creature I had ever known. Brave too. Never complained about her pain, even when it was intolerable."

I knew where this story was going, and it wasn't pretty.

Ken's eyes softened. "Finally, she asked me to help her and of course I did. She passed with dignity and I notified the authorities." He laughed. "Virginia law is fairly specific about that kind of thing, but they didn't prosecute. Just asked me to surrender my law license and gave me probation."

I reached out and squeezed his arm. "What did Ethel hope to gain?"

"Who knows? She hinted about the cash donated to Cavalry Farm being easy to finagle. Said a taste of it would keep her quiet. I told her my crime was a matter of public record and she could just do whatever she liked, but she'd not see one penny of those donations. That cooled her down fast." He pointed toward the paddock. "Speaking of which, your girl is waiting for you. I'll saddle her up for you. Let her try the new gear."

By the time I carefully placed each new item in its appointed bin, Reedy had beautiful Raza saddled and ready for me. She stood on tiptoe, pirouetting in her excitement, her perfect shell ears alert and her lovely eyes alight with mischief. I had longed for an Arabian since my childhood days spent crouched on the library floor, imbibing Walter Farley's tales of *The Black Stallion*. Now, for a time at least, my dream was fulfilled as Raza and I cantered gracefully with Keats and Poe nipping at our heels.

Melding as one with a creature like Raza was such a magical experience that I yearned to share it with Ella. Pruett was unlikely to join us but with Ella, I felt a kinship that was hard to define. The little girl would understand as her devoted daddy never could. She took lessons of course in the formal, somewhat sterile venue sanctioned by her mother, accompanied by other little girls with perfect gear and rigid posture. Things were different here. Riding at Cavalry Farm, floating over less than perfect trails with abandon was the most liberating experience I had ever had. For one brief shining moment horse and rider were as one and it was as close to heaven as an earthbound human could get. I realized then that Raza would be mine—had to be—already was. Ella needed this same experience.

As we headed back to the paddock, I watched Ken, arms folded, and brow arched, smiling and shaking his head. Very little escaped him, and my obsession with Raza certainly did not. He had me hooked and he knew it. After I dismounted, he took Raza's bridle and offered to cool her down for me.

I called the Mals and ambled back to my truck, wondering how many victims Ethel threatened to destroy and who had finally stopped her.

* * * *

Parking spaces were scarce for this Saturday horse show. Fortunately, I managed to snag an exhibitors' slot at the far end of the parking area not far from that dastardly dumpster. Giving it a name somehow lessened its power to inspire fear. In daylight, it looked innocuous enough just a rusty hunk of metal. Nothing to terrorize me. Keats and Poe hugged my sides as we made our way through the spectators. In the far-left corner of the area Sheila waved merrily at me from ringside. I sent her a snappy salute and crossed fingers. Dog shows demanded tenacity and unbridled optimism from owners, breeders and handlers but horse shows demanded that plus a hearty infusion of cash. There was very little profit involved. Pride and bragging rights counted for plenty. Ask any parent who slogs along to little league games even when her child rides the bench.

It was still early, but a knot of customers led by Babette was massed at my stall. Most needed emergency services to replace lost or broken items but Babette had other things on her mind. Makeup couldn't conceal the shadows under her eyes or her limp curls. Looked like she'd had another sleepless night.

"There you are," Babette grunted. "You disappeared yesterday without a trace. I was worried, but Pruett was frantic. Why didn't you answer your phone?"

She sighed when I explained the mix-up. "For heaven's sake, Perri, get a land line. You know how unreliable cell service gets around here."

It was a matter of money, but Babette would never understand. Not in a million years. Saving a few bucks each month meant something to me. My friend and I inhabited very different worlds divided by a vast economic gulf. That was why I understood Ethel, or whatever her real name was. I thoroughly disapproved of her methods and was appalled by her disloyalty, but I understood the impulse. Babette had never in her life wanted for anything except common sense. She meant no harm. She just didn't understand.

"Are you listening to me or dreamin'?" she asked. "Did Pruett ever get hold of you? Lord that man was jumping out of his skin." She looked up at me and grinned like a Cheshire cat. "Oh! He got hold of you all right! Tell me everything."

Dignity flew out the window when Babette got started. No amount of snubs or hints had any impact. Only a sudden influx of new customers derailed her.

"Go cheer Sheila on in ring five," I said. "She needs encouragement."

She shrugged. "I can't stay long anyway. Just had to check up on you, Missy, but I see that you are doing fine!" On her way out, she paused. "Guess you're not interested in the latest about Ethel straight from the horse's mouth. Bascomb being the horse in question in case you didn't know."

She gained the upper hand with that remark. I was as nosey as the next person and Babette knew it.

"Stop fooling around and spill." I stood with my hands on my hips, glaring.

"Well. Bascomb got bank records from that account in the Cayman Islands. Apparently, Ethel was squirreling away five grand a week, if you can believe it."

I thought it over for a moment. "In one deposit or smaller ones? That could tell us how many victims she was squeezing."

"Must have been a couple because he wanted to see my records too. Guess he thought I was paying off that heifer. Naturally, I was clean. Believe me, no one would get twenty grand a month from me no matter what I did." She stuck out her chin. "Publish and be damned as they say."

I bent down pretending to rearrange some belts. Only one of the Croys had something to hide and it wasn't Babette. Had Ethel been blackmailing Carleton the serial philanderer? That seemed unlikely given her obsession with deep pockets. She probably zeroed in on several of his admirers who craved respectability and would pay handsomely to maintain it. Carleton was a lost cause.

"Too bad you have to leave," I said with a snarky grin. "Jakes is scheduled after lunch. You could cheer him on too."

Babette snarled a response. "Not funny. Besides Bascomb set up round three for this afternoon. The cops found a loose floorboard in Ethel's digs and they think she kept blackmail stuff there."

No wonder someone was prowling around Ethel's house. I wondered if Carleton had been searching for the blackmail loot when he got clobbered.

"How is Carleton?" I asked.

"Bearing up quite nicely. Lots of visitors, all female. Plenty of gifts."

I recalled Carleton's fan club from Hamilton Arms. "Anyone from the school?"

"Oh Lawd," She rolled her eyes. "That sleazy Charlotte Westly was front, and center, let me tell you. She tried that sweet as honey stuff on me and I backed her off but quick." Babette tapped her foot like a castanet. "Varmint! Carleton isn't much but he's living in my home. I demand a little respect like the song says."

A resurgence of the old Babette spirit was a good sign. I knew that despite everything she would survive and thrive. Carleton wasn't worth even one hair on her superbly coiffed head.

"See you later," she said. "Remember. I expect you to spill everything about Pruett. Everything! No exceptions."

I fought valiantly to block all thoughts of Pruett, but it wasn't easy. Friends stopped by, customers admired my wares, and sales were brisk. One bright spot occurred when Sheila burst into the shop waving a blue rosette. Sheila was jubilant. She danced around, hugging herself as if she had just won the lottery. Forget about sugarplums. Visions of the winner's circle ran through her head. "I love winning," she announced. "People don't realize how competitive I am, Perri, but it's true. One is the only number that counts in my book."

Now I understood Sheila's attraction to Ellis. He wasn't much to look at and he apparently flunked the stud test, but when it came to wheeling and dealing, Ellis was a titan of industry, confidant of presidents and a very big deal. Sheila reveled in the perks of being Mrs. Ellis Sands, and who could blame her. In a world of planned obsolescence and disposable trophy wives, corralling a rich husband who adored you was nothing to sneeze at.

I shared the titbits that Babette had gleaned.

"Wow! Can you imagine that?" Sheila shook her head. "Ethel had me totally fooled. She hung around like the good and faithful servant, but she must have despised all of us. You know I offered to pay her when she helped out with that fundraiser at our house."

"Really? Did she accept?" I was on autopilot, one ear listening for Pruett.

"Nope. Said it was a pleasure to be of service or some such crap. People get pretty liquored up at those events, Perri. You know that. Sometimes they're indiscreet. Hell, often they are. With a vulture like Ethel hanging around, it was the perfect set-up."

Sheila tossed her platinum bob and sailed for home. Ellis had apparently scheduled a very special treat to celebrate her victory.

Later that afternoon I slipped out to watch Jakes. I should have avoided him but the need to return was akin to a gravitational pull. Hunters were a popular event and the competition attracted a sizable crowd. Fortunately, I was able to wedge myself between a doughty matron and a family with three small children. Despite Jakes's cloddish ways, when Cleopatra entered the ring, she owned it. I almost felt sorry for the other competitors, all sound specimens who simply couldn't measure up to such perfection. Her pace and movement were perfect, and her manners displayed what a regal lady she truly was. Unfortunately, her rider lacked those social graces. Although I am no equine expert, even I could see some of the miscues from Jakes. His rigidity and excess body language detracted from Cleo's stylish performance. Still, her victory was a slam-dunk—until it wasn't. As the competition ended, the judge awarded the top score to Fortunato, a black gelding with an impressive pedigree. The scores were close—Fortunato had an 87 to Cleo's 80—but the results were final.

A ripple of applause sounded in the audience. Obviously, Fortunato had his own set of admirers. Unfortunately, the triumph was marred by a menacing growl from Jakes that quickly turned into an explosion. His outburst startled both horses and humans alike. The rules of the Equestrian Federation didn't allow for boorish conduct and the penalty for such would be steep. I leaned in to avoid missing a single syllable.

"You cheated!" Jakes screeched, pointing at Fortunato's rider. "How much did you pay that crone?"

Outraged squawks emanated from both the rider and the judge, but Jakes outshouted them both. Before the fracas turned violent, a steward stepped into the ring and took charge.

"That's enough, Mr. Jakes. Come with me." He pointed to the official area in the center of the grounds.

Jakes dismounted and reared back to throw a punch, but his opponent sidestepped him. The biologist sprawled on the ground in an ungainly heap while poor Cleo sped toward the open gate. I stepped forward and grabbed the reins. Even the best-behaved horse can panic during a volatile situation and I vowed to do everything to keep her from getting hurt or trampling anyone.

"He attacked me," Jakes yelled. "You all saw it. I'll sue him and the organizers." When two security officers approached, Jakes was escorted from the ring still protesting.

"You okay?" I asked the steward. "Better brush off your combat skills."

He shook his head and grinned. "Not quite what I bargained for. That guy's a menace. Too bad about his horse though. She'll be the one to suffer." He gave me a wave and sauntered off toward the admin tent as several volunteers took charge of Cleopatra and led her toward the barn.

The crowd was bug-eyed, particularly those with kids trailing after them. Horse shows were supposed to be wholesome family fun, not a blood sport. Apparently, Jakes had not gotten the message.

Chapter 18

Poor Cleo. She kept her tail down and lowered her head as if she were traumatized by her owner's downfall. Horses, like dogs, are sensitive, intelligent beings capable of giving unqualified love to even undeserving owners. It is one of the strengths of the human-animal bond. Felines are far less forgiving and more discerning. Witness Thatcher's elaborate system for keeping me firmly in my place.

I followed the steward as he attended to the mare's needs and found a vacant stall for her to rest in while Jakes straightened out his feud. He probably wouldn't get arrested although it was likely that a stiff administrative penalty would dampen his show career. Hers too, unfortunately. What a fool!

As word of the fracas filtered through the show community, a number of visitors agog with curiosity flooded into my shop trolling for information. Violence at these events was mostly verbal—deathblows to careers were administered through innuendo or falsehoods rather than fists. Boorish conduct and brawls were virtually unheard of in a genteel sport that valued decorum above all else. As the day wound down, I put up the closed sign and prepared to leave. Officials would ensure that Cleo was safe until Jakes was able to claim her.

Just before I locked up, the man himself flung open the door and confronted me. Keats and Poe were outside, and I could hear their growls of protest as they sensed danger.

"Where is she, bitch?" Jakes's face was contorted with rage, his fists clenched. "Just can't mind your own business, can you?"

I fought to remain calm and slowly unhooked my belt. The narrow aisles of the shop restricted room to maneuver, but I refused to panic. The heavy silver buckle could land a painful blow if needed. One false move and Jakes would feel its sting.

"Your horse is fine. Check with the stewards or the show officials if you're interested."

He gave a mocking laugh. "Oh, she is, is she? Is that part of your blackmail scheme?"

I was genuinely perplexed. Admittedly, Jakes was a nutcase, but I must have missed a vital clue, something that connected to Ethel. I had no idea what he was blabbering about.

"What did Ethel want from you?" I asked. "What was worth murdering her for?"

Jakes stepped closer, backing me against a rack of show collars. I clutched my belt waiting for the right opportunity.

"Murder?" he bellowed. "Lady, you are delusional. I have a solid alibi for that hag's murder. Just ask the cops." His eyes glittered with malice. "But I have a pretty good idea who killed the little twist and I plan to make it pay."

He didn't frighten me. Maybe he should have but he didn't. I had handled far worse cases than a maniacal biologist. Instead of fear I felt disgust. Jakes was nothing but a puny worm masquerading as a man.

"You love calling women names, don't you? Back off!"

"If the shoe fits… You need someone to teach you a lesson."

I swung the belt—buckle first—at his face. At that distance I couldn't miss, and it struck him squarely in the nose. Blood spurted everywhere on him, me, and my precious products. Jakes howled in pain and I lunged past him toward freedom. Unfortunately, he grabbed my shirttail, and spun me around. He deflected a kick toward his genitals and put his hands around my throat.

"Not so brave now are you," he snarled, pressing harder. "You broke my freaking nose!"

My training kicked in as I jabbed him in the eye with my right elbow. Sadly, it was a glancing blow that only infuriated him more. I was perilously close to losing consciousness when suddenly the door swung open and my guardian angels arrived.

First came Keats and Poe in full military attack mode, followed by the agile form of Pruett. Jakes loosened his grip just enough to allow me to breathe and fall backwards. We both tumbled to the floor of the narrow aisle. I was relatively unscathed, but it was lights out for my assailant as Jakes hit his head hard against a metal rack. Pruett overcame his fear of my dogs and leapt forward to help me up. Jakes was down for the count.

"Are you okay?" he asked, wrapping his arms around me. I must admit it felt good having someone to lean on even though I was confident that I could have saved myself without his help. That was my narrative, born from years of independent living and I stuck to it. Only Pip had pierced the barrier that encapsulated me. Pruett was late to that party, but he was closing fast.

I nodded to him as I gulped blessed lungsful of air. Pruett kept one arm around me as he whipped his iPhone out and dialed 911. "What the hell happened?" he asked. Keats and Poe loomed over Jakes, watching his inert form for any signs of activity.

I summarized the day's activities ending with Jakes's strange behavior. "He knows something about the murder," I croaked. That sound was the best that I could manage. My vocal chords were still recovering from the trauma of Jakes's attack and my neck felt tender.

Pruett brushed my bangs out of my eyes and squeezed my hand. Once again, his tenderness overwhelmed me. "Your neck has bruises all around it. Such a pretty neck too." He winked to show me that he was kidding. "Ah well. Attempted murder should keep him out of circulation for a bit while the cops sweat him for details."

My wits were still scrambled, and any lucid thoughts were banished by the simultaneous arrival of paramedics and the imposing figure of Titus Bascomb. The medics immediately bundled Jakes off to the hospital. After examining my throat and asking some basic questions, they cleared me to face Bascomb.

He took one look at Pruett and motioned toward the door. "Out, Mr. Pruett. Unless you are her attorney or her husband you don't belong here."

Pruett grinned. "Can't claim to be her husband yet but I am her legal representative. So, ask away, Lieutenant." He smothered my outraged squeak in another hug.

Bascomb rolled his eyes. He had the jaded look of a cop who had seen it all before and wasn't fooled. "Fine. Now take me through it. Slowly." Bascomb wedged his ponderous frame into a corner of my shop. Since his sergeant wasn't there, he used his phone to record our conversation. "I assume you have no objections, Counselor." He nodded toward Pruett and received a curt nod in return.

My narrative started at the show ring and continued to Jakes's sudden onslaught. When I mentioned blackmail and innuendos about Ethel's murder, he switched off the phone and held up his hand.

"Stop. He knows the identity of the killer? Who is it?"

"He didn't say but I think he plans to blackmail him or her. Jakes said there were big bucks involved."

Bascomb's expression was snide. "Mrs. Croy has big bucks."

"So do half the people in this area," I retorted. "We should focus on Ethel. Her character and behavior encouraged all kinds of blackmail."

I knew immediately that I'd said something wrong. Bascomb's face contorted and he wagged a meaty finger my way. "There is no 'we' in this, Ms. Morgan. The murder is a police matter. Butt out." He swung toward Pruett. "And that goes double for you, Mr. Pruett. I better not see anything in the media about this. Do you understand? And don't give me any of this first amendment crap either."

Pruett's expression was nothing short of angelic. "Absolutely."

Persistence was my middle name. "What have you found out about Ethel or whatever her real name was?"

Through gritted teeth, he spit out the answer. "Until she moved here two years ago that lady didn't exist. No trace in any of our databases. Now what does that suggest to you?"

I could almost feel my eyes widening. "Witness protection. She was probably a mob informant or involved with a drug cartel. I guess that clears Babette of suspicion."

Pruett had a different theory. "I vote for identity theft. The real Ethel McCall was probably a child who died young many years ago. Funny that her prints weren't on AFIS though."

Smoke doesn't literally spew from someone's ears, but Bascomb gave a fairly good imitation of it. "You both must have a hearing problem. What about the term 'butt out' don't you two understand?" Before I said one word, Pruett spoke for me, an annoying habit that I vowed to nip in the bud as soon as possible. "Of course, Lieutenant, but how else can you explain the money in her bank accounts? Ethel was obviously up to no good. Someone around here was paying to keep a mighty big secret from getting out." He helped me up. "May I take Ms. Morgan home now? She's had one rough day."

Bascomb's snort was world class and highly unprofessional. "Get out of here. Both of you." He thrust his arm out and stalked off.

To Pruett's credit he didn't flinch. "Sounds like good advice. I better drive," he said. "You still seem kind of shaky."

"What about your car?"

"No problem. I'll leave it here overnight. They have security."

I didn't argue. Frankly I welcomed the thought of having company for the evening. My brush with death made me yearn for the solace and safety of my home and pets. Pruett's presence was an additional bonus.

Chapter 19

On the way home, I phoned Babette to tell her the latest about Jakes. Bad news travels fast and I wanted her to hear it from me first. After Jakes's claims, I was also worried that Bascomb would confront her with one of his crackpot theories. Spontaneity was a problem where Babette was concerned. If she were taken unawares, she could easily combust and blurt out all sorts of ill-advised comments that later backfired. In this instance forewarned was definitely forearmed.

"What! You have got to be kidding!" Babette unleashed a string of oaths and imprecations that no true lady would even think of. Considering the circumstances, I had to admit that she was justified. Jakes was a vile creature who deserved no better. "Don't say another word," she said. "I'll be right over."

I couldn't stop her even if I tried. When Babette was on a mission, only an act of God deterred her. Even though that quashed any hope for an uninterrupted evening with Pruett, I didn't care. My emotions were spiraling out of control and that frightened me. I studied his profile as he wrangled my Suburban through the traffic squalls. He was perfect, too perfect. That was the crux of the problem.

"Something bothering you?" he asked.

Of course, something was bothering me! After suffering two assaults, finding a bloody corpse and facing police threats, things were just hunky dory. Afghanistan was a war zone, but it seemed like Disneyland compared with Northern Virginia. Instead of howling at him, I took a deep breath.

"Just Babette. She'll be joining us soon and she's all fired up. Too bad Ella didn't join you."

"Maybe we should pool our information and see where that takes us. If Jakes knows something he might tell me. You know, one guy bragging to another. Of course, if you press charges he'll be cooling his heels in jail."

I yawned, leaned back against the headrest and closed my eyes. Damn. My throat ached something fierce. If only a celestial being would zap this whole mess and make it disappear. Something about Pruett's company induced me to doze off again. When I opened my eyes, we were home, just in time to hear Zeke's angry greeting. No rest for the weary. Unavoidable chores awaited me and tending to a cranky pygmy goat was first among them.

"Sorry I zoned out on you again," I said. "It's not like me."

"Give yourself a break. You don't always have to be strong." He smiled. "Not around me."

I bit my tongue to staunch the tears that threatened. All my life I ruthlessly repressed any trace of vulnerability. It signified weakness, something I simply could not afford, except with Pip. He was the only person—male or female—who let me feel safe. Pruett's kindness lured me closer and closer to him and our bond had strengthened over the past year. Yielding and then losing it was too great a risk. Another loss would break my heart.

I pasted a plucky, can-do grin on my face. "Better do my chores before Zeke kicks down the fence."

"Hold on, warrior woman. Let me help you." He hopped out, opened my door and offered me his hand. "You put on quite a show today," he said. "I was proud of you. Impressed actually. Scared too. Whew! Jakes came out the loser in that one."

I blinked, trying to dislodge the sleep from my eyes. My contact lenses felt grainy and sore and I found myself squinting.

"I forgot to ask you. Where's Ella? I thought she was coming with you today?"

"My plans changed," he said. "Her mother swooped into the city and just had to see her little girl. She plans to take Ella shopping or some such nonsense. Everything's a big event with Monique. Normal life bores her silly."

I kept my opinions to myself. Obviously, anything to do with Monique, super photog and absentee parent, was a very sensitive subject. "I'm glad Ella missed all the excitement though," I said. "Kids should be shielded from violence. It would have frightened her."

Pruett raised his eyebrows. "She's safe with me and she knows it. No one will ever harm that child, so long as I have one breath in my body.

I'd kill anyone who got in the way." He lightened his words by holding out his arm and flexing his muscle. "Come on. I have a way with goats."

We spent the next half hour feeding and grooming Zeke and the dogs. Gradually, Pruett overcame his wariness and approached all of them. Poe and Keats accepted his advances and after eating they curled up in my living room with Thatcher in companionable silence.

By the time Babette swung into the driveway, our entire household was at peace. Pruett learned through his police contacts that Jakes had been charged with assault and jailed for the night. One less thing to worry about.

Babette and the ever-faithful Clara joined our party bearing gifts. "I figured you might get hungry," she said. "Behold. Pollo a la Brasa— Peruvian style chicken."

The aroma was maddening. Suddenly I realized that I had missed both lunch and dinner. I was famished!

Babette got down to basics. "Okay. Now tell me everything."

Between mouthfuls of delicious poultry, we did so. To her delight, Pruett embroidered upon my clash with Jakes by touting me as a cross between Wonder Woman and the goddess Athena.

"You're a hero, Perri. Just think. You trapped a murderer." Babette threw her arms around me, heedless of chicken bones, green salsa and upholstery.

I held up my hand. "Not so fast. I'm not sure Jakes is the killer."

"But he knows something," Pruett said. "He definitely knows something or thinks he does."

Babette snorted in disgust. "Horsefeathers! Ethel was blackmailing him, and he killed her. Plain and simple. I called Sheila, but she was out on the town. I bet she'll agree with me."

Pruett and I locked eyes. The connection was so intense that for an instant, time and place stood still. I gave myself a mental shakedown and returned to the rational world.

"Bascomb made it clear that amateurs were not welcome on his turf. That definitely included you." I pointed to Babette.

"Big deal." She folded her arms and stuck out her lip like a petulant child. Babette never allowed legal niceties to thwart her plans. "As a sovereign citizen, I have every right to ask questions. He can just pound sand or deal with my lawyer. How would Bascomb like being the star of my cable show playing America's most unwanted?"

"Suit yourself." After enduring a difficult day, I had neither the mental nor physical strength to battle Babette. Instead, I curled up in a ball and pulled the afghan up to my chin. My kind-hearted friend reacted immediately. "Perri, forgive me darlin.' I've been so wrapped up in this feud that I forgot how you must feel."

"Let's discuss this later," Pruett said. "The idea of leveraging your cable show has promise. It might be a way to get information. You could change the entire trajectory of the discussion. Repurpose Cavalry Farms as a community resource."

Babette glanced over at Pruett and smiled. "I'll just take off and check back with you in the morning. Come on, Clara."

And with that, Pruett and I were suddenly alone. I didn't ask him to stay even though I hoped he would. Loneliness was an acquired habit, one that I had yet to master even after two years. I yearned for companionship and comfort but feared rejection. I yearned for him.

"Looks like you could use some rest," he said. "Come on. I'll lock up and help you to your room." He led the human-canine procession to the bedroom and tucked me under the covers. "Anything else you need?" he asked.

I summoned my courage and met his gaze. "Just you."

His smile was all the answer that I needed.

Chapter 20

Sunday was a day of rest—unless you were part of the show world. Early that morning I soothed my aching muscles under a scalding shower and gingerly dressed myself. Pruett raised his head for a moment then wordlessly plunged back into dreamland.

My morning chores included feeding, exercising, and placating two dogs, one cat and a goat. For some reason, Zeke was particularly irascible that day. He consumed precious time running around the pasture, hurdling over jumps and generally refusing to enter his stall until I trapped him into it. The triumphant look in his eyes told me that the little beast had enjoyed every second.

My own grooming rituals on show days were usually minimal, but with Pruett around I felt compelled to up my game. The man was accustomed to Monique's standard of perfection, something I neither would nor could attain. Still, I sped to the shower, rid myself of every trace of Zeke, and applied a light cosmetic touch. For once, I let my hair down both literally and figuratively. A silk scarf added a dash of color and hid my neck injuries. It took some effort, but the reward awaited me in the kitchen.

"Wow!" Pruett said, giving me a faux leer. "Hot stuff, Ms. Morgan." He handed me a coffee mug. "Here. Have a caffeine fix."

My cheeks warmed even though I was much too old to blush. "Thanks."

Pruett lifted the scarf and ran his fingers lightly over the welts on my neck. "Poor thing. Your skin still has his fingermarks on it. Bastard!"

I shrugged off his comment and reached for the toast stacked neatly on a plate. For a playboy, Pruett had a pronounced domesticated side.

"I'm tougher than I look. Like they say, you should see the other guy."

Instead of laughing, he took my hand and kissed it. "Don't make a habit of that kind of stuff, Perri. Next time you might get really hurt and how would I ever explain that to Ella?"

"I promise to be careful. Besides, Jakes has been banned from the show grounds so I'm safe there at least. Despite everything, I still don't think he's the murderer. It all leads back to Ethel and her blackmail scheme. Jakes didn't have enough cash to interest her. I think she was only toying with him. Look what she tried with Ken Reedy."

Pruett suggested several theories that I had never considered. We knew very little about Jakes other than his occupation. He might be the frugal type or have family money. Ethel, who apparently loved to twist the knife, might well have taunted him about some secret worth killing for—at least to Jakes. Perhaps her sadistic game was one of power and control as much as money.

"When it comes to blackmail, money may not be the only motive. Love, prestige, position—they all have importance too." Pruett stroked his chin. "Think of that gang Babette assembled in her parlor. Carleton risked his career by messing with other men's wives. Ken Reedy values respect and he could sacrifice that. Sheila and Charlotte have cushy lives that depend on their husbands. And Jacqui—her social connections are all she has. It may sound trivial to us, but that spells motive to me. Ethel was playing with fire and she got burned." Pruett checked the notes on his phone. "Back to this cable show of Babette's. What if she arranged a program about Cavalry Farms and invited some of Ethel's circle to it. People like that Hamilton Arms crew for instance. A couple of those women were hot to trot. Maybe they were afraid their husbands would find out."

I gave that idea some thought. A program about the murder would be too obvious, but a fundraiser for Cavalry Farms might just work. The guest list could include everyone from the original committee as well as any Hamilton Arms patrons who were friendly with Ethel. Bascomb would have a fit but it just might work.

Pruett agreed immediately. "Great! That would give me an excuse to show up too. I'm not sure how Babette will feel about including Jakes, but he was one of the original group." He shrugged. "Who knows? By then he might still be in jail."

Pruett agreed to discuss details with Babette and to do some more digging about Jakes and the other committee members. He had sources and techniques for eliciting information that ordinary mortals lacked. I knew that very few mortals could resist the blandishments of DC's sexiest man alive. Sad to say, I included myself in that group.

I packed up the Suburban, herded my dogs into it and prepared to leave.

He lingered at the driver's side window and tapped it. "Hey! My ride is at the showgrounds. Remember? Shove over."

It was too early in the morning to jockey for driving rights, so I climbed into the passenger seat and let Pruett do the honors. No one had fussed over me in a long time—over two years in fact. I'd forgotten how comforting it could be.

When we arrived, Pruett leapt from the truck after urging me once again to be cautious and to text him when I was safely in my shop. We made no plans for the day, nor did we discuss anything about the evening. I looked in the mirror and wiped a goofy grin off my face. It felt both weird and wonderful to be connected to someone, even as caution lights flashed in my head. Monique was in town, I reminded myself. This was a woman he had once cared for and had a child with. Most men would prefer spending the evening with a celebrity over the dull domestic routine of a farm. That, as they said, was a no-brainer.

Babette had other thoughts. She called just as I unlocked the shop and immediately peppered me with questions about Pruett. I deflected as many as possible and downplayed our involvement. When I mentioned Monique, she pivoted with the grace of Pavlova.

"Don't sell yourself short, Perri. After all, you have substance. You're not just another pretty face." Babette realized what a backhanded compliment that was. "You have inner beauty too," she said. "Anyone can tell by the way he looked at you that Pruett is totally smitten. Definitely smitten."

"He's looking for you by the way. You two can discuss the television bit," I said. "Put your heads together."

Babette sighed. "Don't I wish. Unfortunately, Bascomb is a more likely candidate for head bumping than our golden boy. Okay. Take it easy today. And Perri—leave the heroics to the cops. Bascomb gets paid to dance with murderers. You don't."

After so many warnings, I prowled around the grounds, seeing Jakes behind every barrel. A stop at the barn to check on Cleopatra calmed my emotions. Straightaway, the beautiful mare nudged my pockets cadging for treats. I rewarded her with apple slices and a stray carrot. No sentient being could stroke that soft nose or scratch between her ears without sighing. Fear was simply not my friend and had to be banished. I gave myself a vigorous mental shakedown and steadied my nerves. Sunday show days were relatively peaceful, and this was no exception. After the final hunter class concluded I began the procession toward the Suburban accompanied by Poe. Keats remained in the store guarding my products. I walked slowly, vigilant but not paranoid—not with a Malinois at my side. Even Jakes would think twice before taking on Poe.

"Need some help?" Ken Reedy was a welcome sight. He patted Poe and helped load the stock into my truck. "Got another load or two, I presume?"

I nodded.

"Well, come on then, girl. Get moving. I just left the farm but news travels fast. After yesterday you need to be extra careful." Ken was a man of few words, an extraordinary thing in a lawyer. When he did speak, however, he made every syllable count.

"Don't suppose they'll give Jakes jail time unless you push it," he said. "Most likely cop a plea and order counselling and anger management training." He hooted. "Like that makes a difference with a nutbag like him. He's threatening to sue the show and you personally, Perri."

"Me?"

"Yep. Says his head injuries are all your fault." Like most lawyers, Reedy had a bizarre sense of humor. He patted my back and walked ahead, chuckling all the way.

I was conflicted, unsure how to feel about the whole thing. Obviously, Jakes needed professional help, but a prison sentence might be overkill. Overkill—an interesting choice of words, especially if Jakes really had murdered Ethel. I shivered even though the temperature was moderate for Northern Virginia. Times like this made me yearn to be home cuddling my pets with the down comforter over my head. The unease didn't subside until I swung into my driveway and saw Zeke, flashing his fey, malevolent grin my way.

* * * *

The next week passed quickly and productively for me and my pet family. Work had always been an antidote to worry, so I put myself to the test by working feverishly to complete the belt order. Pruett and I texted but had no substantive contact. Thanks to Babette, however, I kept abreast of the planned cable showdown an event whose level of secrecy surpassed the Manhattan Project.

When it came to relationships, I was no risk taker. Dealing with a man like Pruett was doubly difficult since he was understandably wary of any attempts to entrap him. Still, I took a risk and fashioned a custom set of half-chaps for Ella. Pruett mentioned that her birthday was coming up and a small token seemed appropriate. It was a labor of love and her initials on the finished product made it seem extra special. In order to send it to her, I phoned Pruett's landline, hoping, praying, that Alma the genial housekeeper would answer. Sometimes, prayers actually work.

"Miss Perri," Alma said. "Como estas?"

"Muy bien, Alma. Gracias."

I explained that I had a gift for Ella and needed her mailing address. Alma had a better idea and suggested that I just drop it off at the house.

"Will you be in town this week, Ms. Perri? Bring it over and I will give it to Ella. No problema."

We arranged a time that next morning after the meeting with my client, and I went back to work with a smile on my face.

Traffic was horrific that next morning as I plowed through the maze of DC streets. My nerves frayed and to complicate matters, the Suburban's temperamental air conditioner went on strike. By the time I wrangled a parking space in Georgetown and hauled my sample case up to the office, I resembled a stable hand more than an entrepreneur.

None of that detracted from the meeting. It was pleasant, productive, and best of all, lucrative. My client and the buyers from several large retail outlets loved the belts and clamored for more. I floated out to my truck on a cloud of optimism. With any luck, I could drop off Ella's present and beat the rush hour traffic back to Great Marsh.

Thanks to my GPS, I found Pruett's "P" street roost without too many false turns. I had wrapped Ella's gift in horse themed paper and affixed a small milk bone to the top. The child probably had designer everything, but this handmade gift was still unique and worth having. I was proud of my work. After ringing the bell, I waited for Alma, oblivious to my windswept hair and faded lipstick. The transaction would take only a minute, so I had no need to primp. Finally, the door opened a crack and a woman's throaty voice asked. "Yes? What do you want?"

It may be a cliché, but my heart truly did sink. Every insecurity from childhood welled up within me as the door opened and I glimpsed the flawless face and form of Monique Allaire, the woman Pruett had once loved.

I had always comforted myself by thinking that airbrushed magazine images were artificial and improbable. How wrong I was. Unadorned and clad in an oversize tee-shirt, Monique was the most perfect looking specimen I had ever seen. She was tall, lean, and beautifully put together with silky streaked hair and bright blue eyes. Maybe that perfection explained her arrogance.

"Do I know you?" she asked, giving me a casual onceover. I considered my options: flee, feign ignorance, or pretend I was at the wrong address. Since none of them were feasible I opted for truth.

"Is Alma here?" I asked. "I have something to give her."

Monique gave me a hard stare as if my story rang false. Although we had met before, she either forgot or chose to ignore that fact. "She's at the market. Come back later."

I nodded and turned to leave. No need for a scene. Unfortunately, at that moment Ella appeared and flung herself at me. "Perri! Are the dogs with you?"

I shook my head. "Not today. I know your birthday is next week, so I made you a present." I handed it to her. "From me and all the pets."

Ella's sunny smile warmed my day. "Perri has dogs and a cat and goat too. She's Daddy's girlfriend."

Monique's eyes flashed as if she were still very much in Pruett's life. She pushed open the door and sent a semi-smirk my way. "Wing is at work, but he'll be back for lunch. Come in if you'd care to wait." Her manner was icy, her gaze insolent.

By force of will, I managed to maintain my composure. My simple, spontaneous gesture had suddenly become the source of incalculable humiliation. If Pruett found me there, I simply could not bear it.

"Thanks, but I have to get back. Nice seeing you again, Monique." I gave Ella another hug, took my leave and shed not one tear until I was safely in the Suburban.

* * * *

Babette sized up the situation immediately. She listened to my tale of woe and broke out a bottle of aged brandy.

"Kind of early to drink," I said. "After all nobody died."

"Darlin,' when invincible Perri Morgan falls apart, no time is too early. Here. Bottoms up. Think of it as medicinal."

She waited a decent interval before peppering me for details about Monique. Like most people, Babette was intrigued by the famous beauty and hoped to hear of some flaw. We'd last seen Monique a year ago, but time had not marred her beauty. A mole, errant hair, or chunk of cellulite would have made Babette's day. Alas. I could only report the truth: Pruett's former lover was perfect, lovelier in the flesh than I remembered.

"Sounds like a bitch though." Babette brightened at the thought. "Just think. They're not together so there must be a reason."

Time to dispel her fantasies and mine. "She was wearing a tee-shirt—his."

Babette mounted a spirited argument about the ubiquity of such shirts until I hit her with the showstopper.

"It had his name on it. Wing."

My caring friend enveloped me in a tight hug and immediately turned on Pruett. "All men are bastards, Perri. You know that. They take turns."

My problems were no cause for lamentation. I survived Afghanistan and I would survive this. Carleton was once Babette's husband and he had publicly disgraced her with who knew how many women. That was real pain. Tears were superfluous and unworthy of a warrior woman. Wasn't that what Pruett had called me?

We shared another drink of brandy and chatted about her forthcoming television show. Once word got out that Pruett would make an appearance, the acceptance rate zoomed to one hundred percent. Taping was scheduled for the following Monday at ten a.m. at Babette's place. No word yet on Jakes, although he had been officially charged, freed on his own recognizance and ordered to stay at least one hundred yards away from me. Cleo had been transported to Cavalry Farms where she remained happily camped out.

"When is that sidewinder gonna pick up his horse?" Babette asked. "We're having a dry run over at my place. Before the taping, you know."

I shrugged. "He has to make arrangements through his attorney, so the ball is in his court. More to the point will he attend your show's taping?"

Babette evaded my eyes, a sure sign of trouble. "I'm not handling that detail," she mumbled. Even without mentioning his name Pruett was the center of conversation. I could live with that. The important thing was narrowing the suspect list in Ethel's murder. Anything else was irrelevant.

Tasks awaited me, so I gathered my things to head home. When Babette's cell phone rang, I knew by the furtive look on her face who was calling. That was my exit cue.

"See you later." I strode out the door and jumped into the Suburban. Let Pruett spread his charm elsewhere. He owed me nothing, not even an explanation. Besides, I was a willing participant. More than willing, actually. No doubt he was now on the run, wary about yet another predatory female—me.

Chapter 21

Sheila was waiting for me when I arrived home, pacing around my driveway with Cecil in tow. Since she was wearing boots and breeches, I realized she had recently finished riding. To her credit, she had kept busy by feeding Zeke and frolicking with my dogs. I was officially in her debt and glad to be so.

"Finally," she said. "I thought you'd never come home. I cut short my ride because I had to see you." This behavior was odd for Sheila who typically was one very cool customer. It was obvious that she had some big news to share.

"Come on in and have a drink," I said. "You've got me very curious." Sheila and the entire menagerie save for Zeke followed me into the living room.

"Perri, you won't believe this," she said. "Ellis had his security guys do some sleuthing and guess what they found? Our little community is a nest of crime and corruption! A virtual den of iniquity."

That bombshell required an explanation. Sheila yawned, stretched out her long legs on my couch and spilled her secrets. "Okay. This one will blow your mind. Ken Reedy didn't retire from practicing law. He was disbarred! Actually, he surrendered his law license but it's the same thing. Can you believe it?"

I bowed my head. "I just found out. He didn't try to hide anything."

She nodded. "Yep. He admitted it, lost his license and got a suspended sentence."

I refused to condemn Ken's actions, not after seeing how Pip had suffered. He insisted on bearing the pain even though as a veterinarian, he had access to plenty of alternatives. Had he asked me, I would have done anything to help him.

"What else?" I asked, dreading the answer. Everyone, even a potential murderer deserved a zone of privacy. It felt sordid to pry into their secrets.

"Jacqueline Parks—you know that woman who screwed around with Pruett. Babette's pal."

"Yes?"

"She has a conviction for shoplifting. Can you believe it? She swiped a box of condoms from the CVS. Now that's just nasty!"

I took a perverse pleasure in picturing Pruett using purloined condoms. Served him right. "Don't they usually hush up that kind of stuff, especially in a wealthy community?"

Sheila winked. "Right. But apparently, this was not her first offense. Mrs. Parks clipped a bunch of things from Walmart and Sam's Club too. So lowbrow! She probably got a sick thrill from slumming."

"Anyone else?" Babette's entire committee was apparently mired in corruption and vulnerable to a shark like Ethel.

"This won't surprise you one bit. You met Charlotte Westly and that Neanderthal she married, didn't you?"

"Yeah."

"Charlotte apparently frequents most of the hot sheet motels in the area and has the receipts to prove it. I think she's some kind of nympho."

At least that wasn't illegal. Ill-advised, sleazy, and grounds for divorce, but not illegal unless her partners were underage. I studied Sheila's expression for a clue and decided that she looked guilty as hell.

"Okay. Out with it."

"At least one of her 'friends' was a kid from Hamilton Arms and he was eighteen. The school hushed it up and he was of legal age, so the cops let it slide. I understand that Charlotte settled big time with the kid's family though."

Either the alcohol or the insights into my neighbors made me feel queasy. I prayed that Sheila had finished describing things.

"You mean her husband found out and didn't divorce her?" Most men would have dumped a straying spouse, especially if her offense went public.

Once again Sheila hesitated, as if for dramatic effect. "You got that right. Ellis would dump me like a hot potato. Charlotte was cagey though. She let it be known that if he divorced her, she would spread the word that hubby had performance issues! Think what that would do to his power in the boardroom! No man wants that."

Sheila turned away and busied herself with hugging Cecil. She didn't fool me for a second. That ruse meant that she had something even more unpleasant to share.

"Okay. What aren't you saying?" I gave her my flat-eyed, military stare.

She waited and heaved a big sigh. "Carleton's name came up. He and Charlotte apparently were an item. Jacqueline too. A scandal just might mean the end of his cozy little berth at Hamilton Arms. That's why Bascomb keeps his beady little eyes on Babette. He thinks she had motive, means and opportunity. For a cop that's the trifecta."

I blinked ferociously while trying to process everything. All four suspects were also members of Babette's committee and on or near the premises the day of Ethel's murder. Add Jakes to the list and you had a quintet of potential killers. Everybody had plausible motives although my first reaction was to exclude Ken Reedy and Babette. Carleton was far more likely to strike back than his ex-wife if his livelihood was imperiled. He was so egotistical that I could easily envision the little creep bashing in Ethel's brains if she taunted him. As for Ken and Babette, they were good people, gentle souls at heart who loved animals and abhorred violence. That counted for something, didn't it? A devilish voice within me sneered that even good people could be driven to violence.

Sheila jumped up and brushed off her slacks. "Talk about a quagmire. Even if Ethel deserved it, most of these things were simply no big deal. Certainly not worth a stretch in the big house or Virginia's version of the needle."

I thought back to the murder scene, bloody and savage but somehow impromptu. Ethel's murder was unplanned; I was positive of that. The fire extinguisher was a weapon of convenience, one of sheer chance. There was passion involved but not premeditation. Maybe Ethel upped the ante or taunted her victim. If the killer went berserk, that would explain the ferocity of the attack. According to Bascomb, she was struck on the back of the head, probably while preparing to don that stupid horse costume.

"Babette doesn't know this, I assume?"

Sheila shook her head.

It felt like the ultimate betrayal, keeping vital information from a friend. If only I could bounce my theories off someone. I winced knowing that Pruett was the one I needed but would never contact. Even for Babette.

"Look, hon, I have to make tracks. Ellis has tickets to some charity thing or another tonight and he expects me to dazzle the donors." Sheila preened and did a half pirouette. "Who knows? Maybe I'll see Pruett there. Monique Allaire is co-sponsor of the shindig. Promised to snap some photos too."

My smile was weaker than day old tea. "Good luck. Knock 'em dead."

On second thought, considering our current dilemma my choice of words was unfortunate.

* * * *

Good thing I wasn't a drinker. Even in the throes of Pip's final illness when escape was tempting, I kept my mind clear and my body alcohol free, more from indifference than virtue. I gave myself a quick pep talk designed to ease angst and elevate my spirits. No pun intended. After all, bringing that gift made a little girl happy. I had no ulterior motive. The encounter with Monique was a minor blip in my romantic saga not a tragedy.

Keep telling yourself that Perri. Maybe you'll believe it.

I spent the rest of the evening in my workshop, filling orders and poring over my accounts. Before long, Poe and Keats nuzzled me, and I saw to my surprise that it was nearly ten o'clock. Bedtime for a working stiff like me.

When my cell rang, I answered without checking caller ID, confident that Babette had yet another detail to discuss. His voice, deep, dark, and dreamy, jolted me out of my stupor.

"Sorry I missed you today," Pruett said. "You really hit a home run with my daughter. Couldn't get her to take off that thing without bribing her. Chaps—who knew?"

"I'm glad." I didn't trust myself to say much more. Anything else would have betrayed the depth of my anguish. Chasing men was something I simply did not do.

Pruett hesitated. "Are you mad at me or something, Perri?"

My legs felt weak and I quickly eased down on the sofa. Might as well clear the air right away. "This is so embarrassing. I'm sorry about today. I wasn't stalking you at home or checking up on you. I thought Alma would be there to take the gift."

He laughed, a hearty, masculine sound. I expected to hear voices and other party noises in the background but there was total silence.

"Aren't you at that fundraiser? Sheila said …"

"Are you kidding? I'm babysitting. Those things bore the pants off me, so I avoid them like the plague."

I spared a brief thought for Pruett without his pants then forged ahead with the conversation. "Oh. Just so you know." For some reason, I was close to tears.

"You are welcome at my place anytime, Ms. Morgan, even without a gift." He was laughing again. "Hey, I know it's late but how about having a drink? I can scoop up Ella and be at your place in twenty minutes."

"Tonight?" With no makeup, Pip's ratty old robe and dog themed pajamas, I was scarcely a fashion plate. Truth be told, I was an early to bed, early to rise kind of gal and always had been. Suddenly I got a brainstorm. "We could Skype if you want. Sheila found out a bunch of things that I could run by you. Some of them are pretty wild."

He waited before answering, just long enough to make me sweat. "I guess so, but nothing beats having my arms around you. You're in my head big time, lady. I don't mind telling you."

I gulped, thinking of the glamorous woman at his house and her comely predecessors. Pruett was a practiced lover. A casual affair was *de rigueur* for him but not for me. Disposable partners were the preserve of cynical society fixtures prowling the cocktail circuit, but I was a country mouse. I shrugged off the drama and returned to the impersonal business of death. "Use your imagination. Come on. Let's get started."

Skype had some advantages over direct contact. We spent an uninterrupted hour discussing suspects, communicating in modern mode about murder, society's oldest taboo. Pruett listened carefully as I cited their names and the evidence against them. He bit his lip and scribbled notes on what looked like a legal pad.

"Quite a list," he said, "but my money's still on Jakes. The guy is a nut and we know what kind of temper he has. Ethel might have taunted him, and he just lost it."

"What about Ken?" I held my breath, hoping that Pruett would understand as I did what a decent man Reedy truly was.

"I don't know him, but I sympathize with his actions. Besides, his secret was out in the open, so the cops would already know about it. He really had nothing to hide unless he didn't want his friends to know."

The others were not so lucky. Both women relied on their social status and perceived reputation for fulfilment. Would they kill to conceal relatively minor offenses? Jacqueline was a tall, powerful woman who could probably overwhelm Ethel with no problem. Charlotte was no Amazon but if her rage was fueled by passion she could surprise her victim.

Pruett must have read my mind. "Jacqui Parks plays a mean game of tennis," he said. "Check out the muscles in her forearms sometime. Formidable."

"I'll take your word for that."

Pruett sipped his wine and wisely confined his comments to our suspect list. "We need to at least consider Babette too. Just for the sake of form."

I had already rehearsed the pros and cons of that argument. True, Babette had motive and means but why choose a time when she was hosting a group and might be discovered? She could easily have faked a robbery or lured Ethel to another spot. Plus, she had no illusions about Carleton and I doubted that she cared about his liaisons.

Based on his body language, my arguments fell flat with Pruett. He set his jaw and folded his arms. "Anything else?" he asked. "I know Babette is your friend but when it comes to emotion you just can't predict anything. Hamlet said love leads to desperate undertakings. You gotta admit that nothing is more desperate than murder."

I shrugged it off. "Who am I to dispute the Bard? Just think. Ken, Jacqui, Jakes and Charlotte all had their cars in the driveway and the cops searched them. Wouldn't some forensic evidence have been there? Afterwards, they cordoned off the area. Sheila was late and almost didn't get in."

Pruett hesitated. "Maybe someone hiked or ran in from the highway."

I shook my head. "Doubtful. It's five miles from the road and the timeframe's too narrow. Babette was only gone a short time. I suppose a bicycle might work though."

Either way, the murderer was bold, someone who was willing to risk everything to silence Ethel. I considered the five likely suspects and decided I just didn't know enough about their characters to make a judgement.

"We may learn something at that meeting of Babette's tomorrow." Pruett grinned. "What if I drop by your place tomorrow before the meeting and give you a wakeup call? I promise to bring sustenance."

"What's on the menu?" I asked. "Stale bagels just won't cut it. I have a big appetite."

Pruett was a master of snark. "Trust me. I can satisfy your needs. All of them."

"Not scared of my dogs anymore?" My insouciance surprised even me.

"Nope. We've reached détente. Wait and see."

"Sounds like a plan."

Chapter 22

Sleep eluded me that night. I tried not to fuss about trivial things—no frilly silk negligées or lacy lingerie. Come to think of it, I didn't own any sexy sleepwear. Oversized cotton t-shirts were more my thing, cheap and washable. I had just dozed off when Zeke sounded the alarm, Thatcher bolted out of bed and the Malinois assaulted my ears with frenzied barks. So much for sleep—my guest had arrived.

I quieted my herd and whisked Pruett into the house, hoping that the light was too dim for him to observe me closely. Bed head and morning breath were an unappealing combo. Pruett carried a thermos and a wicker basket that emitted a mouth-watering aroma. "Alma fixed us a feast," he said. "Dig in."

"Have some coffee while I get ready. It won't take long. Promise."

Accompanied by my posse, I zoomed up the stairs and jumped into the shower. Fortunately, my hair was shiny clean, and my jeans were neatly pressed. No sense in trying for glitz. I toweled off and fumbled for Pip's robe. When I emerged from bathing, a surprise awaited me. He had arranged our breakfast on the side table and positioned himself under the bedcovers. He held out his arms and said in a soft, sultry voice, "Come here, lady. Let's have that wakeup call."

* * * *

There was something special about Pruett. It went beyond physical attraction, although that was potent enough. According to the gossip columns, most of his romances dissolved within two months. We'd been an item for well over a year, so I was on borrowed time.

Pruett ran his fingers through my hair. "So lovely, and it's real."

"What?"

He chuckled. "Most models and actresses today have that fake hair—extensions they call it. Looks okay until you touch it. Ugh!" He helped himself to espresso and a heaping plate of spinach quiche ala Alma. "Yum! Wait'til you try this stuff. It's the best."

I couldn't wait to devour that quiche. No sense in pretending, he already knew that I ate like a lumberjack. Besides, wasting food was a sin. All the preachers said so. We satiated ourselves and rewarded the dogs with the remaining scraps. Pruett cleaned up while I attended to Zeke and poured water and kibble for the pups. Thatcher was an exception. She refused to eat any pet food except kitten chow although she had long passed any claim to kittenhood.

We drove separately to Babette's, part of a plan to divide and conquer her little group. Pruett agreed to charm the ladies while I played hostess with my friend. That way if Jakes showed up, I could count on back-up. My neck bruises attested to the man's strength when angered.

By the time we arrived, the others, with the exception of Jakes, had already claimed their spots. I surveyed them with a jaundiced eye: Sheila, long, lean, and cool; Jacqueline blonde and leonine; Charlotte, notable for too much scent and an inordinate amount of jewelry, and Ken Reedy, watchful and poised. Was one of them hiding the ultimate secret?

Babette immediately hugged me, and clasped Pruett's hand. Her cheek was ice-cold despite the blazing fire, and the quilted cashmere outfit she wore. Perhaps the presence of her ex-spouse explained her condition. Carleton sat alone on the oversized chair adjacent to the fireplace, grim and forbidding, with his arms crossed. The man radiated disapproval.

"Why don't we get started," Babette said with forced cheer. "So much to do, so little time. I think you all know each other."

Carleton held up his hand. "Wait. Since Mr. Pruett is a reporter, how much of this discussion is on the record?"

I noticed that Pruett was wedged between Charlotte and Jacqui on the down sofa. He seemed perfectly at home there.

"Let me know if something is private," he said. "No problem. I thought this was just a brainstorming session."

His claque of admirers nodded and patted his shoulder. Ken Reedy eyed Pruett with that jaundiced stare common to lawyers.

"Wasn't Jakes supposed to be here?" Reedy asked. "I didn't see his truck in the driveway."

I frowned, thinking of the battered van I had seen behind Ethel's old place. Jakes owned a vehicle very much like that, but then so did half the guys in the county.

All eyes turned to Babette. "He texted me last night and said he'd be here." She shrugged. "Let's give him a few minutes more."

"Anything new about Ethel?" Reedy asked. "It fell out of the news headlines after that triple murder in Richmond last Friday. Sexier, I guess."

Charlotte shivered. "At least that Bascomb character has backed down. He gives me the creeps, always asking the same questions three different ways."

I leaned forward and took a risk. "He thinks Ethel was a blackmailer. Can you believe it?"

"Didn't we meet at Hamilton Arms?" Charlotte said, squinting up at me. "Something about your niece?"

Pruett quickly intervened. "Perri was there as my guest. My daughter adores her."

"Well, I still think some thief tangled with Ethel and panicked. She was spunky you know. Nosey too. Would have challenged anyone in a heartbeat." Jacqui folded her arms across her capacious bosom as if that settled everything. To his credit, Pruett averted his eyes.

I moved toward Babette to give her a modicum of support. She had a lengthy agenda typed and ready to distribute, but my normally vivacious friend seemed paralyzed by indecision. "Here," I said. "Let me do that."

After each person had a copy, Babette revived somewhat. She led a discussion about Cavalry Farms and its need for financial support, then asked Pruett to share his experience with other groups whose causes challenged the establishment. I had to admit that his comments were concise, witty, and right on point. Naturally, he had no difficulty in holding the attention of every female in the room. Sheila smiled, Charlotte simpered, and Jacqui gaped. I kept my cool while recalling a few pleasurable scenes from our morning tryst. When he finished, I checked my watch, surprised to learn that an hour had passed with no sign of Jakes. If he intended to show up, Jakes had better make a move soon.

Our hostess called for a fifteen-minute break, and the participants scattered. Soon only Pruett, Babette, and I remained in the room. Even Carleton vanished out a side door.

"This isn't working," Babette groaned. "Nobody said one incriminating thing." She twisted to her right side. "Damn. My strap came undone. Turn your back, Pruett. No woman undresses in front of a man."

I stood lookout while she raised her top, unhooked her bra, and made adjustments. By the time she finished, the group straggled in, one by one. Jacqui had obviously freshened her makeup. She headed straight for Pruett and clasped his arm in a deliberate, proprietary hold. I noticed the muscles in her arms and confirmed what Pruett had said. That woman looked strong! Charlotte filed in a minute later clutching her cell phone. The way she cooed into it convinced me that she had finalized an assignation. I watched her when Carleton rejoined us. He kept his head down, but Charlotte shot a guilty look his way. Poor Babette.

Sheila and Ken were the last to re-join the group. She glided by without breaking stride, but Ken stopped to chat.

"Any decisions about Raza? A couple from Charlottesville are interested in her."

I shook my head but my heart sank. Could I stand losing the mare to someone else?

Another thirty minutes passed during which Babette described the fundraiser and what she hoped to achieve. Most of the participants wore that glazed expression of polite indifference that meant their minds had wandered elsewhere. Charlotte stared furtively at her phone; Reedy checked his watch. Even Sheila looked distracted as she fumbled in her purse. When my phone pinged, I rose and read the text. "Come over to Ethel's place in ten minutes if you want to know who killed her. G. Jakes."

How like that varmint to inconvenience someone else to suit his own needs. It was doubly insensitive to meet at a murder victim's former home. I passed my phone to Pruett without saying anything to Babette. He leaned back against the sofa and nodded. I was no coward but with a madman like Jakes I was intelligent enough to get backup. Besides, Jakes hinted that he had solved Ethel's murder and I wanted a witness present when I questioned him.

My heart pounded as I envisioned another confrontation with Jakes. This time at least I was prepared for anything that came my way. Finally, Babette ended the meeting and thanked her guests. I vaulted out the door before the others, but Pruett was detained by Jacqui and Charlotte, both of whom vied for his attention.

I freed Keats and Poe from my truck and sauntered toward the guesthouse. Ethel's place might be locked, although knowing Babette I doubted it. Just as Ken Reedy had said, a battered Ram pickup was parked in back of the house almost out of sight.

I cautiously twisted the doorknob and entered the house, wary of an ambush. The foyer was deserted so I padded on to the living room. That's when I saw his body. Glendon Jakes lay face-up on the living room rug, his mouth open wide in a silent scream. A belt was wrapped tightly around his scrawny neck—one of the special belts I had made for Babette.

* * * *

Keats and Poe immediately went on alert, ears pricked, hackles raised. I summoned my dogs with the Schutzhund command *Pass auf* and carefully backed out of the room. No sense in contaminating another crime scene. As I did, Pruett appeared at the door. I pointed toward the living room but said nothing. Words failed me. I felt shock, not sorrow for Jakes, this deeply troubled man who alienated everyone he encountered. Babette's loathing of Jakes was no secret and Bascomb might well add up motive, means and opportunity, and again arrive at the wrong conclusion. Come to think of it, I was a potential suspect as well.

Pruett soon joined me, cell phone in hand. He took one look at the corpse and pulled me toward him. Despite the circumstances, he stayed calm and cool, preternaturally so.

"Have you called Bascomb yet?" he asked, his voice rocksteady. "Better back out of here and go to Babette's while I handle that."

I shook my head, numbed by unimaginable possibilities. Someone had murdered the unlovely Jakes, someone who recently sat amongst us at Babette's meeting calmly eating snacks and sipping tea. No one would believe otherwise.

Before the other guests cleared the driveway, Pruett stopped them. I hurried inside to prepare Babette and alert her to the coming storm. The scene was emotional and awkward—one step short of hysteria. Females were often tagged the weaker sex but, in this instance, emotion was generated by Carleton Croy whose volcanic rage dwarfed Vesuvius. He stalked over to Babette, fists clenched, and demanded an explanation.

"Are you trying to destroy me," he shouted. "How do you think Hamilton Arms will react to yet another murder on these premises?"

I edged toward my friend in case Carleton got violent. Before I reached her, Pruett intervened.

"Calm down, Croy. We're talking murder here, not some minor faux pas. Now, chill. Bascomb will be here any moment."

All trace of defiance drained out of Carleton like air from a punctured tire. One look at Pruett apparently convinced him that in this instance silence was the better part of valor. Babette swallowed hard and bit her lip. I knew she was close to tears but who could blame her? When the rest of the committee filed in, I observed them closely for any telltale signs of stress. Sheila entered first looking puzzled but composed. Not so, Charlotte Westly. She made no secret of her displeasure and wore a scowl that was fierce enough to melt steel.

"What's going on here, Babette? Some of us have a life, you know."

"Stop complaining," Jacqui said. "Something must be wrong." She turned to Pruett, the source of wisdom. "Tell us, Wing."

Ken Reedy pointed to the window. "Why not ask the cops. They just got here."

Sure enough, flashing lights announced the arrival of our nemesis, Lieutenant Titus Bascomb accompanied by a contingent of underlings.

Pruett and I locked eyes. "I'm afraid there's been an incident," I said. "Glendon Jakes was found in Ethel's living room. Dead."

"Murdered, actually." Pruett scarcely moved a muscle. "Strangled."

Chapter 23

Pruett's words provoked plenty of reaction. Charlotte gasped and collapsed onto the sofa, Jacqui opened her mouth but emitted not a single syllable, and Sheila stood frozen in place, clutching her purse. Only Ken took the news in stride.

"I guess that means we're all suspects," he said. "Makes sense."

A pounding on the door announced the arrival of the authorities. Bascomb, looking more disheveled than ever strode angrily into the foyer and confronted Babette.

"What in the hell are you running here—murder incorporated?"

Pruett interposed himself. "Perri found him, Lieutenant, in Ethel's old house. That's his truck around in back. I can show you if you like."

Bascomb's tree trunk arm barred his way. "Sit, Mr. Pruett. You certainly land in the middle of things. You too, Ms. Morgan." He gave us a flat, hard cop's stare. "While the forensic team handles things, my sergeant and I will interview you. One by one." He pointed my way. "You first, Ms. Morgan. Seems like your name should be Calamity Jane, the way you turn up bodies."

I was unamused by Bascomb's foray into comedy. Everything had happened so fast that I had no time to process the enormity of the situation. Jakes, chief murder suspect, had himself been eliminated. Possibly—no probably—by someone in this very room. I dreaded telling Bascomb that one of my custom belts was the murder weapon. Considering his volatile temperament, he might slap the cuffs on me post haste.

Babette resumed her hostess duties by leading us into the study. I had always loved that room although today its charm eluded me. The old-world style was accentuated with reclaimed walnut paneling, deep, down-filled couches and bookshelves lined with leather-bound classics. Some of the luster dimmed as I faced Bascomb's version of the third degree.

"Why did you go over to that house, Ms. Morgan? Spoiling for another fight, were you?"

He forgot that I had taken those same classes on interrogation and knew all the tricks. Bascomb must have aced Bullying 101 though. He was a natural. I explained as calmly as possible about the text from Jakes. It sounded reasonable to me but Bascomb wasn't buying.

"What time did you get that text?" His sneer was masterful.

"Right before the meeting ended. I showed it to Mr. Pruett. Just ask him."

Bascomb frowned. "So you say. Funny how ten minutes later you found Jakes dead. Do dead men send texts these days, Ms. Morgan? Not that I heard of."

I knew that he was bluffing, trying to force some damaging admission from me. Until the forensic team finished their work, no one knew for sure when Jakes died. I kept calm and merely shrugged.

He pulled out his phone and shoved a photo toward me—a photo of one of my beautiful belts. "Look familiar?"

"Yep. It resembles the belts I make. Most of the stores in Great Marsh stock them. Some in DC as well." I was positive that the belt in question was one of my earlier designs available only to a select clientele. However, my previous encounters with the police had taught me to neither volunteer nor withhold information. Stick to the facts and just tell the truth.

Bascomb trotted out his avuncular act. "Jakes hurt you. I understand that. Maybe he attacked you again and you tried to protect yourself. Any jury would sympathize. You'd probably get off with probation." His toothy grin was grotesque.

"You're wasting your time and mine as well. I can account for my whereabouts from six this morning until I discovered his body. When we took a break, Mr. Pruett and I didn't even leave the room. Now, unless you plan to read me my rights or charge me, that's all I have to say." I folded my arms and met his steely gaze with one of my own.

Bascomb was bloodied but unbowed. "Naturally I'll need your phone to verify your statement. That's it for now, but don't leave the area. You're still on my radar, missy."

I nodded and strolled away slowly—straight, tall, and slightly defiant.

* * * *

My dogs were happy to be freed from the Suburban. One of Bascomb's men watched warily as I opened the hatch and put them in the fenced yard with Clara. A forensic team wearing white coveralls and booties immediately descended on my truck to conduct their search. Despite my act of bravado, Bascomb had rattled me. This was Great Marsh, Virginia, for heaven's sake. How could any of the average citizens assembled in Babette's living room overpower a reasonably strong man like Jakes? And what about that text? It clearly had come from Jakes's phone after his death. That meant that the murderer probably still had his phone. Would Bascomb's guys find it somewhere?

I felt a need to see Pruett, a dangerous compulsion for someone like me who valued independence and zealously guarded her tender heart. It seemed like an eternity before he appeared. I watched him glide toward me, with the peculiar grace of a jungle cat. My heart lurched as he smiled my way and stretched out his hand.

"How are you holding up? Did Bascomb use the old rubber hose on you?" He patted my shoulder.

"He took my phone and I forgot to remind him about what Jakes said the other day."

Pruett raised his eyebrows.

"You know... About how he knew who murdered Ethel and was planning to make a killing. He made a killing all right." I shivered even though the day was warm.

Pruett touched my cheek. "Listen, Iron Woman, you don't have to be tough around me. I told you that before. Anyone would be shaken by seeing one body let alone two in two weeks. Relax."

I have been on my own most of my life, proud to be self-reliant and resilient. I can handle adversity with the best of them, but kindness knocks me out. Something about Pruett penetrated my defenses in a way that only Pip had once done. When he opened his arms, I clung to Pruett like a fragile female in a sappy romance novel. Worst of all—it felt good. I wasn't embarrassed at all.

"I better tell Bascomb again what Jakes said. Not that he'll believe me."

Pruett grinned. "Not the most trusting soul, is he? I'll wait out here for you. Yell if you need backup."

"Coward," I scoffed. The path back to Babette's front door seemed endless as I plodded toward the deputy standing guard. He was suspicious at first but ultimately, I gained entry. Bascomb was ensconced in the library with his next victim, but as luck would have it, Sergeant Avis Stone stood in front of the door. I breathed a sigh of relief—much easier to confide in her than her crusty superior. She listened carefully, noting the specifics on her tablet.

"I'll let the Lieutenant know right away," she said. Her eyes held a spark of mischief. "He'll probably want to talk with you again. Jakes may have set up a meeting with his own murderer."

That made me shiver. "He can reach me at home," I said in a show of bravado. "He has the number." I was resigned to my fate but determined to make a getaway before Bascomb nabbed me. After all, I had a business to run, pets to tend, and a gorgeous male at my side. Let the law come to me.

Pruett was waiting inside the Suburban. "Well. What did he say? Need a lawyer? I heard those women in there, squawking about calling high-powered attorneys. Bascomb's in for quite a tussle when the one-percenters bring out the big guns."

I explained the situation and suggested a quick exit strategy. "You go first, and I'll trail behind. Just show them your press credentials or something."

We made our escape and headed back to my house, leaving the chaos and confusion of Jakes's murder scene behind us. I felt a twinge of conscience when I thought of Babette facing Bascomb and his minions by herself. My poor friend would become fodder for every tabloid on the East Coast with lurid accounts of sex, blackmail, and murder. Pruett advised her to capitalize on the scrum and rail against the proposed closure of Cavalry Farms whenever she was interviewed. That cheered her up immensely and she plunged into the narrative with gusto.

I hunched over the steering wheel during the entire trip home, positive that Bascomb was on my trail. Every flashing light or siren raised my stress level beyond endurance. Only the sight of my fence posts and the looming menace of Zeke brought blessed calm to my mind. Pruett pulled in behind me and leapt out first. He kept a wary eye on Zeke and bravely stayed the course when the dogs emerged.

"How about some coffee?" I asked.

He checked his watch. "If I weren't driving, I'd opt for a stiff drink. I guess coffee will have to do." As we walked toward the house, he put his arm around me. "I wish you could just come home with me until this mess subsides. Doesn't quite work when you have a zoo, does it?"

"I'll get that coffee."

Pruett was right behind me. "No need. I'm not helpless, you know. Feed your pets. I'll make the coffee."

We finished our tasks in record time and settled in around my old walnut table to sift through our thoughts.

"I guess we need to wait for the coroner's report," I said. "Then we'll know when Jakes died. I couldn't tell if his body was still warm but then I didn't touch him either. The look on his face was enough to stop me."

Pruett nodded. "I thought he looked surprised. He wasn't a big guy but still. Most women couldn't take him down."

I considered that for a moment. "I'm not so sure. Look at me. I'm five-nine and fit. If I took him by surprise it might work. Jacqui is certainly tall enough and as you noted, she's strong too. Even Sheila is tall and fit." I excluded Babette from the conversation. No way was my pal a match for Jakes, even if she got the drop on him.

"Reedy and Carleton are on my list," Pruett said. "Carleton is a wimp but if Jakes threatened him, he could be dangerous. Like a cornered rat. Reedy seems like a nice guy but you can never tell. Maybe he snapped if Jakes threatened Cavalry Farms too."

I slugged down my coffee and reached for another cup. Better to risk a caffeine overload than brain freeze. When Pruett's cell phone buzzed, he rose and stepped out of the kitchen. I forgot my manners and leaned forward but couldn't hear one thing that he said.

"That was my editor," he said when he returned. "News travels fast and he wants the scoop on Jakes and his murder. I promise to leave you out of it as much as possible." He drained his coffee cup and gathered his things. "Listen to me, Perri. I worry about you. Stop playing detective before you get hurt. This killer has already murdered twice, one more body won't bother him one bit. Don't let it be yours."

Chapter 24

I think best when my mind is focused on work. That meant dismissing thoughts of murder and returning to my leather business. A girl has to eat after all and if Raza joined our pack that meant another mouth to feed. Correction. I hoped Raza would be mine. For all I knew some upscale yuppies might have already claimed her.

With the dogs cradled on the office floor in their beds, I tackled five orders for lace martingales, my most popular item for smaller dog breeds. Those little beauties had a padded throat piece made of softest leather and slide beading for style in the show ring. Owners of toy and terrier breeds loved them, and their precious pets seemed to agree. During three hours in my workshop, I dismissed thoughts of mayhem and Pruett as well. No good would ever come from obsessing about that man. I knew it, but like all vices, it was easier said than done. Memories of our morning rendezvous stole back into my mind unbidden. Pruett was a hard guy to dismiss.

I stopped working and spent time with Zeke, currying, combing, and feeding the ungrateful little beast until his tummy filled and his coat gleamed. He tolerated my presence as a necessary evil but longed to romp with Keats and Poe. Zeke was a stubborn cuss with firm principles—he refused to settle down until he had his fun.

His truculence stirred a memory of something Babette had said this morning when her bra strap snapped. Something like, no decent woman would consider undressing in front of a man. Ethel had undressed, neatly folded her clothing, and prepared to don that horse costume. Would she have done that in front of Jakes or any other man except a trusted lover? On the other hand, most women disrobed around their women friends and acquaintances without even thinking about it. Was her killer female?

I stretched out on the couch to think but ended up dozing until Bascomb pounded on my door. Since the dogs have extremely acute hearing, their typical cacophony of barks preceded his arrival and prepared me for the onslaught.

As usual, Bascomb skipped social niceties and immediately went for the jugular.

"What's this about Jakes blackmailing someone?" he growled. "Awfully convenient that you remembered it *after* he was murdered."

I sought forbearance. The only path to progress was to humor this cop and ignore his insults. "I meant to tell you but finding his body shocked me. I forgot."

Bascomb had obviously overdosed on Raymond Chandler novels. He curled his lip in a bad cinema noir imitation. That gave me time to interject a question.

"Any idea when he died?" I asked.

Bascomb answered reluctantly using the official terminology. "TOD is undetermined but based on liver temperature, Jakes was dead about two to three hours when you found him." He held up his palms. "That's not precise, just so you know. Any of your little group could have nipped over to Ms. McCall's place and killed him before your meeting. That includes you too, missy."

"You forget—I have an alibi. Mr. Pruett."

Bascomb narrowed his eyes. "You might be in it together. Ever hear of conspiracy? As they say, it takes two. And the murder weapon had your signature all over it."

I remained silent and arched an eyebrow.

"Your belt, Ms. Morgan, your belt." Bascomb looked toward the kitchen. "Any chance of getting some coffee? I could really use a cup."

After I nodded, he stepped warily around my dogs and loomed over the kitchen table. Within minutes, Bascomb was sipping espresso, nibbling biscuits and acting almost civilized. He forced me to repeat, not once but twice, everything I recalled about Jakes's blackmail comment.

"The only thing I surmised was that it was someone wealthy. That scarcely narrows the field around here."

Bascomb decided to be snide. "It eliminates you."

I put a leash on my temper. True, by most objective standards I lacked wealth, but everything was relative. For someone like me, being a self-supporting woman with a home and a good business was a measure of success. I had come a long way and appreciated every leg of the journey. So there!

Bascomb changed his tactics. "Tell me again, who came in the meeting and who left for the break."

I angled for a sliver of information. "You found Jakes's cell phone, I suppose. Any fingerprints on it."

He answered without thinking. "Nope. Wiped clean." His response emboldened me.

"Where was it?"

Suddenly the supercilious Bascomb resurfaced. "Funny thing. We found it wedged under a cushion on your dear friend's sofa. Go figure."

Our conversation went downhill from there. Bascomb sneered and insinuated about Babette and Carleton but got nowhere. I was simply too exhausted to play his puerile games. If only Pruett would call. I couldn't wait to share Bascomb's antics and the latest information. I told myself it was all in the service of justice and solving two murders but even I wasn't fooled. My behavior was juvenile and pathetic. I longed to hear his voice no matter what he said.

After two hours of sheer torture, Bascomb finally decamped. My cell rang just as I was about to abandon hope and go to bed.

"Thinking of me?" Pruett asked. That deep sultry voice quickened my heartbeat.

I decided to play it cool. "Actually, I was thinking of Bascomb. He just left."

"Funny. I didn't think he was your type of guy." Pruett managed to blend sultry and snarky into one salacious sentence. It was a rare talent, one that had probably served him well during his career.

"Very funny. Bascomb is nobody's fool. I worry about Babette."

Pruett dispensed with the levity and immediately grilled me for every morsel of information. We debated the probable time of Jakes's death and implications for our suspects. He gasped when I told him about finding the cell phone under Babette's couch cushion.

"Jacqui and Charlotte sat on the couch," Pruett said. "Could be that collapse was just a ruse so that Charlotte could stash the cell phone out of sight. Maybe they're in it together. Charlotte was on a cell phone when she walked in the room. Who knows if it was really hers."

Before we hung up, Pruett mentioned some pressing engagements that would probably sideline him for several days. I fought bravely to act nonchalant wondering all the while if Monique was one of those engagements. Then I gave myself a stern lecture. Pruett owed me nothing. As long as I accepted that, things would be fine. I attended to my pets, wrapped myself in a ratty tee shirt and drifted into a deep and dreamless sleep.

* * * *

Bascomb haunted me for the next two days, insisting on endless written statements, and repeated conversations. Fortunately, Babette's pricey criminal defense attorney protected her rights by urging both Croys to refuse all requests for interviews. Carleton returned to work and Babette reclaimed her sanity—until the monthly edition of *Capital Corner* hit the newsstands.

I've never subscribed to the thing. Wouldn't have the interest or the time to read sprightly posts about the glitterati or hit pieces on our political overseers. This time was different. My day started with an agitated call from Sheila. The hour was early and the manner so unlike my friend that I scarcely recognized her voice.

"Have you read it?" she asked. "Ellis called a minute ago to warn me. Poor Babette. I mean it's bad enough for the rest of us, but she's right in the middle of things."

I let her wind down before interrupting. When she finished, I felt my world spin out of control.

"The main story is online," Sheila said. "Just plug *Capital Corner* into your computer. How could he do that to us? I thought he was a friend."

Fortunately, I had skipped breakfast. Otherwise, the bile that rose in my throat would have taken me down. I input the information into my computer and gasped. The lead article was entitled "Paradise Pillaged—Sex, Blackmail, and Murder Stalk Suburbia." What followed was an account, letter perfect, of every event since the murder of Ethel McCall and our reactions to it. Participants were named, including me. The author had thoughtfully given my business a plug and even mentioned my pets. The usual weasel words were used to fend off lawsuits: "Alleged," "supposed," "purported." But the message was clear: two murders of prominent Great Marsh residents remained unsolved and the local cops were clueless. Other accounts had appeared in the *Post* and the *Washington Times,* but this had an air of intimacy and contained information known by only a few. Titbits about Jakes's cell phone, his intent to blackmail the murderer and his final text were all included, the same things I shared with Pruett only two nights before. The author's name and photo did not faze me one bit. We had all been duped by Wing Pruett, traitor, Quisling, opportunist and worst of all the man who broke my heart. I should have realized that a hot story meant more to him than relationships. Should have but didn't.

I steeled myself to face Babette and even worse, Bascomb. She would understand but he would not. Bascomb had warned both me and Pruett against leaking any information. I kept that trust not that it mattered much at this point.

Tears were just a wasted effort. I chose to maintain my morning routine by tending to my pets, filling orders and expanding my social media presence. Thanks to Pruett my name was now trending on Facebook but that was notoriety not business. I ignored his phone calls and deleted his texts unread.

Late that afternoon, Babette knocked on my workshop door. Instead of speaking, she held out her arms and enveloped me in a gigantic hug.

"Oh darlin,' I'm so sorry."

I gaped at her, astounded. "You're the victim here, not me."

Babette chuckled, then dissolved into a fit of giggles. "I'm the one who first brought him around, remember? Girl, men are so rotten! Every damn one of them. Get this. Carleton moved into a hotel. Can you believe it? After all the crap he put me through, he decided I was a drain on his reputation. The rat!"

Then we both laughed—long, raucous laughter, until tears streamed from our eyes. Our dogs cozied up to us, trying their best to understand our antics. Thatcher hissed and strutted from the room in high dudgeon.

"What about Bascomb?" I asked. "He'll be out for my scalp."

"Naw. That boy will be busy trying to solve the damn crimes. Doesn't want that clueless label to stick. Besides, the rest of us lawyered up so he's frustrated."

I had no partner now but my determination to solve the murders remained. "You and I have to act," I told Babette. "We have access to all the parties involved. Let's do something."

"What?"

"Let me think about it and get back to you. Just be careful, Babette. That murderer is out there and it's someone we both know."

I spent the evening reviewing motives, suspects, and theories. It was all a jumble, a puzzle with pieces that simply did not fit. It was almost midnight when the dogs sensed something. Keats and Poe rose and charged the door after issuing a warning bark. I reacted by reaching down for my holstered Glock. I abhor violence, but I know how to protect myself. With a double murderer on the loose, I had to remain vigilant.

My cell phone rang; Pruett didn't give up easily. I gave him top marks for persistence, a trait that every good reporter probably cultivated. Pruett pounded on the front door for ten minutes before I finally had enough. After all, he didn't frighten me. Better to settle things once and for all and be done with him. I shoved the Glock behind my back and threw open the door.

My initial reaction floored me. Seeing him melted my anger and fueled an irresistible impulse to kiss him. Fortunately, self-restraint is my superpower.

My voice had an edge but remained steady when I greeted him. I considered that a major triumph. "Hi," I said. "What brings you here? I told you everything I know. Gave you everything I had."

Pruett stared down at me, his eyes burning with intensity. "I am so sorry, Perri. We have to talk. Please. Give me ten minutes."

A glacial calm tempered my emotions and encapsulated my heart. There was no danger now because indifference was the ultimate victory.

I motioned him toward the living room. "Sure. Come on in." I claimed the wingchair. It was Pip's special chair and Pruett had no right to it. He eased onto the sofa and was immediately joined by the traitorous Thatcher. "Would you like a drink, or something to eat?" I played my part to perfection, the hostess offering hospitality to the weary stranger.

"Nothing, thanks." He hesitated. "I don't know what to say. It looks bad, I know that, but believe me I did not deceive you."

I crossed my arms, holding them tight against my chest. My lips stretched into a rictus grin that held no mirth. Body language be damned. It was his show and I was merely the audience.

"Everything spiraled out of control," Pruett said. "I had no idea they intended to publish the article. Not now, at least." He learned forward, hands on knees. "Please believe me, Perri. I wouldn't do that to you. Not ever."

I took a deep breath and channeled my days as an army sergeant. *Pretend this is a standard briefing. Nothing special.*

"What happened?" I asked, watching his eyes, those eyes that captivated me, drawing me into their depths.

Pruett composed himself as he stroked Thatcher's back. "Look. I sent my notes to my editor, my preliminary notes. No conclusions, no salacious headlines. That's standard procedure. We agreed this would be a long piece, five-page article at least. I fought hard for more time, pitched the idea of solving the case first. He agreed. Then Jakes was murdered, and all bets were off. He decided to go with my preliminary draft."

I closed my eyes, trying to sift through an account that pitted emotion against logic. "I feel so bad for the others, particularly Babette. You said some snide things about her. About all of us, actually."

"I typically do character sketches of the principals in my stories, little vignettes, if you will. Kind of theatre of the absurd."

I did not respond. Could not. Emotion was not some salve for hurt feelings. It was volcanic, a world bending ride that I took seriously.

"Do you believe me?" he asked. "I have to know."

I wanted to respond with every fiber of my being. Instead of answering, I posed a different question. "Where do we go from here?"

Pruett stood and stretched out his arms to me. I moved forward, willing myself to avoid the precipice but knowing I would not. Could not. The faint scent of his cologne mesmerized me as the baby soft fabric of his shirt brushed against my cheek. He was probably using me, but I didn't care. For the first time since losing Pip, I felt alive. That alone was worth the risk.

He repeated my question. "Where do we go from here? We find the murderer. Together. Always together."

I couldn't resist making one final gibe. "I hope all that's off the record."

"Count on it," he said.

Chapter 25

Pruett left after we discussed our battle plans. Somehow, he knew this was not the right time for physical contact. Our relationship, or whatever you called it, was fragile. Building trust took time, but satiating lust was easy. Truth be told, while I appreciated sensitivity, I wished he had been more forceful. Sometimes lust is worth considering.

Babette was the ultimate night owl, so I took a chance and called her immediately on Skype. Her voice rose two octaves as she processed everything.

"Good Lord! He had the nerve to face you? I can hardly believe it." She paused then heaved a big sigh. "Of course, any real man would have explained himself in person and like it or not, Pruett is all man!"

Amen, sister.

Her voice softened as she went in for the kill. "Forgive me, darlin' but I must ask. Did you have makeup sex? Ooh, that always feels extra good, doesn't it? Just thinking about it makes me miss old Carleton. I mentioned his assets, didn't I?"

"Stop!" Babette was heading for a major rant and it was time to redirect her energy. "We did not have makeup sex or any other kind. Nothing like that. Our focus was squarely on the murders, where yours should be too. Thank you very much for your interest."

Babette was irrepressible but never stupid. She shifted from carnal matters to the thorny issue of two murders. "I've been scratching my head, trying to figure out who did it. They're my friends, Perri, not murderers. The only ones I ruled out were you, me, and Pruett and that was because we never left the room. The others were all over the place."

As comforting as that was, it was unconvincing. Suppose Jakes had been murdered *before* our meeting started? That expanded the suspect list to include Babette, although Pruett and I were still in the clear. He had never been out of my sight from the time of his wakeup call to our arrival at Babette's. Anyone else could have nipped out to meet Jakes, taken him by surprise, and administered the coup de grâce with my beautifully crafted belt. That told me this was no crime of passion. The killer had arrived with the firm intention of giving the blackmailer the final payment he so richly deserved—death.

"What about your cable show?" I asked. "Still planning on doing it?"

"Absolutely. Not to be crude but think of the audience I'll draw with two murders to talk about. No more local cable. Could be the networks will come a-calling."

At times, Babette astonished and even horrified me. She made no attempt to mask her emotions even when good sense or decorum would have dictated otherwise. Bascomb was busy searching for a suspect and Babette's loose lips might indeed sink her ship. I gave her my mean sergeant stare.

"Pipe down. Until they find the murderer, you have to act as close to normal as you can. Bascomb is just itching to nail someone. Need I remind you that both bodies showed up on your property?"

Babette flashed a sunny smile. Nothing, not even the threat of prison, could dim the light of that grin. "Ah, Perri, chill. With you and Pruett on the case, I don't have to worry." She made kissing noises and signed off for the night.

* * * *

I overslept again. Sun streamed through my drapes flooding my bedroom with a burst of morning light. That awakened my dogs and one fractious feline, who demanded instant gratification. For once, I was thankful to live alone. After a restless night of interrupted dreams, I was certainly no beauty prize. My pups needed a potty break and a certain pygmy goat would soon be braying for food. At times like this, I was a model of efficiency, dispatching my chores in record time. When espresso's siren song beckoned, I finally allowed myself to take a break and read the newspaper. I soon regretted that action. Our local rag, *Great Marsh Gazette*, was filled with tales of Jakes's murder and the resulting drama. The author had cribbed a good deal of his account from Pruett's earlier story.

Today's schedule was horrendous. It was dog show day and as usual I had overpromised and overbooked. I'd agreed to conduct a brief seminar for new pet owners on proper leash and collar procedures, a session encouraged by the AKC. It was essentially a PR stunt but, in this instance, I agreed with them. Anything that encouraged the human-animal bond was a very good thing for both species. Besides, many of those attending would probably spring for a handsome leash or collar from my stock. Not a problem except it was also my scheduled time to exercise the horses at Cavalry Farms.

I battled Beltway traffic for an hour before finally entering the outer Maryland suburb of Timonium where commuters were scarce. Who knew if any of our potential suspects might show up at the event? Ken Reedy almost always did and Sheila seldom missed an opportunity to lead poor Cecil around the ring. Neither of them ranked high on my suspect list but I was anxious to hear speculation from the dog show crowd about Jakes. Had he confided in anyone about his get rich quick scheme? He had few friends but that never stopped Jakes from bragging to anyone in his vicinity. After wrangling a parking spot in the vendor area of the fairground, I freed Poe and Keats and headed for the side entrance. Fortunately, a fellow handler was overseeing the process, and he waved me and my entourage in without a fuss. Strictly speaking, only dogs that were registered for the event were allowed on the premises. Keats and Poe were fixtures, however, and far better behaved than many of their human counterparts.

The moment I reached the stall, my pal Becca swept through the door. She threw her arms around me and hugged me hard.

"Perri. I figured you wouldn't make it after what happened." She averted her eyes. "About Jakes, I mean, and that nasty article by your sweetie. Goes to show you that a man can be hot and devious at the same time."

My own mixed feelings about Pruett surfaced. I wanted to defend him but could not dispute her description. I tried humor instead. "Hot? You thought Jakes was good-looking?"

She reared back in horror. "God, no. I meant the reporter." She scrutinized me. "You're teasing, aren't you? Should have known." Her conversation reverted to animal matters. "I see you have a demo to do today. Saw it in the show program. You seem calm enough so good luck with it. Finding a dead body is bad enough but two—"

That gave me pause. "Say, did you hear Jakes say anything lately about coming into some serious money? I know he hung around dog shows too."

She shook her head. "He was jawing with Ken about something that last day before he went all wacko on you. Seemed pretty smug, if you ask me but I didn't hear much."

After giving me another hug, she disappeared into the crowd to attend to a canine client leaving me with a pressing need to find Ken Reedy.

An influx of customers kept me occupied for several hours. At noon, I grabbed several collars, leashes, and harnesses and headed for the demo ring. This time I took Keats with me. He moved like a dream and would attract a good bit of attention from dog show insiders who would immediately recognize his style.

To my surprise, a large knot of spectators surrounded the ring. Most were parents with their offspring trailing after them, but some were just pet loving adults. I stepped into the ring and adjusted the microphone just in time to note the sinewy form of a certain journalist walking hand-in-hand with Ella. As soon as she spied me, she jumped from foot to foot and squealed my name. I noticed that she was wearing her birthday gift and her dad's engaging grin. I winked her way then started my tutorial. Keats played the perfect assistant by trotting back and forth and illustrating the finer points of each product. The spectators asked plenty of questions and queued up afterwards to purchase collars, leads and even a few belts. All in all, my performance was a profitable endeavor that served me and the dog-loving public well.

Pruett and Ella were the last ones in line. She modeled her chaps by pirouetting back and forth, much to the amusement of her doting dad. "I love my present, Perri," she said hugging my waist. "Thank you."

"Nice job, Ms. Morgan," he said. "Quite a show."

"Thanks." I still distrusted his motives and had no doubt that he knew how disarming Ella was. "What brings you here, business or pleasure?"

His eyes were alight with mischief. "A bit of both, actually. Care to join us later for supper? Tomorrow is Ella's official birthday but we're celebrating a bit early."

"I promised to help out at Cavalry Farms this afternoon. Maybe Ella would like to join me." I checked my watch. "Can you wait a few minutes while I close up shop?"

He touched my arm, just a tap, not enough to explain the surge of sensation that I felt. "No problem. I'll wait as long as it takes."

I got the double entendre although I pretended not to. Was Pruett playing a game with me? If so, he had crossed the line from clever to cruel without skipping a beat.

"Okay." I hurried back to my shop just in time to see Ken Reedy prowling the aisle.

"Hey," I said. "Got a question for you."

He gave me that measured look he had long perfected. "Not for publication, I hope."

I threw up my arms. "Please! I've been dodging Bascomb ever since that stupid article appeared. He wants my head on a post." I asked Reedy about his conversation with Jakes.

"Oh yeah. He was blabbering about buying a new show truck. You saw that hunk of junk he drove. Anyhow, he was fixated on a Dynamax Force, one of those 'Class A' beauties with all the bells and whistles."

That took me aback. "Wow! Those things are pricey, even the used ones."

Top of the line models like Dynamax ran two hundred grand fully equipped. Babette paid that much for her glitzy vehicle we dubbed "Steady Eddie."

"Seemed like a stretch for Jakes," Ken said. "But he was pretty cocky about it."

I evaluated the possibilities. "He had a senior level job with the Government. Pretty good pay. Maybe he saved his money."

Ken shrugged. "Maybe. Jakes said he was expecting a windfall of some kind from a grateful friend. Good luck at the farm today." He hesitated a moment and reached into his pocket. "Thought of something that might interest you," he said, handing me a slip of paper. "This is the fellow Jakes had been negotiating with. About the truck. He's local so you can probably swing around and see him." Ken gave an impish grin. "Unless you're too busy learning the news business."

I seldom blush, but on this occasion I did so. After thanking Ken, I checked my stock, and locked everything up good and tight. No cause for excitement. After all, we were celebrating a little girl's birthday, not planning a seduction. Applebee's was scarcely a romantic spot, especially if we ordered Ella's favorite hot wings. Afterwards, daddy and daughter would head back to Georgetown and I would snuggle up with Thatcher and my dogs.

* * * *

Ella squealed when I told her about our side trip to Cavalry Farms. She loved every kind of animal and was ecstatic about seeing the horses. We pointedly ignored the pained expression on Pruett's face and forged ahead.

Our assignment was simple: in addition to feeding and watering the herd, we agreed to lead the more biddable horses around the paddock for some exercise. I also promised to let Ella share some Raza time with me, just enough for them to get acquainted. The size of the massive Percheron and Clydesdale horses fascinated Pruett. Both were almost eighteen hands high at their withers and since a hand equates to four inches, they were very big boys indeed.

As I suspected, Raza and Ella soon formed a mutual admiration society. The child's reaction to the Arabian mare warmed my heart. Ella threw her arms around Raza's neck, gently stroked it and hugged her. Even Pruett was charmed although he remained cautious. Raza pricked her ears forward, nuzzled both of us, and gently took the carrots we offered.

"She's beautiful, Perri. Is Raza your special horse?" Ella's little face positively glowed while Pruett had the hunted look of a man condemned to equine servitude. I hoisted the child into the saddle, adjusted the stirrups and watched closely as she urged Raza into a trot and gentle canter. To Pruett's relief, we had agreed on a no galloping clause—at least this time. Ella and Raza made a splendid pairing as they traversed the ring.

"Your money wasn't wasted on lessons," I told Pruett. "Ella is a natural."

"I guess," he moaned. "Hamilton Arms encourages all that horse stuff too. Part of good breeding, I suppose."

I signaled to Ella and she slowed Raza down to a walk. "You did great," I said as Pruett helped his child dismount. "Raza loved it. Time for us to rub her down and groom her."

"Why did someone give Raza away?" Ella's little face crinkled with emotion.

How do you explain callous human behavior to an innocent child? I didn't reveal that her prior owners discarded beautiful Raza when they found she was unsuited to competitive hunting, or that they were quite indifferent to her fate. According to Reedy, they planned to sell her at auction if Cavalry Farms didn't take her. That meant a possible death sentence.

"Not everyone takes good care of their pets," I said. "Not like us." I gave her a hug. "Come on. Let's give my girl a good massage."

* * * *

The birthday dinner was magical; there was no other way to describe it. Ella chattered nonstop about her pointer Guinnie, and the entire dog show experience. I enjoyed watching elegant Wing Pruett doing daddy duty. It revealed an endearing aspect of his character that few women, particularly me, could resist. When the staff stood around a birthday cake and sang to Ella, her joy was a thing of beauty. I was growing very fond of the little girl and that was dangerous for both of us. Surely, Pruett would never deliberately expose his daughter to the heartbreak of losing a friend.

Our high spirits dimmed when Pruett paid the check and told his child it was time to go. "You have to leave early tomorrow, Ella. Your mom has something special planned for you."

Ella's smiles vanished as she flashed a mutinous look at her dad. "I don't want to go to New York. I want to be with Raza and Perri."

"Perri has to work tomorrow," he said. "You can see Raza when you get back if Perri agrees."

I dredged up that fake smile adults summon to deceive small children. "And if your dad agrees and if you are really good you can exercise Raza when you get back."

I tapped my iPhone and produced a photo of the beautiful Arabian. "I'll send you her picture every time I go to the farm."

"Perri, she's so beautiful! Just like you." Ella clapped her hands and gave me a fierce hug. That placated her although I knew it was only a temporary fix. Pruett's jaw dropped but he wisely said nothing. Fortunately, children have a short attention span and I was positive that Ella would be all smiles the next day when her glamorous mother arrived.

Pruett walked me to my truck and put his arms around me. "Thanks for today," he said. "You made a little girl very happy. I'm not thrilled about this horse thing though. You know how Ella obsesses about pets. That's all I need."

Something emboldened me. "How about her dad? How does he feel?"

"You made me very happy too," he said.

"Good." I showed him the paper Ken had given me. "The guy lives in Aldie. Maybe he'll know something about Jakes that will help us."

Pruett took the paper. "Let me check it out first. I'll call and let you know. No sense driving there if we can get answers other ways." I drove home in a fog of emotion that was totally unlike me. Hard-nosed Persephone Morgan scoffed at love songs, and never read romance novels. Pip always said my heart was hard outside but mushy inside, like a Mallow Cup. It was one of our little jokes that I never shared with another soul.

Just as I reached the front door, my cell phone shrilled in the night. It jolted me out of dreamland and catapulted me into reality.

Sheila's clear voice rang out in the night. "Where did you disappear to? I wanted you to join me for dinner."

After I explained about Ella's birthday, the phone went silent.

"Sheila? Still there?"

"Yep. I'm just worried about you. I don't want to see you get hurt." Her voice was whisper soft.

"Speak up. I can't hear you."

Sheila paused. "Ellis is in the next room and I don't want him to hear me. You know how he feels about meddling."

Ellis Sands possessed many sterling qualities, but he was a major control freak. If he could manacle his wife and confine her to their mansion, he would gladly do so. It was probably an age thing. Sheila was attractive, a decade younger and much livelier than Ellis. Although she would never admit it, I figured Ellis suffered from a whopping case of performance anxiety as well.

Sheila made a good point about Pruett though. On a whim, I decided to go bold. "Hey. Are you up for some detective work tomorrow?"

Sheila didn't miss a beat. "Sure! But don't you have to work?"

"Phooey. I just got a hot lead about Jakes's killer. Want to be my Watson?"

"You bet!" Sheila cried. "Tell me when and where. Ellis thinks I'll be at the show."

We arranged a meeting time and place and rang off, feeling very smug about our clandestine operation.

Chapter 26

When Sheila reached my driveway the next morning, she had an additional passenger with her. Not Cecil. I was expecting him. The mystery guest was none other than my best friend, Babette.

"Surprised, Perri?" Her grin was wider than Texas. "When Sheila spilled the beans about your little party, I decided to horn in. Three heads are better than two, right?"

Sheila averted her eyes, a sure sign of guilt if ever I saw it.

"We have to be cool about this," I said, giving Babette the fish eye. "If Bascomb finds us meddling he'll blow his top."

Babette shrugged. "Hey, why can't three old friends discuss our options? Besides. I just happen to own one of those fancy rigs. You need my expertise."

Sheila and I rolled our eyes at that one.

"Well, I don't mind name-droppin' if we talk with that salesman." Babette folded her arms and glared. She rarely backed down once she took a stand.

I on the other hand knew when to fold my tent and accept the inevitable. "Okay, ladies. Let's make tracks."

Our spirits were high as we headed to Aldie, an unincorporated mostly rural area some forty miles from Great Marsh. Our strategy was simple but elegant: I would take the lead posing as a potential customer and Sheila and Babette would provide backup. No need to improvise. Babette was famous for spontaneity but on this occasion, it would be a liability and endanger our mission. Since Aldie boasted only one RV showroom, Red's Roadrunners, it was simple enough to find and exploit. Once I parked the Suburban in the muddy parking lot, our adventure began. Babette immediately abandoned or forgot her pledge to remain in the background by leaping from the backseat and trekking toward the sales room.

"Hey," I called. "Wait up for heaven's sake."

Sheila gingerly heaved herself out of the Rover and limped toward the parking lot.

"You sure are slow today," Babette said. "What's wrong with you?"

"Nothing," Sheila said. "I fell off my mountain bike last night and scuffed my knees. Luckily, I was wearing a helmet. Guess I'm not as limber as I thought."

"Don't sweat it," Babette said. "Age creeps up on us all." Her eyes were aglow, and her high spirits had returned. "And before you ask, Carleton is still at that hotel being comforted by God knows who." More defiance by Babette. "I say she's welcome to him. After all that heavy equipment of his won't last forever. Depreciation, you know."

The thought of Carleton, equipment and all, was too grotesque to contemplate. On the other hand, any woman who could stomach his arrogance and constant complaints deserved some physical comfort. Apparently, he could provide it when he was motivated.

"Don't suppose you found out who she is," Sheila asked. "If it were Ellis, I'd be on her trail for sure."

Babette sniffed. "Nope. Don't know, don't care." She looked away and said in a small voice. "I stopped caring about the time that he did. Besides, he vamoosed so fast he left evidence behind." She dangled a man's gold cufflink at us. "He didn't get this from me."

Frankly although it looked expensive but big and clunky too. Babette had far better taste than that.

Sheila pulled out her glasses. "Cartier, I think. Not cheap."

Babette clenched her face in bulldog fashion. "Not hardly. Those babies cost big bucks. Not including tax. I bet his girlfriend doesn't know he lost one of them."

That put both Sheila and me in permanent lockdown. What did one say to the ex-spouse of a cad? Babette continued her monologue.

"Must be someone with big bucks. Of course, that's about everyone we know in this town. Hope she got her money's worth. Carleton knows to put out when it's in his best interests."

I flashed back to my conversation with Charlotte Westly at that Hamilton Arms soiree. She hinted that Carleton only pursued wealthy women. Come to think of it, Charlotte and Jacqui were both women of means. Either of them might be the guilty party.

Sheila proved her social skills by changing the subject. "Either way, I don't think it's relevant to the murders. Affairs are pretty routine these days."

She was right of course. One had only to peruse the Internet to confirm that. Still someone had committed two murders for a reason that must have seemed perfectly sound. Only a psychotic monster would kill out of blood lust. It was far more likely that someone we all knew, an outwardly rational being, had weighed the options, balanced risk over reward and taken two lives.

"Remember," I said before we reached the showroom. "Let me take the lead." I gave Babette my fiercest stare. "We don't want to spook this guy by mentioning Jakes's death."

"How do you know who to ask?" Sheila asked. "This is a big place."

I reached into my pocket and found the slip of paper. "Ken Reedy gave me his name. Walter Johnson."

Babette gave me a snappy salute, but Sheila was leveled by a sneezing fit. She buried her face in her handkerchief and coughed violently.

"You okay?" I asked.

"It's nothing," she said. "Hay fever has been driving me mad this week and I have a migraine that just won't quit. Go on you two. I'll catch up with you."

As it happened, the first salesman who approached us wore a big smile and a name-tag saying "Walter." He was a swarthy man of middle years with the posture of a marine and an infectious air of good cheer. All things considered, Walter Johnson made one heck of a positive impression.

Babette targeted him immediately. She puffed out her chest and shamelessly batted those fake eyelashes. "My friend goes to all the horse shows," she said, "I told her it's time to buy something big. I'm thinking one of those babies that have all the bells and whistles like I got."

Johnson's eyes widened and I swear I saw dollar signs in them. "Were you thinking new or used?"

Babette shrugged. "Show us around. We heard you'd give us a good deal."

I saw him preen a bit. "Well, that's mighty nice. Reputation is everything in this business. Who should I thank for that compliment?"

My pal showed a talent for deception that was truly awe-inspiring. Frightening too.

"Glendon Jakes." She sighed. "His hunter wins everything in sight."

Apparently, news traveled slowly in Aldie. I watched him closely and Johnson didn't react at all to Jakes's name.

"We haven't closed the deal yet," he said. "Mr. Jakes had to win over the missus. Said he was expecting a big windfall soon. He wanted to go for our deluxe model brand new but that is a sizable investment. You know how it is."

We exchanged polite laughs over the power of women to thwart the dreams of their spouses.

"Mrs. Jakes holds very strong opinions. She's really something isn't she," I asked. "So lovely. I think she's the one with the money too."

Johnson looked puzzled, but he gamely played along. "I really didn't get a good look at her. She stayed in his truck with their dog. But that explains it. Money talks."

I traded sympathetic smiles with him. "It always does. Which dog did they have with them?"

He shrugged. "I'm not much of a dog person. Something big."

Both Jacqueline and Charlotte had sizable dogs and to a non-dog person wary of large canines, a standard poodle, pointer or Lab were interchangeable. I gave Johnson a pinch of encouragement. "Maybe you could show us the kind of models Glendon liked. Not that we're competitive, you understand. It's just that he can be a little pushy."

Playing our part required that we traipse through the lot and examine various high-end specimens. Quite frankly, some of those models were damn impressive. Sheila joined us just as we finished our tours. I noticed the acquisitive gleam in Babette's eyes and for a moment I feared that she might sign on the dotted line, and head for home in another motor coach.

Babette did her aw-shucks routine. "I made my own decision, but my friend will have to drag her husband out here." She handed Johnson her card. "I'm kind of stuck on that big baby out there." She pointed to a gigantic class A Thor.

Guilt welled up in me as I watched Walter Johnson's face. No doubt the poor man was already calculating his commission on the big sale.

"You've been very helpful," I said. "Thanks for your time." As we headed back to the car, Sheila frowned. "Makes you wonder where a guy like Jakes would get that kind of dough. Two hundred thousand bucks is hardly chicken feed no matter how wealthy you are. Not so easy to accumulate or disburse without being traced."

One snippet of information had cheered me up. With that sum of money involved, Reedy was now in the clear. Ken was financially comfortable but not wealthy enough to finance Jakes's new lifestyle.

"Sounds like something you should discuss with your planning group," I told Babette. "We'll bring up luxury motor homes and watch their reaction."

Meanwhile, for a number of reasons both personal and professional, I couldn't wait to call Pruett.

* * * *

My calls went directly to Pruett's voice mail. He left a terse message stating that he would be out of town for a few days and would stay in touch. That shouldn't have bothered me, but it did. After all, Wing Pruett was totally free to do whatever caught his fancy even if it involved another woman. Visions of a certain superstar floated through my mind, but I ruthlessly suppressed them. Such thoughts were counterproductive and did no good at all. Work was the perfect antidote to melancholy. I attended to my pets and spent the rest of the evening in my workshop with the dogs and Thatcher curled up around me. Mercifully, Zeke was nestled peacefully in his outdoor stall.

Sales of my custom belts had really taken off. That augmented my income stream and brought in a host of new clients for the dog and horse products that were my mainstay. Based on Ella's reaction, I considered adding a line of custom-made children's chaps. So many little girls adored horses that it might be a great marketing ploy. I hunched over my drawing table, working feverishly to design several eye-catching versions with fringe. Most of my patrons rode English versus Western so chaps wouldn't be worn in competition. Youngsters would still enjoy strutting around in them however. My efforts paid off and the final results pleased me. I considered doing a tie-in with Cavalry Farms and splitting the profits with them. By the time I turned off the lights and rounded up Keats and Poe, I was exhausted, but in a very good way that didn't include Pruett at all.

Chapter 27

Babette had also been busy. True to her word, she had scheduled a televised discussion entitled "Uniting the Community," for a week from tomorrow. The lure of a television appearance, even on a seldom-watched cable channel, had appealed to our little group and all the usual suspects had agreed to participate, even Carleton. No word on Pruett's availability.

To my surprise, I also received an urgent request from Babette to accompany her to a cocktail party at Hamilton Arms. Carleton had begged her to play nice, but she refused to go unless I served as her wingman. I couldn't miss the chance to quiz Jacqui and Charlotte even without the golden lure of Pruett.

I spent time the next morning rehearsing various strategies and subsequently rejecting all of them. My wardrobe was less problematic. Babette assured me that a little black dress, that panacea of the style challenged, would allow me to blend in with the staid crowd of one percenters. I took her at her word and paired it with a lovely Loro Piana stole that Pip had given me. The beautiful garment fed my fantasies, encasing me as his arms once had. I felt loved and protected again; Pruett be damned.

Babette Croy was hard to miss in a red satin pantsuit with a lacy camisole. As soon as I pulled into her driveway, she rushed out to greet me, twirling around for my approval with Clara at her side.

"Very nice, Mrs. Croy. Very nice indeed." I looked around. "Where's Carleton?"

She rolled her eyes. "He left from his hotel. Supposedly had a faculty meeting before the reception but I think we know better."

I locked arms with her. "Who cares? We'll have a better time without him." I explained my plans for Charlotte and Jacqui. "Since you two are friends, you better take Jacqui. I'll try to get Charlotte to warm up to me."

"Too bad Wing's not there. He can warm up any woman." She threw a superior smirk my way. "Heard anything from him?"

I shook my head but said nothing. My cell phone was still in the truck. I'd deliberately left it there as an act of self-discipline or masochism, I couldn't decide which. After all, Pruett was a reporter. A good one. If he wanted to contact someone, he knew how to do it.

Babette dangled the Mercedes key fob under my nose. "Well come on girl. Let's get this show on the road. I'm taking Clara for backup. She won't mind staying in the car." She winked. "See if you can spot my ex's latest conquest while you're at it." Gallows humor had become more typical of my friend lately. I understood that Carleton was a piece of detritus not worth even one of her tears. Still. Rejection was always a bitter pill to swallow.

As we sped down Georgetown turnpike, Babette grew introspective. "Do you really think a woman did this? Two murders? Seems like overkill."

That was one way to look at it. Personally, I was creeped out by the whole thing. My girlhood fantasies of being Nancy Drew had been replaced by a solid feeling of dread. If only things could go back to normal even if normal meant the absence of Pruett.

* * * *

Hamilton Arms was primed for opulence that evening. Every imaginable luxury vehicle from Rolls Royce to Ferrari decorated the vast parking lot of the humble Quaker school. I chuckled at the irony of that scene although I kept my thoughts to myself. When it came to the vagaries of wealth, Babette had no sense of humor.

After surrendering our ride to the parking attendant, we strolled into the entryway, stopping to adjust our eyes to the dim light. Chandeliers supplemented by crystal sconces illuminated the room casting a rosy glow on the participants. I scanned the crowd for signs of Carleton, Jacqui, or Charlotte. What I saw instead left me sickened and sad. Pruett, surrounded by a host of sycophants, stood arm in arm with Monique Allaire, spreading charm and dispensing bon mots. The splendor of that golden duo was so astounding that even I felt their gravitational pull. Pruett wore an exquisitely cut suit that had to be Italian. As for Monique—what can I say? She was luminous, arrayed in a silken confection that showcased her incredibly long legs.

In comparison, my little black dress was closer to a nun's habit than a symbol of sophistication. I turned aside, pulling Pip's stole tightly around my shoulders. What made me think for even one moment that I could compete? Desire must have made me delusional.

Fortunately, a heaping dose of common sense and some tough self-talk rescued me. I was certainly no glamor girl, but I had plenty to be proud of. Pip had loved me and someday so would another man. If not, I could stand on my own with a little help from my friends. Pruett belonged with Monique in another world, a parallel universe where horse shows and leathersmiths didn't exist.

At the far-right corner of the ballroom a discreet illuminated sign marked the ladies' lounge. Sounded like a plan. I glided toward it at a dignified pace, hoping against hope that Pruett had not seen me. Unfortunately, I had not gone unobserved. Charlotte Westly spotted me instantly and hailed me with saccharine smiles and words as poisonous as blow darts.

"Perri Morgan. Didn't expect to see you here tonight. I see Wing has another date." Her mean little eyes glittered with malice.

I stared at her and waited a full minute before responding. Silence made her antsy as I hoped it would. "Oh, you mean Monique Allaire. Isn't she lovely? Their little girl Ella is in pre-school, as I'm sure you know."

Charlotte rocked back on her heels, crestfallen. "Yes. She's a darling child. Just what you'd expect with those two as parents."

I plunged into my prepared narrative with more vigor than I originally planned. "I guess you've heard about the blackmail scheme? With Jakes and Ethel, I mean."

Charlotte's mouth hung open like a gaffed fish. Clearly, this was not the conversation she was expecting. Her completion paled as she sputtered out a response. "I don't know what you mean."

My smile was smoother than Italian silk. "Ah come on, Charlotte. What did they have on you? Jakes bragged about a big pay day."

She craned her neck looking for any eavesdroppers. "Quiet. They'll hear you. Besides I never paid Jakes a damn dime. Ethel put the squeeze on me but not Jakes. When she died, I was finally free." She sniffed. "I never even had a conversation with that dreadful Jakes creature. If you spread any rumors expect to be sued." With that, Charlotte Wilkerson stalked off to join her husband, leaving me curious but not much wiser. I combed my hair, adjusted my shawl and ventured out to join the fray.

Babette was far more proficient at prying information from the unwary. I watched her joke and head toss as she chatted up her old pal Jacqui. To be fair, Jacqui was preoccupied by the many moves of Pruett and his partner.

Who could blame her? I sipped my glass of punch, cursing the abstemious Quakers who had robbed me of an alcoholic lift. A shot of false courage would have really buoyed my spirits under duress.

"I see Babette roped you into coming tonight," said a snarky voice. It could only be one person. Carleton, looking fully recovered from his injuries, slimed his way toward me.

"I enjoy parties," I lied. "You like the spotlight, Carleton, so I'm sure you agree."

He snarled a response and sped toward a Chanel clad matron whose wide grin told me she welcomed his attentions. I glanced at my watch, hoping against hope that this shindig would soon be over.

Then I felt his touch and inhaled a faint whiff of his cologne. "You look lovely tonight, Perri." Wing Pruett said. "Seeing you makes this torture worthwhile." He gently tucked a wisp of hair behind my ear and gave me the full wattage of his smile. I felt rather than saw Monique glowering from across the room.

I took a deep breath to slow my rapid heartbeat. Surely, he could hear it even from afar. By focusing on business, I might spare myself from utter humiliation.

"Nice to see you too. Babette wrangled me an invitation and I couldn't resist knowing that three of our suspects would probably show up. We made some progress recently." My voice was even and my tone polite but not intimate. I was proud of that.

Pruett's frown told me he was puzzled. "Maybe you can fill me in tonight," he said. My eyes widened at the audacity of such a suggestion and Pruett held his hand up. "No double entendre meant. I just wanted to see you. I've missed you, Perri. More than you know."

I'm a country mouse, not a simpleton. Wing Pruett's patent leather line would never sway me.

My smile was wholesomeness itself. "Sure. Let me check with Babette." I turned toward the podium, confronting the stony stare of one displeased photojournalist. "Oops. Looks like your date wants you back."

Pruett grasped my arm. "It's not what it looks like. The school makes both parents show up at least once a year for these extravaganzas. I had to force Monique to show or risk having Ella dropped."

It sounded plausible, perhaps because I desperately wanted to believe it. "How is Ella?" I asked. Just thinking of the little girl made me smile.

He took my hand and squeezed it. "Ella misses you too. All she talked about was horses and you. Drove Monique bonkers. I had to fly to New York to sort things out."

Picturing that scene made me laugh. Before I responded, Babette and her bosom buddy Jacqui barreled into our conversation.

"Thought I saw you," Babette said rising on tiptoes to kiss his cheek. "Jacqui and I were just discussing our television show. You will be there, won't you?"

Pruett nodded. "Wouldn't miss it. Now if you ladies will forgive me, I better get back to Monique. She's going to present some special award to the fundraiser of the year." He locked eyes with me once more, then strode gracefully away.

Jacqui's sigh was loud and deep. "Damn, that man is hot. Just look at his backside. Wouldn't I love to get him in the sack again." She elbowed me in the ribs. "Don't mind sharing either, Perri. How about it?"

I was too startled to respond but Babette saved the day. "Cut that out, Jacqui. You've got enough trouble as it is." Babette dished up her most charming and deceptive grin. "By the way, sugar, did I hear that you're buying an RV? Deluxe model with all the bells and whistles?"

Jacqui shrugged half-heartedly and leaned back. "Hardly. I'm not the camping type. Not practical."

My pal motored on as if she hadn't heard a word. "We heard that Jakes planned to buy one. Said he was getting a windfall from some woman."

Unless she was an award caliber actress, Jacqui was not the woman involved. She yawned and kept her eye fixed on Pruett as he spoke with Monique. "Suit yourself, Babette. You always do anyway." She sailed off headed toward the podium like a guided missile.

"Well that misfired," I said. "What else did you find out?"

Babette held up her hand. "Hush. I want to hear Monique."

Monique ascended to the platform and spoke in a breathy voice with the faintest touch of a French accent. Even I was charmed by her brief remarks that focused on the school and not herself. Afterwards she posed for pictures with the honoree and several of the board members. Pruett stood by her side the entire time with his arms folded. His expression was impenetrable, impossible to determine whether he was enjoying himself or acting a part. I hoped he was miserable but feared he was not.

"She's really something, isn't she?" Babette said. "Damn near perfect." She pointed toward her ex-husband. "Look at Carleton with his tongue hanging out. That hound-dog just won't quit."

I changed the subject before Babette said something else to sink my spirits. "Did you find out anything useful from Jacqui? She didn't react at all to that stuff about the RV."

"Nothing that I didn't know or suspect before. According to Jacqui, my dear ex-husband has more than one honey stashed away." Babette avoided eye contact. She looked straight ahead as she spoke. "I knew or suspected anyway that Charlotte was involved, but apparently he hooked another rich one too."

I squeezed her shoulder. "Not Jacqui? She might be trying to throw you off the scent."

Babette shrugged. "Who knows? According to Jacqui, Ethel caught him kissing someone at one of those posh fundraisers. Knowing what we now do about Ethel, she probably put the squeeze on him and his girlfriend." Babette's stiff upper lip trembled as she said that. "Of course, Jacqui screwed around with plenty of married men, so she might be the one. Wouldn't stop her for a damn minute."

I weighed the options while sipping yet another cup of that anemic punch. Either my taste buds had given up the ghost or the stuff had actually improved. "Wow! This isn't so bad after all."

Her snarky grin stopped me in mid-sip. "Nope. A slug of bourbon improves the taste of almost everything." Babette opened her purse, revealing a tiny silver flask.

"You are incorrigible," I said. "Hey, I was thinking... Jakes said he knew who killed Ethel. That means he saw or overheard something the day she was murdered. Something that made him pretty cocky about getting a payoff."

Babette sneered. "Something that killed the slime bag. Served him right."

"You're not listening," I said. Her habit of jumping in before I finished was irritating beyond belief. "Don't you see? Everything goes back to that group at your house the day Ethel died. The same crowd was there when Jakes bought the farm."

Babette hesitated. "Okay. Four guys were there—Jakes, Reedy, Carleton, and Pruett although Pruett had no motive. You, me, Charlotte and Jacqui were around too."

"Don't forget Sheila. She couldn't get past the cops when Ethel died, but she was there the second time, so we have to count her. She's rich too."

"I guess." Babette sucked in her cheeks and stayed quiet. "Maybe it wasn't a woman after all. Men are stronger and more likely to be violent." She snickered. "Except Carleton of course. That man is a total wuss unless he has his pants down."

I noticed Pruett walking toward us, sans Monique. Apparently, she had disappeared soon after delivering her little speech. Babette immediately buttonholed him and launched into a prolonged diatribe about men and murder. Pruett made a few cursory responses, but I zoned out. We had missed something important and it was bothering me.

Pruett touched my cheek. "Earth to Perri. Still with us?"

Suddenly I recalled the point that had eluded me. "How do you feel about cufflinks?" I asked, pointing toward the French cuffs he wore.

"Neutral. On special occasions I wear them but not every day. Too much trouble."

His cufflinks were simple: heavy golden squares with a monogrammed P. They suited the man perfectly—elegant with a touch of austerity.

"What's that about?" Pruett asked.

Babette jumped in, describing the Cartier cufflink she had found in Carleton's sock drawer.

"I don't like diamond jewelry, at least not on men." Pruett gave me a smoldering look that raised my temperature to the stratosphere. "Mostly old guys wear that kind of stuff anyway. Corporate boardrooms are full of them. Check out the crowd here."

Sure enough, most of the portly senior set around us, including Charlotte Westly's husband, sported glittering cufflinks. I tried not to stare at his hands but couldn't help myself. Unless my eyesight failed me, Mr. Westly wore Cartier cufflinks identical to the one in the sock drawer. He also had the hairiest hands I had seen outside of a zoo. Major gag factor.

I angled my body sideways to distract Babette. "That was our reaction too," I said. "The cost was prohibitive. Someone probably re-gifted them to Carleton." Babette sniffed. "Second hand stuff is all that varmint deserves, even if it is pricey." Her eyes lacked focus, probably a result of emotional distress and too much Bourbon punch. To avoid a scene, we had to make a quick getaway.

"Come on," I said, taking her arm. "Let's go home and talk it over."

"Am I invited too?" Pruett asked.

Babette perked up immediately. "Sure thing, handsome. Let's meet at Perri's place. Mine isn't safe right now with Carleton prowling around."

He looked to me for an invitation and maybe a bit more.

"Fine," I said. "The more the merrier. But won't Monique be bored?"

Pruett shook his head. "Nah. We had a town car drop us off. Monique left for Georgetown as soon as she finished that presentation. Alma's there watching Ella."

That meant Pruett had no transportation home unless he called a car service. My pulse raced, and a full body flush enveloped me. No man—even Pip—had affected me that way. Better to ignore those urges rather than yield to them. Easy enough to think, much harder to carry out. Abstinence was a stern, demanding mistress and no fun at all.

"Hey," Babette said. "You ready, Perri? You look out of it."

Hoist on my own horny petard! If Babette noticed, Pruett might have too. I hastily changed the subject. "I better drive. You're still a bit tipsy."

"Nonsense!" Babette was in her 'never give up' mode, despite being flushed and more than a bit wobbly.

Pruett beamed at her and bowed. "May I chauffeur you lovely ladies? It would be my privilege."

Babette immediately got all girly. "Of course, Wing. Don't listen to us." She grabbed his arm like a hungry trout and flounced toward the door in full view of the crowd.

Chapter 28

Pruett helped Babette into the house while I attended to my pets. The dogs rallied around me with wags and kisses as if I were a warrior returning from a prolonged siege. True to type, Thatcher showed me her backside and scurried toward our guests. Zeke head butted my leg.

I found Pruett and Babette comfortably settled in the living room, sharing glasses of sparkling water. She commandeered Pip's chair and sprawled out in an ungainly heap while Pruett sat cross-legged on the sofa, the perfect poster boy for GQ magazine. I joined him there leaving a respectable space between us.

"Okay," I said. "Let's compare notes." When I shared Charlotte's reaction to Jakes and Ethel, Babette suddenly sat up and clapped.

"So, she was paying Ethel to keep quiet. Very interesting. Perfect motive for murder if you ask me. Her husband would have raised Cain if he knew she was diddling one of the staff. Could cost Carleton his job too." She sputtered when she spoke, realizing that career loss gave Carleton a gold-plated motive for both murders. Babette bowed her head, but not before a tear trickled down her cheek.

Pruett rode to the rescue. "Charlotte's husband knows what she's like. Probably not worth making a fuss about unless it became a major scandal. Who else was on your list?" Babette brightened immediately. "Jacqui. You remember her, don't you Wing?"

He wagged his finger her way and laughed. "That's the spirit! Now Jacqui has that shoplifting problem as I recall. Very dicey if she's slipped up recently. Could be that Jakes saw her coming out of your place the day of the murder. She's a big woman, capable of clobbering you, Perri."

I got a sudden brainstorm. "Hey, Jacqui was wearing black that day just like my attacker. Wasn't she, Babette?"

"I think both of them were," Babette replied. "Sheila wasn't there so I can't say about her, although she favors dark clothing. And Ken almost always wears it."

I knew I was on to something. Something important. I clutched Pruett's arm in my excitement. It felt so good that I didn't let go. "Remember what you said, Babette?"

Her eyes were still glassy from the effects of Bourbon. "Not really. Sometimes I talk so much it's hard to know what I said."

"Come on," I prompted her. "We were talking about Ethel's costume and you said that no woman would undress in front of a man like that unless he was her husband or lover."

"So? Everyone knows that."

"It suggests that the murderer was a woman. We know Ethel wasn't romantically involved with anyone around here. At least I don't think so. Anyway, she took her time, folded her dress up nice and neat, and prepared to step into that stupid horse costume. She probably turned her back to the murderer while they chatted. Ethel was arrogant that way. She underestimated her adversary. Obviously, Jakes did too. That means it was someone who seemed non-threatening."

Pruett nodded. "Sounds plausible but what about timing?"

"The cops only estimate her time of death from around eight am to nine that morning. Very imprecise, according to Bascomb. Someone could have nipped in and finished her off with no problem. After all, the fire extinguisher was right there."

Babette poked her head up in time to comment. "Forget it. You got there at eight thirty and found her body. You were attacked shortly after that. Sort of pinpoints TOD." I could tell by her smirk that she was very pleased with herself. Unfortunately, she was also right. Unless the killer crept back in later, Ethel was probably murdered between eight and eight thirty that morning. Too risky unless of course that same killer happened to live in the house. Then he or she had all the time in the world to set things up. I closed my eyes, refusing to contemplate that possibility. Babette was too kind to kill, and Carleton was too indolent to make the effort.

Pruett moved closer and put his arm around me. "Tired? Try leaning on me for a while."

We exchanged glances fuller of fire than Shakespeare's sonnets. As Pruett's lips touched mine a sound rivaling an air raid siren pierced the air. Babette with Clara at her feet had zonked out, a victim of too many drinks and too few hopes.

Her raucous snores were a mood killer at least for the moment. Pruett and I both started laughing and simply could not stop. I slipped out of his arms, grabbed a coverlet and tucked it around Babette. Something told me she might spend the night in Pip's comfy chair. Toward the end when the pain intensified, he had done that too many times to count.

I held my hand out to Pruett, trying mightily to sound nonchalant. "Want to turn in, or is it too early for you?"

His voice was deep and sensuous, full of unanticipated promise. "Who said anything about sleeping?"

* * * *

I arose early the next day, eager to tend my pets and tame my libido. Babette was still snoozing, and when last seen Pruett had buried himself under a mound of covers. I fed the dogs, inveigled Zeke into eating hay, and tried without much success to interest Thatcher in her kibble. After downing a cup of espresso, I took the unusual step of preparing a spinach quiche and popping it into the oven. Perri Morgan, wonder woman and domestic goddess!

I had an appointment to meet the owner of a pet boutique in Arlington, one of DC's close suburbs. If she showed interest in my products, it would go a long way toward promoting the Morgan Fine Leather brand. That heartened me. Anything that would increase my revenue stream was a big win. Cobbling together pet shows and web sales was time consuming and erratic. Babette thought my concern was silly. Of course, she had never even mastered the art of balancing a checkbook let alone running a business. None of that mattered of course. I loved my big-hearted friend who would have showered me with cash if I needed it. Carleton was another matter entirely.

I busied myself dressing the table with Limoges china, an auction find that elevated any meal to a special occasion. It was a silly, delusional act but harmless enough as fantasies went.

A cacophony of barks and growls brought me back to earth and announced that a visitor had arrived. Unlike many of my neighbors, I had no need for a doorbell. Not with the Malinois crew on the job. The noise roused Babette who reacted like a grumpy bear trying to hibernate.

"What's happening?" she asked rubbing sleep-laden eyes.

"Morning, princess. We have a visitor." I pointed to the doorway where Titus Bascomb stood wearing a major frown and a rumpled suit that had seen better days. I shooed Babette toward the dining table and welcomed Bascomb in. "Morning, Lieutenant. Join us for some breakfast."

He stepped gingerly around Thatcher, all the while eyeing the three dogs. "Those hounds won't bite me, I hope."

"No worries." I poured each of us a cup of espresso, using the large French bowls that forced one to proceed slowly. Bascomb sniffed the brew and cautiously sipped. He closed his eyes and sighed like a very happy man. "Hmm. Mighty fine. Just what I needed."

At that moment, Pruett appeared at the table garbed in Pip's old robe. He yawned and greeted the lawman with a supercilious grin that bordered on a sneer. "On the job early today, I see."

Bascomb eyed the bathrobe and returned the sneer with interest. "You too, Mr. Pruett."

I was too busy sorting out conflicting feelings to absorb the banter. Another man was wearing Pip's clothing. That tatty robe was as much a part of him as the worn galoshes I refused to discard. Was it an act of betrayal or merely the final grueling stage of the grief process? Kübler-Ross termed it "letting go and acceptance." To me it seemed more like abandonment. I had no answer and perhaps I never would. Pip would always be a part of me and I liked it that way. He comforted and consoled me even from the grave.

The oven timer pinged, ending my reverie. I opened the door allowing the enticing scent of quiche to fill the small kitchen and waft into the dining room. Babette was the first to comment.

"Mark this day down in the record books. Persephone Morgan outdoes Martha Stewart."

My cheeks flushed more from the oven's heat than embarrassment. Leave it to my best pal to accentuate the obvious and sow confusion. I grabbed a pizza cutter and spatula, filling each plate with a steaming slice of quiche. "No big deal. Enjoy."

Pruett filled the conversational void with appreciative noises. "Yum! You compete with Alma when it comes to quiche." His eyes met mine. "And in other ways too numerous to count."

Bascomb almost choked on his espresso. "I won't take up too much of your time, folks. Just for the record, Mr. Jakes had his windpipe broken. The doc thinks he was disabled first, probably by a knock on the head."

"Wait a minute," I said. "There was no blood."

"Nope. Just a bump on the base of the skull, hard enough to disorient or disable him but probably not enough to kill him outright. The broken windpipe did the trick."

Pruett stayed silent, but I could not. "What about the belt?" In my haste, I stumbled over the words. "Did my belt kill Jakes, Lieutenant?"

He kept me waiting while he chewed a forkful of quiche. Was Bascomb being polite or merely obstreperous? I couldn't decide. Pruett reached under the table and squeezed my knee, as if urging caution. Babette felt no such constraints.

"Out with it, Titus. Are you here to arrest one of us?"

"No ma'am. Just a friendly chat." Bascomb's cunning alligator eyes stayed half-shut as though sizing up his prey. "And to answer your question, Ms. Morgan, I'm afraid the doc thinks your belt was used to strangle Mr. Jakes. Tell me again which of your guests left the meeting during the break."

Babette heaved a gigantic sigh and repeated the familiar litany of names. "And just like I told you before, Perri, Pruett and I stayed put."

I filled everyone's cup with more espresso, moving cautiously from place to place. None of the precious liquid spilled, which was a major triumph, considering my shaking hands. If Bascomb's goal was to hold our attention and raise the anxiety level, he exceeded all expectations. That cop was definitely up to something.

"Is that all?" Babette asked brusquely, checking her watch.

Bascomb took another long, slow sip. "One more thing." He glanced at each of us before taking center stage. "Those times really don't mean much anymore. The coroner says Jakes died anywhere between two and four hours of the time you found him."

I did some quick calculations in my head. This was eerily similar to Ethel's murder. Anyone, even Pruett or I, could have met Jakes early that morning, grabbed his phone, struck him down, and arrived right on time for the ten am soiree. Using one of my belts provided a touch of whimsy or a hint of sadism, I couldn't decide which.

"Surely someone would have seen a vehicle entering or exiting at that early hour." Pruett's manner was casual as if he were discussing the sports scores or a recent film.

Bascomb matched him tone for tone. "One would think so. We found some footprints and what looked like wheelbarrow or bike tracks. Nothing helpful."

I grew weary of this cat and mouse game, especially since I was the rodent being pursued by a predatory cop. "What's your point, Lieutenant?"

He rose and gave each of us a long, searching look. "This time factor threw a monkey wrench into my scenario. My suspect list just grew longer. I thought you folks should know in case you had any plans to leave the area."

"What about Cleo? She's bunking at Cavalry Farms, you know." I clenched my fists to absorb the agony.

"Cleo? Who the hell is that?" He seemed genuinely puzzled.

Babette scowled at him. "Don't be obtuse for a change, Titus. Cleopatra was Jakes's champion Palomino."

He shrugged. "No clue. Someone will pick her up sooner or later I suppose."

I shivered at the thought of the gentle hunter and her probable fate. Despite his faults Jakes had cared for his horse. "No problem. She's doing fine there. I'll be glad to keep an eye on her."

Bascomb thanked me for breakfast and ambled toward the door with the untroubled gait of a man on a mission.

"What do you make of that?" Babette asked. "Sounded like a threat to me."

Pruett snickered. "Or a promise. I guess no one is in the clear as far as Bascomb's concerned. He does have a point though."

I considered that for a moment. Despite his hints, Bascomb had yet to specify a real motive—something that would lead to two murders. Blackmail could easily escalate into violence, but the stakes seemed way too low. Ethel and perhaps Jakes had taken a dangerous road to perdition and paid the ultimate price. I did a quick mental review of the motives and suspects that I knew of. The case brimmed with infidelity, criminal mischief, and career suicide. In the worst possible scenario, Carleton would lose his post, Charlotte's husband would dump her, and Jacqui would be exposed to the entire world as a low-end thief. Ken had very little to lose. So, what if his part in his dying wife's end was revealed? Most people—myself included—would applaud or at least understand his actions. On the other hand, Ken's sense of justice made him a prime candidate for a justice crusader. As for the rest of us—me, Pruett, Babette and Sheila—I simply could not muster a compelling case for any of us to commit one murder let alone two.

"Dollar for your thoughts?" Pruett said.

"What happened to a penny?"

The gleam in his eyes made me shiver. "Inflation." He squeezed my hand. "Guess I better get dressed and head for work. My editor has a short fuse these days."

I nodded and rose to clear the kitchen table. "You need a ride, remember. I'll take you into DC. Give me a minute to get ready." The truth was that I relished every second spent with him. Not the wisest course of action but one that I was reconciled to.

Babette yawned. "I don't have anything special to do. Not one thing."

I reminded her about her television show. The final showdown was only six days away. It was High Noon and the OK Corral rolled up in one telegenic piece. She pondered it and stifled a yawn.

"No problemo, I've got everything under control. Maybe they have an opening at the salon. A pedicure and massage always soothe my spirits." She fumbled for Clara's leash and sauntered toward the door. "See you love birds later."

Pruett gazed down at me. "Lovebirds? Is that what we are?"

I busied myself with rinsing the dishes. "Babette dramatizes everything. You know that. Just ignore her."

He plunged his hands into the soapy water and clutched my wrists. "I like the idea. How about you?"

I tried to formulate a snappy comeback, but my throat constricted. Washing dishes in Pip's kitchen with a man wearing his robe—way too complicated for me to handle. A trite response was the best I could muster.

"Fine with me. I've always been a bird lover."

Chapter 29

Pruett and I discussed mundane matters during our trip into DC, speculating wildly about Babette's cable program and its probable outcome.

"Why should anyone show up for it?" Pruett asked. "Smarter for the guilty party to lay low."

"That's just the point. No one will want to be a no show, not if it means looking guilty." I was confident about that.

"Maybe you should help Babette with the script." Pruett slipped his arm around me. "Make sure it conforms to your stated goal."

His antics momentarily distracted me and caused the driver of a weathered mini-van to honk angrily. Normally I would have given him the one-finger salute but in deference to Pruett, I summoned a superior smile and drove on.

"Based on what you know, who's your prime suspect?" I was genuinely curious to learn the answer.

He frowned as he considered the question. "Frankly, I haven't a clue. They all had a lot to lose but murder—that's another thing entirely. Only a ruthless competitor would choose that route. You know, a win at any cost person."

I nodded. "Hard to consider friends or acquaintances as sociopaths I guess."

Pruett raised his eyebrows. "Turnabout is fair play. Who rings your bells?"

I bit my lip, unwilling to say the name.

"Come on, girl. Out with it. I promise this is off the record." He winked as if he were only half-serious.

"Carleton." I blurted out. It was a betrayal of Babette, but the man fit every category—serious consequences if outed; hedonistic spirit; physical strength, and amoral outlook. Carleton rang every bell. The only downside was his innate indolence. Professor Croy was hardly a go-getter or risk taker.

As we turned down P Street, Pruett gathered his belongings. "What about your theory that it was a woman? You know, Ethel undressing and all that?"

"I know, but Ethel might well had been taunting him. Disrobing to show he was a wimp or something less than a real man. He certainly had motive, means, and opportunity." I applied the brakes and stopped in front of the townhouse. Before leaving, Pruett reached across the seat and kissed me goodbye.

"We need to talk, Ms. Persephone Morgan. Not about murder either. About the two of us and where this thing is going."

A hairball-sized lump worthy of Thatcher clogged my throat and made me choke. Pruett wacked me on the back until I was finally able to speak. His attempt at the Heimlich Maneuver lacked finesse but it got the job done. I forced myself to face him head-on.

"Okay. After we clear this mess up. Then we'll talk."

He winked and bounded out of the car with an insouciance that bordered on arrogance.

* * * *

The trek to Arlington took longer than I planned. Traffic—the bane of every DC driver's existence—kept me tapping the brakes for almost a solid hour. Fortunately, I arrived at my destination The Soignee Salon, with five minutes to spare. The owner, Nanette Neal, was a refreshing change from the supercilious snob I had expected.

"I'm in love with your beautiful belts," she said, tossing her mane of auburn hair, "especially the mother-daughter angle. Since everyone seems to have a pet these days, a matching leash is more icing on the cake. With any luck, we might get coverage in the *Post's* style section. The editor owes me a few favors."

I was flabbergasted by the prospect, too shy to ask who referred me to her. On an art deco table behind her desk, I noticed a photo of a titian-haired sprite with her mother's wide grin. "Your daughter?" I asked.

Nanette smiled. "Lesley is a student at Hamilton Arms. First grade. Her classmate wore one of your belts to school, and that's all Lesley chattered about. My child was obsessed with getting one for herself."

Ella. The connection finally made sense. I mentioned her name and Nanette brightened. "Oh yes," she said. "You must know Wing Pruett and Monique. What a lovely couple."

I managed a smile and quickly changed the subject back to business. As we chatted about Hamilton Arms and the educational climate there, Nanette sighed. "I get lots of customers from Hamilton but sometimes they're not worth the aggravation."

I plastered a sympathetic smile on my face and said nothing. According to Sheila, Nanette was normally the soul of discretion. For whatever reason, today she insisted on over-sharing, or, spilling her guts to use the vernacular.

"Some women abuse small retailers like me," she said. "You know the drill—purchase, wear the garment then return it the next day. In the trade we call it wardrobing." Nanette reached in to her purse and retrieved a pack of cigarettes. "I stopped smoking last year," she laughed, "but today has been really tough. Upscale chains put those obnoxious tags on garments and refuse to take them back. I can't afford to alienate my customers."

I nodded sympathetically even though I wouldn't dream of pulling a scam like that myself.

"Anyway, today, a mother from Hamilton Arms—one with plenty of cash—came in and dumped over three thousand bucks worth of cashmere sweaters on the counter. Said her husband didn't like them." Nanette exhaled a giant plume of smoke. "Huh! She'd obviously worn them, and it wasn't the first time either. She pulls that with everyone. I swear I'm going to ban that Charlotte Westly from this store."

My mouth dropped open. Feisty vixen Charlotte Westly was a chisler as well as a slut! Could she also be a murderer?

"Forget I said that, Perri. Please. I can't return the stuff, so I'm stuck with it." Nanette grabbed a pile of incredibly gorgeous cashmere and pushed it my way. "Here. Want it?"

It was tempting, but no way could I every pay that much for clothing. "I can't afford them, I'm afraid. They are wonderful though."

Nanette winked. "How about we trade some of those belts for the sweaters. That way I get a chance to recoup something."

When I realized she was serious, I readily agreed. Before I left, Nanette sweetened the deal by placing an initial order for belts with an option for more. The price was a revelation, far more than I had ever dreamed of and enough to raise my spirits. I pinched myself just to prove I was awake and not in a fugue state. I left Soignee Salon cosseted by cashmere and filled with plenty of questions about a certain wealthy matron.

With a bit of luck, I could hop on to I-66 West and beat the rush hour traffic to my house. Ominous black clouds decorated the horizon making me fear for the safety of my pets. Thunderstorms in Virginia tended to be swift and brutal, filled with *Sturm und Drang*. Keats and Poe took them in stride, but I had no idea how Zeke would react.

Had I really tagged Carleton as a double murderer? It sounded fanciful the more I thought of it. After all, Carleton himself had been attacked, and the last thing that self-centered creature would do was injure himself. Ken Reedy was a more likely prospect, although his motive was shaky. I simply could not picture him harming a woman, even a nefarious type like Ethel. When it came to Ken, objectivity was impossible. His kindness to animals left me totally biased in his favor.

The weather gods humored me, and I pulled into my driveway just as the heavens parted. Zeke glared balefully at me as I led him inside to his stall and forked hay into his bucket. The dogs were damp but otherwise untouched and Thatcher who always remained indoors anyway showed supreme indifference to the cloudburst.

Although I was gone for only a few hours, it felt like an eternity—too much emotion, elation and angst for one day. I longed to change into PJs, cuddle up in Pip's chair and kick back. Heck. I might even crack open a bottle of wine.

Too bad I didn't clear my plans with Babette. My cell phone shrilled just as I got comfortable, and her number flashed before my eyes. My thoughts were unprintable and unkind. Being Babette's BFF was often more pain than pleasure.

"Did I interrupt anything?" she asked. I steadfastly ignored the sniffle in her voice.

After counting way past ten, I responded. "Nope. What's up?"

"I'm lonely, Perri. Everyone has someone to love but me."

"Don't be silly. Look at me or your pal, Jacqui. You don't need a man around to be happy, Babette. Besides you have Clara and friends who love you."

This time her sniffles sounded like foghorns. "Big deal. When the lights are out, I need a man. You have Pruett. Sheila has Ellis and even though he's too old to put out, he showers her with affection. Even Carleton had his good points."

Self-pity annoys me, particularly coming from a privileged, pampered member of the elite. I dispensed with tact and opted for tough love.

"Don't you dare! There was no exclusivity clause with your husband. You know that Carleton shared his so-called assets with half the women in town. You deserve better, Babette. Snap out of it!"

The silence on her end was oppressive. Then Babette, my wacky, wonderful pal began to laugh. Guffaw. Bray. After a time, she stopped and got down to business.

"I guess you told me, Miss Persephone. You always were the strong one. Okay, let's chat about my television show. Hot damn! Trapping a killer is hard work. Guess we better work on our ground game."

We spent the next half hour doing just that.

* * * *

I slept in Pip's chair that night. Sweet dreams of comfort and seduction overwhelmed me, lulling me into slumber. Pruett played the starring role in fantasies that were so explicit even in retrospect that they made me blush. Only my dogs' pleas and the irritated howls of Thatcher roused me.

The storm was long gone, and, in its wake, a lovely azure sky enveloped Great Marsh Virginia. Optimism was the mood of the day and I quickly devised a list of chores. First and foremost, I had to finalize and deliver the show gear for both Cecil and Sheila's gelding. I could have sent the order by Fed-Ex, but that was far too impersonal for a top customer and good friend like Sheila Sands. Besides, it gave me another opportunity to pick her considerable brain about the murders.

I inhaled a large cup of espresso, tended to my pets, and got down to work. It was no nonsense, nose to the grindstone time. I admit I kept my cell phone close at hand in case Pruett called. I finalized the order just in time for lunch, packed Cecil's gear and loaded my dogs into the Suburban. Sheila promised to provide both a tasty spread and quality time to chat about Bascomb's bombshell. I felt ravenous, hungry for both food and conversation. Discipline is good for the soul but hard on the tummy sometimes. I vowed to confine my views to munching, murder and mayhem rather than rhapsodizing about a certain media celebrity.

I phoned as usual before approaching Arcadia. Ellis Sands had very peculiar rules about security that even Sheila abided by. No casual visitors for him. No sir. Every visitor was verified and logged in at the gate. It seemed excessive even paranoid to me, but the Sands lived on a different planet than the proletariat. Who else would have a home with a beautifully constructed Orangerie worthy of Versailles itself?

Sheila was waiting with her front door opened wide. When he saw my menagerie, Cecil uttered one anemic woof then hid behind her, very much a baby in a giant's body.

"Come in. All of you. It's servants' day off so we'll have to forage for pot luck." She was impeccably garbed in tones of silver, a color that complimented her platinum bob. Discreet pieces of Georg Jensen jewelry completed the outfit giving it just the right touch. Sheila's social set eschewed flashy symbols of wealth, branding them *nouveau riche*. That summed up someone like Charlotte or even Jacqui rather neatly. Babette was in a category all her own.

We trooped through the vast great room decorated in tones of teal and white. The beautiful space managed to be both soothing and elegant at the same time. Hard to believe that a drooling hulk like Cecil strode the premises with impunity.

"We can use the Orangerie if you don't mind. That way the pups can enjoy their treats as well." Leave it to Sheila to accommodate each of her guests. I grinned since that area was larger than my dining room and kitchen combined. On a lovely autumn day packed with sunshine, the sparkling glass structure was even more impressive. Using a bit of imagination, I could envision Marie Antoinette herself gracing the table.

Sheila must have read my mind. She waved her arm around the room. "Opulent, I know, but Ellis is a Eurocentric fiend. Anything that smacks of the great estates is right up his alley. It's his harmless obsession."

Something told me that his wife was another one of Ellis Sands' obsessions. That too was harmless enough.

"It's lovely," I said. "Everything is perfect."

The table was blanketed with crystal, china, and an impressive arrangement of lilies. I was no expert on luxury goods but the name Herend adorned the china, and Baccarat was etched into the crystal. I settled in, prepared to enjoy a brief fling with the good life.

Sheila's eyes sparkled with mischief. "Okay, Leather Lady. Time to sing for your supper."

I looked quizzically at her. "May I hum a tune instead? A dirge, perhaps?"

"Okay. I give up." She slipped into the kitchen and emerged with an enticing shrimp and avocado salad for us plus meaty marrow bones for the canine crew.

"Yum! Sustenance first." I forked a healthy portion of salad on to my plate, snagged a roll and dove in. Normally I skip lunch or gnaw on a piece of fruit, but life with Pruett had activated all my appetites. As we ate, I described the recent encounter with Bascomb and the bombshell about Charlotte. Sheila neglected her lunch as she absorbed every syllable. Apparently, her Nancy Drew gene was alive and well.

"Let me get this straight. Since the timeframes are out the window any one of us could have done the deed and slipped away." Sheila's perfectly arched brows drew together in a frown. "That's a lot of motive for someone. Does Bascomb have a clue?"

I crunched a shrimp and considered her question. Something told me that Bascomb was a whole lot smarter than he led us to believe. His clueless act was shop-worn but curiously effective, probably designed to trap one of us into a damaging admission.

"You know, he seemed pretty confident considering the circumstances. I'm afraid for Babette." I consoled myself with a sliver of avocado.

Sheila's expression didn't change. That in itself frightened me. By saying nothing, she spoke volumes. She locked eyes with me and sighed. "What does her lawyer say?"

I shrugged. Babette said very little about her attorney and even less about Carleton's situation.

"Think about it from Bascomb's perspective," Sheila said. "Cops like things all neat and tidy with all the loose ends tied up. Babette and Carleton live on the property where two murders occurred. That doesn't look good."

I squeezed my eyes closed and forced myself to concentrate. Ethel was a blackmailer. Pruett had confirmed that much. I strongly believed that Jakes assumed the mantle after her murder. Both of them had probably been struck down by the same hand, someone who had finally lost patience with their schemes.

"Neither of them saw it coming," I said. "Jakes was skulking around the area on the day Ethel died. We know that. I bet he saw our murderer doing something. Something that implicated him or her in Ethel's murder."

"Her? You think a woman would be that bloodthirsty?" Sheila was unconvinced.

"Women have more to lose," I said, "status, reputation, money. Powerful forces. And don't discount love."

"Love? You're kidding." Sheila folded her arms and shook her head. "I don't see it. Someone was paying Jakes and Ethel. Titus probably checked our bank balances for large withdraws unless he's more pathetic than I figured."

"Charlotte admitted paying off Ethel. Maybe she decided to nip things in the bud when Jakes took up the cause." I tried to visualize petite Charlotte throttling Jakes. Somehow it didn't compute.

"She has a husband, doesn't she? Maybe he wanted to avenge his honor or something hopelessly medieval. I know Ellis would react that way if I were in that kind of scrape. Not that he's my idea of Rambo or anything." She laughed. "He'd probably assign it to his second in command anyway. My husband is one big believer in delegating."

I looked down at my plate to suppress the desire to laugh. Ellis Sands was eighty at least. He was intellectually vigorous but physically limited. Of course, Jakes was bashed in the head before the killer strangled him. Anyone could manage that even a small woman or a frail senior. A more likely scenario concerned filthy lucre. Ellis possessed a mighty bank account that could be used to hire plenty of muscle. While it was possible, it still seemed unlikely. Power players like him crushed their opponents in the courts or the boardroom, leaving the tawdry chores to lesser beings.

"What do you know about Jacqui? I mean really know." I watched Sheila squirm as she weighed loyalty to her friend against shielding a potential murderer.

"Jacqui has her demons like most of us, but cash is not a problem. Her ex-husband left her well off. On the other hand, she cornered Ethel at the fundraiser I told you about and believe me, it was no friendly chat. Sparks flew."

"Most women wound with words, not deeds," I said. "Of course, some, like me, have the skills to defend themselves. What about Jacqui?"

Sheila avoided my eyes and busied herself with hugging Cecil. Once again, she appeared to be weighing options. "Jacqui and I both take martial arts classes. Nothing too exotic of course. Just basic self-defense stuff."

Sheila had more to tell and was avoiding the real issue. I could tell by the way she bit her lip. Several things were adding up. Jacqui had the right body type to be my assailant. She was impulsive too with a volatile temper and a mean streak. I recalled the way her greedy eyes devoured Pruett and the hostile looks she shot my way.

"Come on. Out with it. I won't tell Bascomb." I hated to pressure Sheila, but Babette's future hung in the balance. Apologies were for later.

"Okay. It's just that Jacqui earned a black belt in Tae Kwon Do. She's sort of like the class star. The rest of us are dabblers."

One well-placed blow could easily have disabled Jakes. Taking Ethel down would have been child's play. Jacqui was a virtual stranger to me, but she might have purchased one of my belts in town. Implicating me would have been the proverbial icing on the cake for a jealous woman. Major payback for my involvement with Pruett.

"One thing bothers me," Sheila said. "Ethel's murder seemed spur of the moment, but Jakes was a different story. Someone planned that one." She reached down and scratched Cecil's ear. "Maybe we're looking for two killers instead of one."

I had never even considered that. Suddenly I raised an uncomfortable possibility. "What about Ken? Maybe he tried to protect someone. He's such a sweetie, sort of like a knight errant. If Ethel or Jakes threatened Cavalry Farms, I'm not sure what Ken would do."

Sheila put her head in her hands. "It's too much trouble playing detective. No fun at all. I like Ken Reedy no matter what he did. Why not let Bascomb figure everything out? That's why we pay him for crying out loud."

I shrugged and said nothing. For all I knew she might be right. Probably was.

Sheila steepled her fingers and looked up. "One thing I am sure of. Whoever murdered Ethel and Jakes must have had a damn good reason for it, something worth risking life and liberty for. Find that, and you'll find the killer."

Chapter 30

I immersed myself in work that evening, but it didn't help. Crafting leather products requires skill and concentration. There are rules to follow too. I imported sheets of fine English bridle leather for most of my products, custom measured each article and cut and stitched in my workshop. Precision was my watch-word and there was no room for error. Murder was an entirely different matter and once the "thou shalt not kill" threshold was breached, all bets were off. After serving in the military I was no stranger to violence. Soldiers fought the enemy, but they also brawled over sex, money, and status often with disastrous results. I vividly recalled one baby-faced recruit who slit his roommate's throat over a perceived slight, climbed into bed and slept the night away. This was different. An ordinary citizen—cold sober and calculating—had taken two lives. These crimes were personal, far from the battlefield, based in an idyllic setting among friends and neighbors just like me. The mayhem violated my personal space and left me feeling curiously vulnerable.

To discipline myself, I spent a full hour bathing and grooming Zeke. Handling that irascible goat was more punishment than pleasure even though I was convinced that he secretly enjoyed the ritual. It was cozy enough with Keats and Poe gathered 'round, providing a canine support unit for their pal. I was so focused on my task that I ignored the ringing of my cell phone and missed a call from Pruett. Returning his call took more moxie than I ever anticipated. All my insecurities arose and with them questions too dreadful to contemplate. Suppose Monique answered the phone? What if he brushed me off? After gritting my teeth, I vowed to expunge this feckless version of myself from my life and get on with it.

Pruett answered immediately in that warm, smoky voice that drove me wild.

After a few preliminaries, I shared my conversation with Sheila. "Maybe she's right," I said. "Two killers might make sense. Muddy the waters."

"Maybe." Pruett paused. "You realize that you've upped the stakes for Babette and Carleton? Despite their differences, they both had something to lose."

I have a stubborn streak a mile wide. "Not buying that. Not about Babette. She's had three other husbands, so a divorce wouldn't destroy her. Carleton now, he's a different kettle of fish. The man makes egotism an art form, and he's all about the bucks."

Pruett hesitated. "I suppose Jacqui might confide in me..."

"Great! I'll tackle Ken Reedy. We became good friends through the rescue stuff."

"Whoa," Pruett said. "Wait one minute. If Reedy killed two people you'd put yourself in danger. No way."

I chuckled and sidestepped the protection issue. "A show cluster starts Friday. I'm pretty sure Ken will be there so if you happen to drop by, you could keep an eye on both of us."

Pruett sensed a concession and he jumped on it. "Good plan. There's something fishy about that guy. Mr. Dependable. He already had a scuffle with Jakes, didn't he?"

"A minor disagreement. No big deal. If you lounge around Hamilton Arms tomorrow, you might get lucky. Jacqui volunteers there twice a week or so Babette told me."

Pruett muttered several uncouth and unprintable things, but he agreed. "Don't blame me if she tests my virtue. Maybe I'll ask her to lunch. As I recall she has quite an appetite."

That was an opening only a saint could refuse. I am no candidate for a halo, so I immediately pounced. "You're just the man to satisfy all of Jacqui's appetites. She mentioned that only last week."

For once, he was stumped. "I don't drink that much anymore. One night with Jacqui was a better cure than an AA meeting. That woman is a piranha. You can bet I'll stick to mineral water around her."

I was still smiling long after we hung up. Things were so easy between Pruett and me—banter, affection and passion. Who could ask for anything more? I knew I was deluding myself, getting in deeper with each call and kiss. I was philosophical about the situation, substituting analysis for emotion. All told, the pleasure would outweigh the pain.

* * * *

Monday was the busiest day of my workweek. Internet orders were brisk, requiring an immediate acknowledgement to the customer and adjustments to my schedule. No complaints, no sir. My livelihood and identity were intertwined in Creature Comforts and I planned to keep it that way. Romantic fantasies were fine, but they did not pay the bills.

I tried unsuccessfully to process the clues we had accumulated but my brain was on overload and my usual confidant, Babette, was out of bounds. Pruett had sent me a mysterious text saying he had "done his duty" whatever that meant and would report later. There was only one way to escape the mental muddle. I plunged into the monotony of routine chores with a vengeance. It was comforting to feed and exercise my pets, check email, and return phone calls. Physical activity obviated the need for brainwork and left me exhausted but clear headed. When Sheila called after dinner, I gave her a concise summary of my thoughts.

"So, it looks like we were wrong about Charlotte and Carleton," I said. "The cuff link threw us off."

"Who else could it be?" Sheila asked. "She's a chisler. We know that, but it's just so petty. We need a list of Hamilton Arms parents. You can bet Carleton's bit of fluff came from there. Opportunity and all that."

She was right, but I hated to involve Babette any more than necessary. Maybe Pruett had a listing. Schools tended to distribute those things to parents. I fell asleep that night clutching my cell phone with a cat at my side and the dogs curled around the bed. No texts or messages disturbed my rest.

Chapter 31

Horse shows have their own rhythm for both vendors and participants. After years of practice, I mastered the routine, moving seamlessly through the familiar ritual: Wake up, care for the pets, load up my goods, and get my over-caffeinated self on the road. My fondest memories were of sharing the experience with Pip when he was the on-site veterinarian. Every show has one, but he added a special touch of magic to the event. Pip genuinely loved all animals, especially horses, and they reciprocated. Small wonder that show regulars dubbed him "the horse whisperer," a moniker that held more than a grain of truth. In contrast, Pruett, a man with a pathological fear of animals simply couldn't compete in that arena.

I gave myself a mental shakedown. Relationships were not a competitive sport and only a fool would think otherwise. Pip would be the first one to chastise me for putting him on a pedestal. Like all of us he had his faults but try as I might, I just couldn't recall any. Until I resolved that conflict, my life was stuck in perpetual neutral, or neuter in the case of relationships.

By the time I arrived at the showgrounds, prime parking spaces had been snapped up. In recognition of the amount of product we hauled around, vendors were assigned a special area close to the venue. Close was a relative term when it involved navigating through throngs of pets and people carrying cartons of leather goods and two large dogs. As I unloaded the truck, the cavalry arrived in the person of Ken Reedy.

"Need help?" he asked with a wry smile.

"Naw." I struck a pose, hands on hips. "Used to be a teamster. How do you think I got these muscles?"

He reached into the truck, opened the crates, and grabbed the dogs' leads. "Big day. Good luck with sales. Customers can be persnickety."

"Persnickety? That's a word I don't often hear."

Ken shrugged. "Archaic maybe but useful. Hey, made any progress on the murders? Nothing much in the papers."

Although this was the opportunity I hoped and planned for, the triumph felt hollow. Ken Reedy was no killer. I knew that. Still, he was on the scene of both murders and certainly had the physical strength to do the deed. I recalled that Ken had served in Special Forces during the first Gulf War. That meant he also had the resolve to take serious actions if needed.

"Wait till I put this stuff away and I'll tell you everything I know. Your courtroom skills will come in handy."

He flashed that sardonic grin once more. "Okay. I don't mind being your sounding board. Anything to help Babette."

We worked in silence for the next ten minutes, toting my products and setting up the stall. After that, I leashed Keats and Poe, and turned to Ken. "Come on. Let's walk and talk."

We exited out of the side door headed toward the meadow that abutted the arena. At this time of day, very few humans were out and about. That didn't bother me at all. Ken would never hurt me. I knew that. Besides, Keats and Poe provided the best most reliable back up anyone could ask for. They were trained warriors who watched over me at all times and their instinct for trouble far surpassed my own.

"Come on," Ken said. "Tell me everything."

I gave him a concise summary of everything that transpired. Ken was an attentive listener who watched me wordlessly, absorbing every word, nuance and piece of information. Verbalizing my thoughts had other benefits. It helped me to gain perspective as well.

"Sounds like it boils down to four or five points," Ken said. "Ethel was blackmailing a number of folks and one of them ended it. Her murder was probably a spontaneous act rather than planned out."

I nodded. "That's the way we've got it figured too."

He smiled again. "We? Does that include a certain investigative reporter?"

I can maintain a poker face with the best of them, a skill I honed in the army. Things had changed though. Something about the name Pruett wreaked havoc with my self-control. No more Persephone the stoic. I felt the color rise to my cheeks and turned aside.

"Several of us are involved. Babette and Sheila helped out too."

"I suppose most folks have something to hide. Something big to them even if seems trivial to others."

That was the thing that plagued me. Charlotte's fondness for young men and her penny-pinching ways were reprehensible, but not criminal.

Returning worn clothing was vile and dishonest, the hallmark of a shady soul, but none of these misdeeds shouted murder. I also doubted that Charlotte had enough ready cash to support Glendon Jakes in his new lifestyle.

"You okay, Perri?" Ken asked. "Got something on your mind?"

I shook off my misgivings and turned to him. "What's your take on Jacqui and Sheila? They're the only other ones who were close enough to the crime scenes."

Ken chuckled. "Except for me, you mean. Don't exclude any suspects, my girl. First law of criminal defense. Anyone is capable of committing murder under the right circumstances."

"I trust you, Ken."

He tightened his grip on my arm. "Don't. By now, you know about my wife's death. Some folks called that murder."

"Not me. I would have helped Pip cross over if he had asked." I gulped to avoid choking on unshed tears. Guilt and pain my long-time companions, welled up in me. Should I have ended Pip's suffering? Was I so greedy for every minute with him, that I put my needs before his pain?

Ken moved closer, to comfort not menace me. Keats and Poe followed suit.

"I hate to mention this, Perri, and I know you love Babette..." Ken hesitated, "but she has one heck of a motive. Carleton has an even bigger one. If Hamilton Arms dumps him, he won't find another slot. Somehow, I can't see him teaching in a DC public school. Not an entitled guy like him."

Brainstorms can come anywhere, even in the middle of a meadow. I pounded Ken on the shoulder for emphasis. "It comes down to that fundraiser at Sheila's place last year. I wasn't there, but the others were."

Ken's eyes widened. "I was there. We all were. Not Jakes of course. Sheila would never invite a low-life like him. Babette and Carleton showed up though. So, what?"

"Sheila told me there was some sort of problem, a fracas between guests."

He stopped short, bent down and patted Keats. "Something like that."

"Ethel was there, wasn't she?"

"Yep." If Ken was auditioning for an old time Western, he won my vote. Unfortunately, a laconic cowpoke wouldn't help solve the murders.

I stood tall, balancing my weight evenly on both feet. "If you won't tell me, let Bascomb know. You just might stop a murderer."

Ken shook his finger at me. "Leave it, Perri. They don't deserve your time. Both of them—Ethel and Jakes—were just no good. They fed off other people's misery. I tried to warn Ethel, but she laughed in my face."

My heart rate accelerated dramatically. Was he confessing to murder? I kept my voice calm and casual. "Ethel fooled most of us but not you. How long did you know about her?"

"Lawyers get pretty good at judging people," he said. "Ethel's humble act just didn't sit well with me. I pegged her for a phony. Maybe it was her eyes. Windows to the soul they call them, don't they?"

I closed my own eyes, trying to visualize Ethel's face. Come to think of it, those glasses she wore obscured her eyes very effectively. From what I could recall they were fairly average, nothing spectacular. I frowned, puzzled by his point.

"Every once in a while, the mask dropped, and the real Ethel emerged." He rubbed his forearm absently. "Blackmail."

This time Ken seemed genuinely amused. "She miscalculated. I had already surrendered my law license, and anyone who did internet research would know the whole story about me. I wasn't ashamed of what I did. I'd do it again if my wife were suffering."

This was the oddest confession I had ever heard, and believe me, I had heard plenty of them. The field was filling up with horses, riders, and owners now. Ken couldn't hurt me if he tried. "Why did she do it—money?"

"Nope. Ethel didn't care about money. Didn't you tell me she left it all in her safety deposit box?"

"What then?"

"Power. Ethel, or whatever her name was, loved power, especially over rich people. It tickled her to see them grovel. Jakes was another kettle of fish entirely. He was greedy. Wanted money however he could get it and thought he was smarter than everyone else."

Ken patted Poe's soft coat and gave him a nose kiss. "He sure didn't deserve a princess like Cleopatra. I wasn't surprised at all when he bit the dust."

Something weird was going on. Ken wasn't the murderer. No way. But he sure as hell knew who was. "You know who did this, don't you?"

Ken gave me his trial face, the impassive look that had made him a courtroom star. "I'll say it again. Stay out of it, Perri. No good can come of meddling."

He was probably right but if Bascomb got frustrated he still might try to pin the murders on Babette. Worse still, if no one were charged, the stigma would surround her like a noxious cloud and ruin her life. I refused to let that happen.

"Sorry. Can't do it. You have to go to the police. Please, Ken."

I'll never know what his response would have been. Before he said one more word, a gleeful voice rang out. "Perri! Poe. Keats."

The children's crusade, led by Ella Pruett, accompanied by her father, had arrived.

After hugging my dogs, Ella threw her arms around my waist and gave me some love too. Pruett put his arm around me and extended his hand to Ken.

"Good to see you again, Ken. Ella and I decided to check up on Perri. Cheer her on." His eyes were a truth detector scanning our faces without saying a word. I tried to meet his glance but could not.

Ken turned toward the ring. "Looks like reinforcements have arrived. I'll be on my way folks." He strolled off, arms swinging as if he had not a care in the world.

I was aching to share my information with Pruett, but time was short. I bent down and whispered in Ella's ear.

"Come on. Let's put Poe and Keats in their crates." I sped toward ring nine, with Ella and Pruett trailing in our wake. Ken Reedy's words bounced through my brain. He knew who the killer was but for reasons of his own refused to tell me. Why? What would prevent a law and order type like Reedy from doing his duty? Perhaps the danger was over, and the killer posed no harm to anyone else. But that didn't excuse the offenses already committed. No matter what the provocation, murder times two equals a big-time capital offense.

Knowing that secret put Ken in danger too, not that he seemed to care. His wife's death had stripped him of something vital. Now Ken drifted through life, going through the motions without much emotion or enthusiasm—except when it came to animals. His devotion to dogs and rescue horses sparked a renewed purpose in Ken. Those thoughts struck a chord with me. Since Pip passed, I had been much the same, existing not living. My pets, even the irascible Zeke, had saved me no matter what the future held. Pruett and Ella had changed me too, by showing their love. I now knew that I could reclaim my life without betraying or discarding Pip.

"Alma packed a picnic lunch for us," Pruett said, pointing to a wicker hamper. "Bet you could use a snack." Over smoked salmon and salad, Pruett shared his encounter with Jacqui.

"Brrr." He shivered as he described their meeting and subsequent lunch. "The things I do in the pursuit of truth. That woman almost devoured me."

Ella's puzzled look reminded him that little ears were remarkably perceptive. Pruett ruffled her hair and quickly changed the subject. "Poe looks thirsty, Ella. Go fill his bowl." The little girl sped away to a water fountain while staying within eyeshot of her dad.

"So, what happened?" I low-keyed it even though my curiosity was boiling.

Pruett's expression hovered between smile and smirk. "As you predicted, Jacqui couldn't resist my fatal charm. We spent two hours at La Chaumiere, while she sampled everything on the menu including me. Man, that woman can eat."

Silence was a powerful weapon under the right circumstances. I plastered a neutral look on my face and waited patiently.

"You are one tough case. Okay. After much cajoling and some false promises, Jacqui finally confided in me." He pinched my cheek. "She doesn't like you by the way. Thinks you're not my type. Way too serious."

Taunts from a jealous woman like Jacqui shouldn't have bothered me but they did. "Thanks for the news bulletin," I growled. "Learn anything useful, Romeo?"

After several glasses of wine, Jacqui apparently opened her heart and who knew what else to Pruett. She admitted her little problem with shoplifting and protested that her therapist told her it was a disorder not a fault.

"Tell that to the police. I'm sure her mugshot looked lovely."

Ella filled Poe's water bowl and proceeded to do the same for Keats. That allowed Pruett to continue his spiel.

"She described that fundraiser you're so keen on. Sounded pretty tame to me but she did recall some sort of fracas between Ethel and one of the merrymakers. Apparently, Ethel got a drink thrown in her face and asked Jacqui to help her clean up."

I clenched my fists until they were numb. Pruett was deliberately drawing out this tale for effect and driving me crazy in the process. Since there were witnesses about including a child, I resisted the impulse to scream or pummel him.

"Names?" I asked through clenched teeth.

"Nope. One thing though. According to Jacqui, Ethel laughed about the whole thing. Said something about people who lived in glass houses, adultery, and storming the moat, whatever that means."

I pondered that one for a second. My childhood had been a hodgepodge of different religious training although my foster family was ardently Catholic. After a second, I recalled that the sixth commandment is a major bummer that forbids adultery and anything that smacks of sexual pleasure. Jacqui qualified as an expert witness when it came to licentiousness.

"We only have Jacqui's word for all this," I said. "Maybe she threw the drink in question herself. Wouldn't put it past her."

Pruett's smile lit up the sky. "Jealous, are you? Don't worry. I saved my virtue just for you."

"Don't flatter yourself. Come to think of it, Sheila said everyone was well lubricated that evening. Loose lips lead to trouble." Considering Ellis Sands's circle of pals, any number of guests were fabulously wealthy with plenty to lose. Unfortunately, they weren't part of Babette's planning committee. As painful as it was, there were only six possibilities.

Pruett donned his mask of inscrutability. He monitored my expression as closely as a handsome hawk without giving anything away. I clutched his arm as a sudden thought consumed me.

"Think carefully. Did Jacqui say a woman mixed it up with Ethel?"

He pursed his lips as he thought. "Not really. Come to think of it she didn't. I just assumed…"

I turned aside to hide the superior smirk he so richly deserved. Journalists were trained not to assume anything and the exquisitely educated Pruett knew that. All along I had suspected Carleton, the ultimate narcissist. If threatened, he wouldn't hesitate to lash out at anyone especially a woman. Ethel would have relished his loss of control. It represented another power trip for a woman who loved gaining the upper hand over her supposed benefactors. Carleton would brush me off if I broached the subject. Only Babette could answer that question.

"Hello in there, Perri." Pruett tapped my forehead, making Ella giggle. The little girl flung her arms around his waist and hugged her dad.

"Just like Pinocchio, Daddy. Perri has a wooden head!" Wooden head or not, I suddenly realized that by neglecting my shop, I was short-changing myself and the customers who depended upon me.

"Got to run," I said. "I promised to open the shop by noon."

Pruett decided to play peacemaker. "How about this? After work, I'll swing by your place." He snapped his fingers. "I've got it! We could grab some dinner at L'Auberge. It's right in Great Falls and very romantic." He rolled his eyes in a failed attempt at a leer.

Pip had taken me there and Pruett was correct. L'Auberge Chez Francois was both romantic and expensive, not the ideal place for someone who had spent her day at a dog show. "That's so formal," I said. "Maybe some other time." It was a feeble excuse but the best I could muster on short notice.

His middle name may well have been "persistence." Very little deterred Pruett when he was pursuing something or someone he wanted.

"No problem. They opened a brasserie next to it. Chez Jacques, just the kind of place you will love." He took my hand and gently kissed it. "How about it, Mademoiselle? Pick you up at eight."

Resistance was futile, so I chose to yield, finding a curious satisfaction in sweet surrender. "It's a date, Monsieur."

Chapter 32

We never made our dinner date. Just as Pruett pulled into my driveway, I received a hysterical, undecipherable call for help. I barely understood Babette through her storm of tears, hiccups, and sobs.

"Calm down," I said. "What happened?"

"They took her," Babette sobbed. "They said they'd kill her."

"Who?"

"Raza. Someone with a muffled voice called me. Just like in the movies." Babette took a breath. "Perri, she's been horse-napped. If you don't back off, bad things will happen."

"Where are you now," I asked. My voice remained steady, but it wasn't an easy task.

Babette's frustration exploded into a tirade mostly directed at obtuse people like me. "I'm at the farm of course. Cavalry Farms. Today's my volunteer day, remember?"

My heart sank at the thought of my beautiful Raza in the clutches of a double murderer. This killer wouldn't hesitate to act and there was no time to waste. Pruett, Keats and Poe hopped into the Suburban with me as we barreled toward the highway.

"On our way," I told Babette. "Stay calm."

* * * *

Pruett frowned as he pondered the situation. "Weird," he said. "Why threaten Babette instead of you?"

I had already considered that. "Soft target. Let's face it, until the murders, Babette barely locked her doors let alone tangled with murderers. Someone knew that she was alone and unlikely to ask any probing questions." I looked at my dogs through the rear-view mirror. "Besides, who would tangle with warriors like Keats and Poe? Remember. They're Schutzhund trained."

Pruett patted my knee. "It could be anyone you know, any of the people at Babette's house that day."

He was right of course. Evidence trumped negative feelings every time. All of them, even Jacqui and Charlotte were animal lovers so there was hope for my beautiful Arabian. Anyone with a heart—particularly a woman—would never hurt an animal. I blocked any thoughts that told me otherwise. After all, the murderer had already killed twice. Would he or she hesitate to eliminate a horse?

"I just hope whoever did this won't hurt her," I said. My stomach clenched every time we rounded a curve. The culprit could eliminate the problem simply by shipping Raza to one of the many food lots. I squeezed my eyes shut to suppress the tears that threatened. Hiding a horse was an easy proposition in a place like Great Marsh. All that acreage with barns and outbuildings. If you included Loudoun County, the possibilities were endless. Loudoun had more horses than any other county in Virginia and many of its estates were vast. No wonder it was called hunt country.

Pruett's strength was comforting. For once he didn't say much but his presence helped to steady me. I had to be stoic for Babette's sake. If I fell apart, my friend would totally disintegrate. I needed to project confidence and stability the way I had in my previous career.

The gate to Cavalry Farms was wide open, another sign that portended trouble. As soon as we neared the barn, Babette burst out of the door, heedless of the tears coursing down her cheeks, or the mascara tracks marring her eyes.

"Oh, my Lord," she cried. "What can I do?" In typical Babette fashion, she flung herself into Pruett's arms, seeking male comfort. I was frankly tempted to do the same thing. To his credit, he did the manly thing, stroking her hair, patting her back and murmuring softly. I released the Malinois and grabbed my torch from under the seat. Keats and Poe both excelled in tracking. With any luck they might be able to pick up Raza's scent.

"Okay," Pruett said. "When did you see her last?"

Babette dithered for a moment before answering. She backed up a few steps and got defensive. "Wednesday is my spa day, so I was just a bit late. Ken Reedy knows all about it so I figured he'd have it covered. It's fenced after all. I got here right after one. I never had any trouble before."

I immediately thought of her absent spouse. "Where was Carleton?"

Babette bristled. "How should I know? He doesn't live with me anymore, Perri. Plus, today was a school day."

Pruett had a different thought. "Do you have a standing appointment every Wednesday?"

She spent an inordinate amount of time explaining the various spa services and how often she used each of them. To avoid pinching my pal's cheeks, I focused on Pruett's question. Anyone familiar with Babette would know about her spa habits. Lord knows she broadcasted her schedule to anyone who would listen and a few who refused to. That confirmed what we had already surmised: Raza was taken by an insider, someone who knew my pal's vagaries and took advantage of the window of time.

"Let's see the note," I said. Babette fumbled in her pocket and extracted a wrinkled piece of paper with a very clear message. Crystal clear.

"I wrote down everything. Just like they said." Thankfully, Babette's penmanship was a tribute to her private education.

"'Stop meddling or Raza dies. Tell the leather lady that,'" I read aloud. "No ambiguity there."

"Have you called Bascomb?" Pruett asked Babette.

"How crazy are you? Bascomb can't solve two murders. Think he can find a horse? He wouldn't even try." Tears dripped down Babette's cheek. "Ethel and Jakes were blackmailers who deserved to die. Let 'em rot, but Raza doesn't deserve this." She turned to me and clutched my arm. "Promise me, you'll quit, Perri. Please."

Words are sometimes inadequate. I hugged my friend without bothering to mislead or correct her. Sadly, odds were that Raza was already gone, dead or shipped to those horrific food lots that slaughtered horses. In general criminals were a ruthless and self-centered bunch who tended to quickly eliminate anything that might compromise their safety. I said a silent prayer to Francis of Assisi, patron saint of animals, a relic from my theologically muddled past. Maybe the culprit had a soft spot for animals. If Ken Reedy or Sheila did it, they would never hurt Raza. I'd stake my life on that. Unfortunately, I was less confident about Carleton, Charlotte, or Jacqui. Each was a blatant narcissist who looked out for number one regardless of consequences.

We started in the fenced pasture where Raza had last been seen. The dogs immediately picked up her scent and surged toward the rear gate with Pruett and me in tow. Babette stayed behind, clutching Clara's lead.

Before long, the promising lead grew stone cold. Tire tracks made by some type of large SUV pulling a horse trailer were imbedded in the mud. Raza's captor had obviously led her to a van and driven away.

"Know anything about tire tracks?" I asked Pruett.

He made no apologies. "Nope. Not a thing. I'm a sports car guy. One SUV looks pretty much like another to me. Sounds more like your department."

Defeat left a sour taste in my mouth. At least one thing was certain: Carleton neither drove nor owned an SUV—far too pedestrian a vehicle for a self-styled hottie. That didn't absolve him from the crime, however. He was fully capable of urging a confederate—likely female—to do the deed. Charlotte and Jacqui both owned SUVs and might easily own or rent a horse trailer as well. To be fair, so did Ken and Sheila. Almost every household in Great Marsh had one or more of those metal beasts including Babette and me. I headed back to the barn feeling dispirited and helpless.

"Maybe tomorrow things will look brighter," Pruett said. "It's too dark to see much now." He looped his arm around me and squeezed my shoulders. "Ella is staying with Alma tonight. Let's go to your place and discuss strategy as soon as the other volunteers get here."

My hormones immediately warred with my obligations to Babette. Her carefully manicured world had been totally upended in the past month and she needed me. Before I answered him, Pruett glanced at Babette and eked out a grin.

"Okay. I get it. We'll probably end up bunking at your place tonight." He turned toward my pal. "If you'll have us, that is."

She tried to be brave, biting her lip, and fighting back tears. "Don't worry about me. You two go on. I'll stay in case the kidnapper calls me. You never know."

Despite her protestations, the end was inevitable: three adults and three canines trooped over to Babette's house and gathered around the stone fireplace. Pruett made himself useful by pouring brandy while I whipped up an omelet. Fortunately, I had fed both Zeke and Thatcher before leaving so they were good to go until the morning.

We spent the evening discussing pleasant topics and avoiding any mention of Raza's fate. Pruett entertained us with tales of Ella's antics and her obsession with Guinnie.

"She practically sleeps in that belt Perri made her," he said. "Only takes it off to bathe. And those chaps, weird as they are. Kid loves them."

That triggered a niggling thought in my brandy-soaked brain that slipped away before I could capture it. Shortly after midnight we clambered up the stairs in search of rest. I didn't sleep right away, however. Pruett explored his very precise brand of strategy with me until we both drifted off to slumber land.

* * * *

Something roused me very early the next morning. After I quietly showered and dressed, Pruett mumbled garbled, unintelligible gobbledygook and quickly sank back under the covers. A quick trip back home would allow me to care for Zeke and Thatcher, feed the dogs, and zip back before Babette or Pruett even realized that I had gone. With any luck, it would also clear my head of extraneous matters and allow me to focus. I was missing something, a critical piece of evidence. If only I could dredge it up.

Navigating through Sunday morning traffic was a breeze since the good citizens of Great Marsh took their day of rest very seriously. Most, even the churchgoers, didn't stir from their homes until late morning. At six am even the crickets were nestled all snug in their beds.

I hustled the dogs out of the car and steeled myself for a confrontation with Zeke. The irascible goat got lonely even when his stall was well stocked with fresh hay and oats. He wasn't shy about expressing himself either. Fortunately, Keats and Poe served as a distraction. They surrounded him, chased him for a while and calmly accepted his head butts and nuzzling.

A few chores still remained undone. Thatcher required sustenance and attention, despite her feigned indifference to anything human. I also needed to shed last night's finery for more practical garb. The search for Raza might well lead through difficult terrain.

While deactivating the alarm system, I thought again of the kidnapper's words. There was something strange yet familiar about that word choice. Obviously, the author knew both Babette and me. No surprise since he or she was part of a small circle of intimates, someone who knew of Babette's schedule and my passion for Raza.

Keats and Poe stood on alert, their fur bristling.

"Hey you guys, calm down. No need to be upset." I followed them into the living room puzzled by the soft growls coming from their throats. Thatcher was sprawled out on the couch, unharmed and purring loudly. She was not alone.

When I saw my visitor, everything fell into place. I stifled a gasp and reverted to my prior training. *Remain calm. Pretend that everything is fine.*

"I didn't know you would be here," I said. "No wonder Zeke was so happy. Good thing I stopped by. Where's your truck?"

"In your garage."

Keats and Poe maintained their position, never taking their eyes off our guest.

"Keep them away from me. I'd hate to hurt them." The deadly nose of a Glock peeked out at me. Oddly enough that sleek instrument of death had a red snakeskin base.

"That's some Glock. What is it—a 26?"

"Yep. Customized to make it pretty and easy to conceal. Powerful though. Your dogs' heads would explode."

"No problem. They won't move without the command." I took a deep breath. "Raza's okay, isn't she?"

"So far. I'm not a monster you know."

The surreal conversation continued. Obviously, this murderer sincerely believed that. It was my job to feed the illusion.

"True. Ethel and Jakes were miserable human beings," I said. "But surely I don't fit in that category."

"I've always liked you, Perri, but I made a mistake."

"Ah. The message. That wording bothered me, you know. Leather Lady. Only you ever called me that. I just refused to believe it." I eased into a wing chair.

"It won't hurt. I promise that. Believe me I'm an excellent marksman. You won't suffer."

I grimaced. "Small consolation under the circumstances. Ethel dropped a clue too, you know. That thing about people who live in glass houses. At the time I thought it was a cliché, but she was being literal. Tell me about it. Before you end things. Please, Sheila."

Chapter 33

Sheila Sands bit her lip as she pondered my request. "The Orangerie. I should have known. It fascinated that stupid slag." She locked eyes with me. "Oh, why not. I saw Pruett's Jag in the garage, so I expect he won't be joining us. Not for a while at least. Be a shame to destroy a beautiful specimen like him."

She remained perfectly composed and exquisitely attired while discussing her crimes. We had played this scene so many times before—just two gal pals shooting the breeze.

"Ethel." Sheila spat the name. "A small time grifter who thought she hit the big time. I hadn't planned to kill her, but she taunted me. The fire extinguisher was there and boom. The bitch deserved it. She was on the lam, you know. Ellis's security guys got the scoop on her. Pure poison."

"And Jakes?"

"Pathetic! He saw me riding my mountain bike the day Ethel died. Hadn't counted on that. That's how I got to Babette's without leaving tire tracks. Anyhow, Jakes saw me, so he had to go. I got there early and finished him off. Grabbed his phone too."

No wonder. Jakes was long dead by the time I got that text. "And Carleton," I asked. "Why clobber him?"

Sheila grimaced. "Now that was pure pleasure. Should have finished that creep off as a public service. I knew you and Babette were in Georgetown, so I gave Ethel's digs a once-over in case she really had stashed something there. Carleton interrupted me and paid the price."

I marveled again at her composure. Murder and mayhem didn't faze her at all.

"You have everything, Sheila. What in the world was worth risking that?"

It was the wrong thing to ask. She glared at me through the slitted eyes of a stranger.

"For Christ's sake, Perri, Ellis is eighty-two. No amount of Viagra can hoist up his flag. I'm a passionate woman. You may not care about sex, but I do. Ethel loved snooping. She overheard something indiscreet and followed me. End of story."

Was it really that simple? A cheating wife defending her turf? The whole thing seemed so pointless.

"Surely Ellis would forgive you. He loves you."

"Status means everything to men like Ellis. More than any wife, for sure. Ten years ago, I signed a prenup that would send me right back to the trenches. I'm too old for to restart my nursing career, Perri. Not a chance." She motioned to me with the Glock. "Let's get this over with."

I was almost out of time. "Let me crate the dogs first. Please Sheila. That way they won't give you any trouble and you won't have to hurt them." I bet my life that she was first and foremost a person who would never harm an animal.

"Okay. Nothing tricky, though. I'm a crackerjack shot."

I stepped back, just as a piercing shriek filled the air, jolting both of us. Zeke at his most vociferous. When Sheila turned toward the window, I saw my chance.

"*FASS!*" I called to the Malinois. Those brave boys hadn't forgotten their training, or the Schutzhund command for attack. They leapt at Sheila as one, dislodging the Glock from her hand and throwing her to the floor. I moved swiftly to capture the gun and signaled my dogs, with *Pass auf!*, the guard command.

Sheila didn't move a muscle. She was motionless, ossified, the ultimate stone sculpture. I watched her closely as I dialed Bascomb's number.

* * * *

Everything after that was anticlimactic. Police cruisers, sirens and one highly perturbed police Lieutenant arrived within minutes. Babette and Pruett were right behind them.

"Good Lord," Bascomb cried. "That's Mrs. Sands. There must be some mistake. Do you know who her husband is?"

For once, the power of the fourth estate came in handy. Pruett stood at attention taking in every word and recording each detail. Despite the gods of commerce and money in Great Marsh there would be no cover-up this time. Not today.

Babette sidled up to Bascomb and clutched his arm. "She's got Perri's horse, Titus. Please let me go with your guys to get her."

I strode over to Sheila before he could stop me. "Tell us, Sheila. Where is Raza? It's the least you can do."

She tossed her stylish bob and grinned, making me forget for a moment that this was a double murderer not my friend. "Really, Perri. Use your imagination. Raza is enjoying my barn. Stall right next to my gelding. I truly love that horse. Promise me you'll find him a good home. Ellis might have him put down."

Bascomb nodded at Babette and signaled to his officers. "Go on. I can always say we have Mrs. Sands's permission."

Pruett had disappeared into the bedroom, smartphone in hand. I knew he was contacting his editor, phoning in the biggest scoop to hit DC that year. It was his job after all and he was good at it.

* * * *

Sheila Sands was booked for two counts of aggravated murder but didn't go to trial. Her husband dispatched a battery of high-powered attorneys who descended upon the Fairfax County police with all the impact that money and influence can bring. A team of eminent psychiatrists testified that Sheila suffered from paranoid delusions and was not competent to face her accusers. A plea bargain was arranged, and Sheila was confined to a luxurious facility to receive the treatment she so badly needed. When their schemes came to light, no one mourned either Ethel or Glendon Jakes. They were soon forgotten as more sensational crimes captured the public interest.

Pruett received accolades for his expose and I got a valuable prize as well by becoming the proud owner of Raza, the beautiful mare who captured my heart. That was one love match that would never fall asunder and even Pruett admitted that he was slowly warming up to the equine experience. Despite Sheila's murderous intent, I also felt obligated to safeguard her horse. With Ellis Sands's agreement, his wife's beautiful gelding was gifted to Hamilton Arms where he would receive lifetime care and love. Throngs of horse-crazy little girls would see to that.

Cecil got a happy ending too when Ken Reedy welcomed him into his home and his life. Under his tutelage, the Ridgeback pup gained confidence and points toward his AKC championship. Something magical happened when those two joined forces, the odd confluence of canine love and human need. Ken suddenly exuded a zest that I had never seen in him before. By saving Cecil, Ken had reignited his own passion for life and something more. Although we never discussed it, I knew that Ken was the secret lover Sheila had cherished. Sometimes things work out after all.

The future of Cavalry Farms was also safeguarded. A coalition of veterans' groups, animal activists, and children's advocates combined to repurpose the facility as a haven for abandoned horses and human souls damaged by PTSD or physical ailments. The powers-that-be in Great Marsh proudly touted it as a crown jewel in the town proof positive that the affluent community had a big heart.

Pruett and Ella now spent most weekends at my place. We continue to take our relationship slowly, caring more for each other day by day. For the first time since losing Pip, I felt whole again, freed from the crushing burden of doubts. A brush with death can do that to you.

By circulating a vastly inflated account of our heroics, Babette enhanced our reputation as amateur sleuths and solidified her claim as a change agent. Although I downplayed the entire incident, she eagerly sought opportunities to showcase our detective skills. According to Babette, our next adventure is right around the corner. I've learned to never bet against her.

If you enjoyed *Homicide by Horse Show*, be sure not to miss Arlene Kay's first Creature Comforts mystery

Army vet Persephone "Perri" Morgan has big plans, as her custom leather leashes, saddles, and other pet accessories are the rage of dog and horse enthusiasts everywhere. But when murder prances into the ring at a Massachusetts dog show, Perri must confront a cunning killer who's a breed apart.

Accompanied by her bestie Babette and four oversize canines, Perri motors down to the Big E Dog Show in high style. Perri hopes to combine business with pleasure by also spending time with sexy DC journalist Wing Pruett. Until a storm traps everyone at the exposition hall...and a man's body is found in a snow-covered field, a pair of pink poodle grooming shears plunged through his heart.

Turns out the deceased was a double-dealing huckster who had plenty of enemies chomping at the bit. But as breeders and their prize pets preen and strut, the murderer strikes again. Aided by her trusty canine companions, Keats and Poe, Perri must collar a killer before she's the next "Dead in Show" winner.

Keep reading for a special look!

Chapter 1

Road trips always rattled me. They carried me back to my army days in an airless transport truck, where I sat wedged between raunchy guys with mixed motives. I had to admit that they were expert practitioners of that international game—Russian hands and Roman fingers. In those times, a woman needed sharp elbows and an even sharper tongue to survive and thrive. Out of necessity, I had acquired both. They weren't a bad bunch. Like me, most of my fellow warriors were actually scared kids buoying their courage with a show of false bravado. As soldiers, we served our country and learned invaluable life lessons that strengthened us—if we survived.

Things were different now, of course, but those memories still hovered about the recesses of my mind every time I took a road trip. I closed my eyes and made a wish.

Please. Whisk me away on a magic carpet and make me vanish.

Naturally that didn't happen. We barreled down the highway in Babette Croy's super-duper Class A motor home at top speed without missing a beat. Then, for the hundredth time that day, I wondered how in the world I would ever survive the coming week. Seven whole days in close quarters with my best friend and several thousand dog enthusiasts. The possibilities for mischief were endless.

"Are you okay, Perri?" The dulcet tones of seven-year-old Ella Pruett revived me and brought me to my senses. A mini-frown marred the sweet face of the moppet I had grown to love, flooding me with guilt.

"Of course. Don't worry about me. I was just dreaming." I winked to show her that everything was fine. Hunky-dory. Peachy keen. My trusty Malinois Keats and Poe immediately went on alert. They were canine truth detectors who could sense lies—particularly mine—at ten paces. That was their job during a three-year stint in the army, and retired or not, they hadn't lost a step. Most people confused Belgians like my boys with either German shepherds or shepherd/collie mixes. Nothing could be further from the truth, as police forces throughout the world now realized. Belgian Malinois are a distinct breed—streamlined, tireless workers with an unending appetite for action. I reached for them, looked into soulful doggy eyes, and gave each a nose kiss. In times of stress, nothing surpassed a furry embrace.

"Don't mind Perri, sugar. She's just a stick in the mud." Babette, my best pal and our designated driver, twisted around in the driver's seat and rolled her eyes, ignoring the threat of oncoming traffic and the blaring horns of outraged drivers. "I know," she said, "let's sing a song. Road trips are supposed to be fun. Look at it this way. By leavin' today, we'll beat the snowstorm and avoid all that nasty winter traffic. Plus, that gives us plenty of girl time together."

Babette was a guided missile—locked, loaded, and ready to fire. Fortunately, I distracted her by mentioning one of her favorite subjects: dogs. After all, canine competition was what had sparked our little caravan. Why else would two adults, one child, and four large dogs abandon Great Marsh, Virginia, and drive for six hours to the sooty embrace of the Big E Coliseum, also known as the Eastern States Expo Center, a carbuncle on the foot of western Massachusetts.

I didn't mind roughing it. Four years in the US Army had cured me of needless luxuries, but Babette was a different story entirely. My friend considered anything short of full cable, Italian sheets, and catered meals an unendurable hardship. Great wealth does that to a person, I'm told, although in my case it was strictly a rumor. My business, Creature Comforts, provided me with a decent livelihood and a satisfying creative outlet. I left the opulence to Babette and most of my neighbors in Great Marsh. That explained the luxury motor home. There were more modest models available, but Babette wouldn't hear of it. Second class was simply not in her vocabulary. This latest acquisition, the behemoth dubbed Steady Eddie, sported granite countertops, plush leather furniture, two steam showers, and accommodations for eight. At first, I'd been wary, but Babette surprised me. After all, not everyone could maneuver a metal monster through heavy traffic. My friend was petite but surprisingly adept at doing just that. Rule number one in the Croy friendship manual—never underestimate Babette!

"Miss your daddy, Ella?" Babette's coy tone gave her away. "I know Ms. Perri does."

Ella was the much-loved daughter of Wing Pruett, investigative journalist, hottie supreme, and my main squeeze. How to describe Wing Pruett? Sculpted features, thick dark hair, and a body most women (and men) could only dream about. No doubt about it. All six plus feet of my honey were as close to perfection as mere mortals could ever get. He was absent today but planned to join us later in the week after wrapping up his current assignment. He'd been uncharacteristically vague about the project, and that made me wonder. Despite Babette's prompts and none too subtle hints, Pruett refused to spill the journalistic beans. I surmised, however, that it had something to do with dog shows. That was a real puzzler. Wing Pruett, the man who fearlessly confronted evildoers of all stripes, was terrified of dogs. Cynophobia was the clinical term for an ailment I simply could not understand. Still, he had made great strides, mostly due to Ella and his interaction with my own menagerie. Few men would admit, let alone address, such a malady, but then Pruett was not most men. I missed him like crazy but kept that feeling to myself.

I turned toward my dogs to avoid Babette's scrutiny. Damn that woman. She sometimes knew me better than I knew myself. Truth be told, I missed Pruett every second that we spent apart. Simple logic told me that a country mouse like me was unlikely to hold his interest long-term, but raw emotion kept me firmly anchored to his side. After almost a year, things had only gotten better—for me at least.

"I see him every night on Skype," Ella said with that unassailable logic small children often use. "He blows kisses to me and Guinnie." Lady Guinevere, a champion pointer, was the love of Ella's life. "Ms. Perri too. Daddy always saves a kiss for her." I loved that child as if she were my own little girl. She wasn't, of course. She was the offspring of Pruett and renowned photojournalist Monique Allaire and had the black curly mane and soulful blue eyes to prove it. Monique was mostly absent from her life, but Pruett was the ultimate Mr. Mom. I knew that allowing Ella to join our merry band proved his trust in me, but it also conferred an awesome responsibility. That's what shattered my nerves and led to sleepless nights. Dog shows were busy places, and the Big E was cavernous—so many nooks and crevices where a little girl might wander off, get lost, or worse. Add a potential blizzard to the mix, and anything might happen.

"You won't go anywhere without me or Ms. Babette. Right, Ella? Remember. We promised your dad that."

She nodded solemnly. "I promise. Besides, Guinnie will protect me too." Her eyes shone as she stroked the pointer's silky coat. "And all the other dogs will help."

I crossed my fingers and took a deep breath. Babette and her border collie, Clara, were focused on agility contests. Babette was obsessed with winning agility competitions, and border collies—those bright, stealthy herders—won top honors in most agility contests. My friend tended toward extremes, especially in times of emotional stress. Since she had recently divorced the cretinous Carleton Croy, Babette was temporarily man-less, and a lonely Babette was a fearsome thing indeed. Thank heavens for the presence of an innocent child. That shielded me from hearing a litany of praise for Carleton's manly parts that Babette so desperately missed. She conveniently forgot that her ex had shared his largesse with any number of her friends and a few enemies as well. When it came to men, Babette had a fond but very selective memory.

Ella had her own dreams. She yearned to be a junior dog handler, a member of that select group of youngsters that dotted every dog show. After discussing the issue with Pruett, I promised to introduce her to some of the kids who participated in the sport. Fortunately, all juniors had to be at least nine years of age, so Pruett had two years to go before confronting the situation. Wing was ambivalent about animals, and I was certain that he hoped Ella's interest would fade.

"Remember," I told Ella, "I'm counting on you to help me with my store." I am a leathersmith by trade, an occupation that requires both creativity and precision. After careful study at art school and an apprenticeship with a master craftsman, I focused on designing products for the creatures I most loved. The majority of my customers were dog and horse fanciers, although lately I'd branched out to custom belts with mother-daughter themes. Any event at the Big E was bound to bring in a slew of business. Snowstorms and other weather mishaps encouraged even more potential customers to attend the show. They chose to brave the elements rather than risk a bout of cabin fever. That pleased me since by necessity I kept my eyes firmly trained on the bottom line.

The little girl beamed. "Yep. See, I got my belt on."

I nodded in appreciation of Ella, a truly wonderful child. I had never married, although I came close one time. Being childless wasn't a problem for me since my biological clock simply did not tick. Before meeting Pruett, I lacked the maternal gene, or so I thought. An affinity for animals came naturally to me, and my menagerie included two dogs, one cantankerous feline, and an ornery goat with bad manners and a temper to match.

Once Ella stepped into the picture, that all changed. At thirty years of age, I had finally embraced the role of child nurturer and caregiver. Go figure.

Babette slowed the trailer and pulled into a rest stop parking lot. "Let's take a break," she said. "I need to stretch my legs, and I know the pups could use some potty time."

Fortunately, we had the coach fully stocked with every possible type of provision, so food and drink were plentiful. Babette had made sure of that. After leashing the dogs, we stepped into the bright sunshine and walked toward the pet area.

"Heard they had some fireworks at last week's show," Babette said in a stage whisper.

I raised my eyebrows.

"Yep. A real dustup." She watched as Ella disposed of Guinnie's waste. "Yael Lindsay almost came to blows with that Bethany. You know her."

My goal was to sell products, not become mired in scandals. "Nope. Can't place either one."

Babette puffed out her cheeks in a pout. "Oh. You're no fun at all, Ms. Goody Two-shoes. Bethany is that slutty one. Slinks around the arena in super-tight duds that show everything and pretends to be a pet psychic. Don't see how that heifer can even move, let alone mentally communicate with dogs. Thinks she's the queen of agility too."

Something she said piqued my interest. "That's odd. Yael rules the pointer world with an iron fist. Strictly conformation events. Why would she bother with an agility person? Besides she's rather elderly for a fistfight."

"Aha!" Babette pounced immediately. "You know more than you let on. I knew it."

What could I do? I shrugged and gave her a guilty grin. Babette, master of trickery, had trapped me fair and square. "You know I steer clear of these feuds. At least I try to. Remember, I need to sell stuff to both camps."

Sales were a foreign language to my pal. She never even bothered to balance her checkbook, whereas I accounted for each penny with nuclear precision. Call it a legacy from my life as a foster child or just plain business acumen. Either one worked for me. Pip had always urged me to ease up and enjoy life without going overboard. Balance was his watchword.

I snapped a leash on further memories lest tears flood my eyes. Pip, my late fiancé, was gone. Had been these three years since melanoma had stolen him from me. He still resided with me in the home we'd shared, in the pets we both had loved, and in the memories I cherished. Those were the hardest things to suppress because I simply refused to. No matter where things went with Pruett, the late Philip Hahn, DVM, owned a part of me and always would. I told myself that he wasn't really gone. Pip had just left ahead of me.

"Hey, Earth to Perri." Babette tapped me on my forehead. "Stop mooning and get movin'. We've got a show to get to." She clapped her hands for Ella. "Right, Ella? Let's roll."

The remainder of our journey was uneventful, and we exited the Mass Pike and approached the Big E without incident. To my surprise, Babette had researched everything pertinent to parking and maintaining her motor coach right down to electronic and cable television hookups. Many dog show veterans chose the convenience of recreational vehicles over the rigors of motel life since upscale establishments banned or severely restricted dogs. The remaining "dog hotels" simply didn't measure up to Babette's high standards. Thus, the luxury coach—an inspired, if pricey, solution that paid dividends to me too. I groused about needless spending when my pal had purchased Steady Eddie, citing depreciation, inconvenience, and the numerous animal charities that needed the money instead. Opulence made me uncomfortable, a throwback to my hardscrabble childhood. Still, I was secretly pleased by the comfort and ease of our accommodations. Friendship with Babette conferred many benefits, and chief among them was sharing the spoils of wealth. Money aside, her loyalty and sweet nature were the primary attractions for me.

Although the Big E reserved a sizable area for large vehicles and trailers, choice slots close to the show venue were at a premium. I worried that our late arrival might relegate us to the far reaches of the fairground—Siberia, as the regulars termed it. If that were our fate, juggling dogs, leather products, and one lively child would present quite a challenge, especially during inclement weather.

Once again, Babette read my mind. "Don't fret, Perri. We've got a primo spot. I already arranged it." Try as she might, she couldn't hide the smirk that covered her pretty face.

"How'd you manage that?" I asked, mindful that a small child was within earshot.

Babette fluttered her eyelashes. "Charm and wit."

I crossed my arms. "What else?"

"Suspicious little twit, aren't you? Okay. You caught me. A well-placed bribe didn't hurt either. Just a generous cash gift to the guy in charge of the area." Babette stared me down. "Don't be an old prig, Perri. It's the American way. Once that snow starts, things will get crazy here."

"What's a prig, Ms. Babette?" Ella proved yet again that her hearing was exceptionally sharp.

Babette swung into a reserved slot closest to the show area. "Don't worry, pumpkin. Ms. Perri is just a stuffed shirt. We have to loosen her up."

Ella's big blue eyes sparkled. "My daddy says Ms. Perri is perfect."

Now it was my turn to blush and change the subject. I hated to acknowledge the firm grip that Wing Pruett and his darling moppet had on my heart. Orphans like me fear loss more than most folks. After being wrenched from my parents' arms and watching my fiancé slip away, I tried mightily to steel myself against further pain. Through a concentrated stealth campaign, Pruett had managed to penetrate those defenses and unleash my fondest hopes. Love does that to a body, but it's a deep and dangerous game.

"Come on," I said, dusting off my jeans. "Let's hook up this baby and walk around the grounds. I see a few familiar faces already."

Babette clambered out of the driver's seat and immediately made a connection. Our near neighbor, a muscular, middle-aged man with a thick crop of gray hair, held out his arm and helped Babette alight. She sized him up and went all girly on him.

"Why, thank you, kind sir. I can always use a little help." In true Babette fashion, she simpered. I really hated when she did that, but it was straight from the Croy playbook, with a bow to Scarlett O'Hara. Most men fell for it, especially when she showed her dimples. This guy was no exception.

I did a quick appraisal of Prince Galahad. He was tall, tanned, and neatly dressed in a pressed pair of jeans and checked shirt. There was nothing wrong with his body either, but I was more concerned with his motives. Call me protective, but Babette had zero judgment when it came to men. The unlamented Carleton Croy, husband number four, was an opportunist who was more interested in her bankbook than her loving heart. Similarly, any con man worth his salt would assess Steady Eddie and quickly realize the bucks that went with it. I leapt out of my seat, clutched Ella, and unleashed my dogs.

"Forgive me, ma'am. I should have introduced myself." Babette's admirer ignored me and kept hold of her hand. "Rafael Ramos at your service. Most folks call me Rafa."

Ramos's vehicle was a poor cousin of ours, a rusted Airstream that had seen better days. Naturally, Babette seemed oblivious to that as she zeroed in on our neighbor. I knew the signs and decided to immediately nip young love in the bud.

Babette was still in dreamland. "Rafa? Ooh. Just like the tennis player. That's fascinatin'!"

He shrugged and shook his head. "Don't I wish. Unfortunately, I'm not much of an athlete." His faux modesty aroused my suspicions. The muscles on this guy proved that he did some serious physical training.

"Hi, Rafa," I said, extending my hand. "I'm Perri Morgan, and this is Ella. Excuse us while we exercise our crew. We've got four hungry canines on board."

Ramos unhanded my friend and switched into helpful mode. "Of course. Be glad to help you with the connections on this big boy if you need anything. Sure is a beauty." He then proved that he was also a dog person. "Wow! Speaking of beauties, your dogs are phenomenal." He approached Keats and Poe with the palm of his hand open and lowered.

When they acknowledged him, he patted their silky heads and did the same to Clara and Guinnie.

"Do you have a dog, sir?" Ella asked.

He bent down and smiled. "Call me Rafa, honey. And the answer is yes. My breed is standard poodles. Don't have any with me this trip because I'm judging."

"You're a judge," Babette trilled as if he had said "brain surgeon." The throb in her voice sounded authentic and probably was. "How excitin'."

Rafael lowered his head in an "aw shucks" routine. "I just love doing the show circuit. Being around beautiful dogs and lovely ladies—doesn't get much better than that."

"Guinnie is a Grand Champion," Ella said proudly. "She's almost at bronze level." In dog show parlance, there were five levels of Grand Champion, and Guinnie was new to that elevated crowd. She had bronze, silver, gold, and platinum levels yet to conquer, but that didn't concern me one bit. With Guinnie's perfection, Ella's persistence, and Pruett's pocketbook, no obstacle was insurmountable.

Rafa nodded. "I can see why. Didn't I see her written up in the latest issue of *Canine Chronicles*?"

Ella's smile was luminous. She nodded and reached down to give Guinnie another hug. In deference to the little girl, I hoped Rafa wouldn't probe any further. Grand Champion Camelot Kennel's Lady Guinevere had come to us under tragic circumstances that were best forgotten. Like most pointers, Guinnie was a gentle, loving companion with plenty of brains. The important thing was the immutable bond between Ella and her dog.

"Let me take these guys for a run," I said, whistling to my dogs. "Ready, Ella?" We loped toward the backfields, leaving Babette to her new suitor. I know from experience when to fade from the scene, particularly when it involved a man. Their animated conversation told me that our absence hadn't even been noticed. No surprise there. Babette was a loyal friend, but any presentable man with a pulse could easily turn her head.

Ella, on the other hand, saw only Guinnie and the other dogs. Her big blue eyes shone with happiness as she romped with our pack of pups. Loving animals came easily to most children, and I harbored grave suspicions about kids who felt otherwise. Indifference to animals was just plain unnatural—serial killer material.

A sudden cacophony of noise rudely interrupted my thoughts. I clutched Ella's hand, steering her toward the trees and to the left of the warring parties. Neither combatant acknowledged us, but I suspect that, in the heat of battle, neither of them noticed us either. To my chagrin, these disturbers of the peace were adults, grown women, not marauding teens. Yael Lindsay, a well-preserved sexagenarian with seriously teased hair and an eye-popping diamond ring, shook her fist. "You listen here, Bethany. I run this show. That means no shenanigans by the likes of you. Hussy!"

Her antagonist, agility master Bethany Zahn, was the seductress so vividly described by Babette. Maybe it was the black leather blanketing her from stem to sultry stern that gave Bethany away or the mane of unnaturally black curls that she twirled. Either way, she radiated sex appeal, snark, and a dollop of dominatrix.

"Run?" she sneered, hands on hips. "Honey, at your age you couldn't run if your life depended on it. Join a gym, why don't you? Better still, muzzle that horny hubby of yours. He's into agility in a big way, or so I hear." Bethany smirked at her own wit and sauntered off toward the show entrance without a backward glance.

I normally eschew gossip, but that little tiff fascinated me—until I recalled the urchin who clutched my hand. Ella Pruett trained her baby blues on me and asked, "Why were those ladies fighting, Perri? Daddy says that's not right."

Honesty was the best policy, especially when it involved a bright, inquisitive child like Ella, who was not easily fooled.

"Your daddy was right. Shouting never solves anything, honey. Some people never learn." I clapped my hands, causing Poe and Keats to snap to attention. "Come on. Let's run a race with these pups."

We sped down the field, trailing four dogs that easily outpaced us and leaving the snarling women behind. Canine quarrels were typically sparked by competition—dominance, food, territory, or sex. Humans were no different. Based on the scene I had just witnessed, one or all of those factors might have caused the dustup. I never dreamed that tragedy awaited us.

About the Author

Photo by Kim Rodriques Photography

Arlene Kay spent twenty years as a Senior Federal Executive where she was known as a most unconventional public servant. Her time with the federal government, from Texas to Washington DC, allowed her to observe both human and corporate foibles and rejoice in unintentional humor. These locations, and the many people she encountered, are celebrated in her mystery novels. She is also the author of the Boston Uncommons Mystery series as well as *Intrusion* and *Die Laughing.* She is a member of International Thriller Writers.

Visit her on the web at www.arlenekay.com.

www.ingramcontent.com/pod-product-compliance
Lightning Source LLC
Chambersburg PA
CBHW050520260626
47157CB00004B/1410